# Finding
# *Mr. Wrong*

## Stella MacLean

Cataloguing and Publication information is available from The Canadian ISBN Service System, Library and Archives Canada.

ISBN: 978-0-9878295-9-7
Website: www.stellamaclean.com

Editor Services: Patricia Thomas
Cover Artist: The Killion Group, Inc.
Interior Formatting: Author E.M.S.

*To the wise women in my life.*

*Tory Leblanc*
*Julianne MacLean*
*Deborah Hale*
*Shirley Hailstock*
*Linda Hersey*
*Lina Gardiner*
*Norah Wilson*
*Pat Thomas*


*Thank you.*

# Chapter One

———— ⬧ ————

"Life sucks," Maggie muttered. She leaned against the counter in Sean O'Toole's kitchen, shuffled the stack of bills and sipped the last of her coffee. Time was running out. With her lousy luck, in a couple of days her father would want to learn more about the great job she had been pretending to have, a job she'd touted as being far superior to the one she'd left behind in Boston.

On top of worry about her investment, she missed her four-year-old son Jeremy. She'd confided her problems in her mother who promptly offered to keep Jeremy while she sorted out the repayment of the money Sean O'Toole owed her.

She had to find Sean or face her father's scorn when he found out she was working in a steakhouse as a waitress, and that her money and her business partner, Sean O'Toole, were nowhere to be found. She sighed, a sigh that turned into a groan at the unfairness of it all.

Of course, if she were flawlessly honest about it all, it was her unwavering attraction to bad boys that had caused the real problem. While still under the influence of Sean's O'Toole's exotic appeal, she'd let him sweet-talk her into thinking that Harry's Place was one hell of an investment deal. At least she'd drawn the line where sex was concerned…one giant step forward in her life.

Later, excited about being part owner of what she thought was a thriving restaurant business, she'd come home to Portland to see how her investment in Sean's business was going. She discovered that Sean had left town without a word of explanation, and no one knew where he was or when to expect him back. And she'd learned that Harry's Place, her great investment, was on the financial skids…and Maggie's money had vaporized.

She'd lain in wait for Sean to return. Well, not exactly lain—more like hidden out at his house…except when she worked at Harry's Place. Since her arrival, she'd thought of little else except what she'd do when she caught up with the creep. Her fingers itched to grab Sean where it hurt most. His wallet.

Her shift at the steakhouse started in less than two hours, and she'd be damned if she'd let her money troubles ruin the rest of her free time. She planned to sun herself on Sean's patio and let the sun's warmth smooth away her worries.

She dropped the stack of bills on the counter and strolled through the living room into the sunroom. Sean might be a master con when it came to taking other people's money, but he knew how to build a house with character.

Maggie planned to have a house like his some day, when her current rash of financial troubles were a distant memory. As she unlocked the patio doors, she gazed out over the perennial gardens and boxwood hedge that framed the lawn. At the edge of the lawn a man, decked out in black leather, stood talking to Edna Cotter. Maggie stared. *Was he patting Edna's pet skunk?*

Nobody in his right mind patted Galahad.

Nobody in his right mind gave Edna Cotter an opportunity to ask questions either.

She should know. Maggie had learned that lesson the hard way. Her hastily constructed story about being Sean's long lost cousin would not stand up under the most casual scrutiny. Certainly not under Edna's ambush interrogation techniques. Maggie moved back from the door and watched. Edna seemed to be telling the stranger a story that required a lot of arm waving and hand movements.

A quick check of the man showed he had a high cuddle factor starting with a body that filled his black leather pants and jacket to perfection. Her pulse kicked up ten points at the mere thought of what his arms would feel like.

*Give your head a shake!*

"But it can't hurt to window shop," she murmured as she continued her perusal. His black hair flirted with the edge of his leather collar as he gave Edna a smile that would melt icebergs. Even with the door closed, Maggie could hear Edna's giggle.

*Not good.* Edna probably hadn't giggled since Richard Nixon resigned.

If this was the stranger's doing, he was a man to avoid. God only knew, she'd had enough experience with sexy men in black to last her a lifetime.

Maggie steadied her stuttering pulse then turned away. The patio was definitely not a good idea.

A peel of laughter made her turn back. *What now?* She peeked one eye around the doorframe.

Despite her best efforts, her gaze moved to the stranger, up his broad chest to the links of gold at his throat, along his jutting jaw line and up to his eyes—that stared directly at her.

He smiled at Maggie and said something to Edna who promptly pealed off another loud hoot of laughter.

Unease swam in Maggie's stomach as she watched them walk toward the patio, Edna clutching his arm while his broad smile ploughed into Maggie's resolve. Should she sneak away, and not answer when they knocked? Something told her that this stranger wouldn't be put off that easily.

Might as well face the situation head on. She opened the sliding glass door.

Edna warbled excitedly. "Maggie, come out here this minute. Have I got a surprise for you!" She swept across the patio and grabbed Maggie's arm. "Your half brother just arrived. He didn't want to disturb you. He thought you were sleeping. I told him you work some pretty strange hours at that saloon."

Maggie stared in disbelief. *Half brother.* She had no half brother.

"Oh, Sis, I've missed you so much. How have you been? That horrible hospital, those ugly white jackets and those strange padded little rooms. It must have been awful! You poor thing," the stranger said as he left Edna's side and rushed to scoop Maggie into his arms.

This man was a lunatic if he thought he could imply something like that in front of Edna and get away with it. Maggie ducked his outstretched arm, turned and slid her foot in his path, hoping he'd land on his ass, or crash into the patio door. The last thing she needed was another smart-mouthed con artist with a Tom Cruise smile and a Brad Pitt body.

He recovered easily, and before she could get out of harm's way his arms enfolded her, pulling her into his chest in one sweeping move. "Say you missed me, Sis. I've missed you *so* much."

His arms held her in a vice-like grip as his words slid into the space between them. "Play along with me. I've had a rough morning."

"It's about to get a whole lot rougher," Maggie hissed as she stepped on his instep.

"Ohhhhh! That's my favorite sister for ya." The handsome stranger laughed and slid into a deckchair and plunked her down on his lap. His lips brushed her earlobe in a move that felt suspiciously like a kiss. A tingle rippled through her body like an ice cream soda's fizz on a hot day.

"Try that again and I'll put you over my lap and spank you," he said, his lips hot against her cheek.

Maggie smothered the starburst sensation his lips had sparked, and glared at him. "Take your best shot, buster, but

I wouldn't give a girl like me such easy access to your family jewels. Know what I mean?" She glanced down in the general direction of his crotch. "You try spanking me, and I'll have you singing soprano."

"Don't make promises you can't keep," he whispered close to her ear, his words punctuated with a look that would make a nun strip.

*God, he was gorgeous!* And the creep knew it! "Are you willing to take the chance?"

"Always. I love a woman who knows what she wants." His fingers started caressing her butt. Her pulse tripped skyward along with her temper.

"If I were you, I'd be real careful around me. I don't play fair." She dropped the words just at the end of his nose and leapt out of his lap.

He crossed one leather-clad ankle over the other, leaned back in the chair and let out a long sigh. "This is heaven, Sis. But what a shame. Edna tells me our cousin Sean is away and has left you to housesit." He winked at her. "And you not feeling well. What a bummer."

A sharp retort, clarifying who was the real bum around here, flew to her lips, but she blocked it. He obviously knew her story about how Sean had asked her to housesit, thanks to loose-lips Cotter. At least the version she'd given Edna, minus the lock-picking stuff, of course. The mental hospital bit was his fabrication, and if he dared to stick around long enough, she'd make him pay.

But with her dismal luck, he also knew she wasn't Sean's cousin. Her mind scrambled over the possibilities, discarding all the options that came to mind. There had to be a way to send this man packing without making him too curious. She just needed time and a clear head to think about it.

In the meantime, she'd play along, and find out what the stranger was doing here. Besides, any hint that her story wasn't true, would have Edna asking questions again. "Yes, our dear cousin Sean had to leave in a hurry." *Just ahead of the police, no doubt.* "He asked me to look after things."

"When do we expect him back, My Sweetness?" he asked, a cheeky grin on his face.

She resisted the urge to smack him one for his arrogance. That would come later—after Edna left. She shrugged as she gave Edna a quick glance.

The old dear's head was going back and forth like a tennis ball at Wimbledon. Maggie couldn't afford to tell the stranger to get lost with Edna taking in every word. It would make her neighbor suspicious and Maggie couldn't risk that. Edna's modus operandi was to call the police at the drop of a leaf in the yard. Maggie wouldn't be the least bit surprised to find that Edna had 911 on speed dial.

On the other hand, if the stranger had any idea where Sean might have gone, Maggie had a right to know. But first she needed to get him away from 'big ears.' Like a woman about to pick up a snake, Maggie reached toward the stranger and extended her hand. "I'm sure you have a lot to tell me. Why don't we go inside?"

Surprise flickered in his eyes. "Sure, Sis. We have a whole lot of catching up to do." He reached for her outstretched hand, a come-get-me look on his handsome face.

She gave him a don't-fool-with-me glare, the one she reserved for certified cads. And in her mind, the stranger who sprawled on the deckchair, with his many physical charms on full display, was a Charter Member of the Certified Cad Club.

"I'll leave you two young people to catch up," Edna said as she turned to leave the patio. "But I'll expect you to join me for supper one of these nights. I've gotten to like that young Sean, and want to know all about him. He's quite the charmer."

"That's our Sean," the stranger said, his gaze doing a long, heated assessment of Maggie…from her wedge sandals to the mass of red hair framing her face. A sexy smile tipped up the corners of his lips.

Maggie's body pinged in response. *Mind your business,* she mouthed in his direction.

*You are my business,* he mouthed back.

Edna stopped at the edge of the patio. "Now you two promise me that you'll come together."

"We promise," they said in unison.

With that, Edna made her way across the grass, her rubber boots making a plopping sound as she entered her own yard, Galahad close behind. She picked up a rifle of some sort off the ground and walked inside. Maggie shook her head.

"God, for a minute there—"

"Shh. She hears better than an owl. Wait until she's gone inside her house."

"Whatever you say. You're in charge, Sister Dear."

Maggie ignored his comment as she waited for the familiar clunk of Edna's screen door. Then she waited a while longer, hoping that Edna would close her inside door. With Edna safely out of the way, Maggie would be able to deal with this leather-clad lothario on the patio instead of letting him come inside.

Silence radiated from Edna's back door, which meant that the old dear was in eavesdropping mode. Maggie had no choice but to move the conversation inside. "Shall we?"

"Shall we what?" The sexy challenge in his eyes had her hormones scrambling to line up like so many iron filings along a magnet.

"Follow me." Without looking back, Maggie opened the patio door. She scanned the room for the most advantageous spot to set this man straight about the situation. She did not intend to have him hanging around the house making her life more difficult than it already was.

Being a partner in Sean's business was her chance to secure Jeremy's future—a plan in jeopardy with Sean's disappearance.

If this man had plans to try and beat her to Sean, he'd

better think again. She had no intention of letting anyone find him ahead of her. This man could not stay here.

Settling into an over-stuffed wicker chair, Maggie let out a long, exaggerated sigh…one designed to show the stranger that all of this was old hat to her. "So, what's your angle? You've got ten seconds to tell me your Sean-done-you-wrong story."

The stranger prowled around the room like a caged animal. Her eyes kept dropping below his waist to where his leather pants barely disguised his well-muscled thighs. He made one last lap and came to a full stop in front of her chair. Resting his hands on his hips, he looked down at her. "Lady, I don't know who you are. But you're not Sean O'Toole's cousin."

To Maggie's dismay, she felt the truth of his frank appraisal all the way to the tips of her magenta-painted toenails. "Says who?"

He slid onto the sofa, stretched out his sexy body inches from hers—his penetrating gaze leading a searing charge through all her body parts. "Says me. So do I throw you out, or are you going to tell me what you're doing here?"

The woman pretending to be related to his friend was one of the most enticing redheads Tom had ever seen, with a fiery personality to go with the hair. There were times when he liked a little verbal sparring with a woman. Today wasn't shaping up to be one of them.

He'd parked his Harley in Sean's back driveway and was trekking across the grass, still damp from last night's rain, when he tripped over a lawn hose and fell face down in the grass. Then when he raised his head and faced a woman named Edna Cotter holding a shotgun, while a skunk named Galahad looked on, he figured it was all over. With his thoughts scrambled by the idea that he might be shot…or face a drenching with Eau de Skunk, he'd babbled on about coming to visit Sean.

When Edna told him she was being neighborly and looking out for someone named Maggie he'd tried to come up with a plan. Playing for time, he'd gotten Edna to tell him a little bit about the woman living in Sean's house. It seemed that Edna really liked Maggie, a less-than-reassuring notion, given Edna's shotgun and her choice of pets.

Nothing this redhead said or did could top the rush of fear and finally relief when he'd managed to charm Edna into putting the shotgun down and getting her pet skunk out of firing range.

"I'm waiting," he said as he settled farther back into the cushions of the sofa.

"You got it all wrong. It's you who owes me an explanation."

Not sure which tactic to use, Tom continued to size her up as she braced her back against the wicker chair. Red hair rained down around her face in large unruly curls. Her long, lean body curved in all the right places. Her defiant glare washed like ice and fire over his skin, daring him to challenge her.

He knew he could slip past her cool edge, and fan the flame smoldering in her eyes. It would be easy. He knew, because he'd had plenty of experience. He'd always known how to make women want him. Hell, he'd made a career out of it—a career he no longer wanted.

In the beginning his plan had been to get the money Sean owed him, and get back on the road to Boston, but that wasn't going to work now. If Sean had skipped town, Tom would have to get to Sean's business establishment and try his luck there.

Tom's instincts told him the woman sitting in the wicker chair would know all about Sean and his business. "You're right. You deserve an explanation. Sean owes me money." He gave her a grin designed to tweak her interest.

"So, get in line. Behind me." She sniffed, tucked one long leg under her and settled deeper in the chair.

"He owes you money too?"

"Yes," she said, her beautiful lips drawn together in a pout.

Gut instinct told him this woman was up to something… Exactly what he didn't know. But he would make it his business to find out. "This isn't getting us anywhere. Can we call a truce? My name's Tom Rawlins and I'm a friend of Sean's. I might be able to help you."

"I doubt it. Sean and I were supposed to be business partners. I gave him my money and got zip in return."

Her gaze met his, just long enough for him to see a sudden flash of uncertainty in her eyes. Had Sean also run out on her? He was more than capable of it. Sean's idea of a long-term relationship was two dates in a row. "Were you supposed to be buying into his steakhouse?"

"Yeah, or so I thought."

"Were you aware that Sean has a gambling problem?"

Surprise widened her eyes. Her gaze slid past him toward the floor. "He's going to have more than a gambling problem when I catch him." She thumped her balled fists on the arms of the wicker chair.

How much money had this woman given Sean? It had to be a sizeable amount, if the look of desperation in her eyes were any indication. "I understand how you feel."

Her gaze snapped back to meet his. He smiled encouragingly.

She let out a long sigh. "Not that it matters, but I'm Maggie Kincade."

"Nice to meet you." He nixed the idea of shaking hands with her. By the look in her eyes, it was clear the lady wasn't into the niceties of life at the moment. He didn't blame her. Financial difficulties had a way of changing a whole lot of things. He ought to know. "We have to come up with a way to get our money back."

She straightened an unruly curl and tucked it off her face. "The only way to get our money back is to find Sean."

"I agree. Have you been living here very long?"

She sighed in resignation. "Seven days."

"Did Sean get any mail that would help us?"

"Not unless you count bills."

"Was there a credit card statement among them? It might tell us where he is, maybe even the name of the hotel where he's staying."

She fired a suspicious glance in his direction. "Are you in the habit of going through other people's mail?"

"And did Sean leave you a key?" he asked.

She flushed and he knew the answer. "So, no credit card statement?"

"No."

"Too bad." Tom rubbed his jaw, trying to remember some of the places Sean might have gone.

Maggie looked at her watch and jumped up. "I have to get ready for work."

"Can we talk about Sean when you get back?"

She turned—her shoulders set, her amber eyes dark with determination. "I beg your pardon?"

"I said, I'll be here when you get back."

"We'll see about that." She spun out of the sunroom, and he heard a door close somewhere in the house.

From past experience, Tom knew his best strategy to get more information was to sit and wait her out. She was a redhead. She didn't want him here, which meant she'd be back to argue with him.

Tom looked the room over as he waited. On a wicker wall unit in the corner, he saw the ceramic cat Sean had always considered his good luck piece. He and Sean had been close friends once and it had been Tom's money that had helped Sean restart his business after his first run-in with gambling. He'd paid that back and borrowed again. But if Sean had taken Maggie's money the way she said, he'd changed. He and Maggie stood to lose all their money if they didn't come up with a plan to find Sean before he gambled it all away.

Maggie strode back into the room, her cheeks flushed. "You can't stay here."

"How do you plan to stop me?" he asked, keeping his tone neutral.

Her eyebrows snaked together. "I'll think of something."

"Take your time."

Giving her watch a quick glance, Maggie shifted her weight from one foot to the other. "You have to leave with me."

"If I do, I'll come right back in." He pointed at the patio doors. "I happen to know where Sean hides an extra key."

"You're bluffing."

Tom got up and walked over to the patio door, opened it and extracted a key from a hole over the middle of the door. "I'm not." He held the key out to her.

"I'll have that, if you don't mind." She attempted to grab the key.

He blocked her. "I do mind."

She was so close he could see the freckles on her nose and feel the warmth of her skin. "If you're willing to negotiate, we might be able to reach some sort of compromise."

"Yeah? Let me guess. I'll ask you to leave and you'll stay anyway."

"What would make you say a thing like that?"

Maggie scowled. "Past experience with men like you."

He didn't have to ask what she meant. Her eyes held more distrust than he'd seen in a long time. "You can trust me. This key will be given back to you tomorrow—if I'm allowed to stay here tonight."

He waited, knowing she was trying to decide if she could trust him—a stranger in the house. "I'm completely harmless. Edna trusts me, and Edna hasn't trusted very many people in her life. I got the condensed version of *Life According to Edna* after I met Galahad."

A smile started in Maggie's eyes, easing the tension in her face. "Edna loves to terrorize strangers with Galahad.

He can't really spray you. He was fixed years ago."

"Yeah, I found that out *after* I told her my life story. I can tell you my life story, if you'd like."

She flipped her hair off her shoulders and placed her hands on her hips. "You can get up close and personal with Edna all you want, but I'll pass on the offer. Besides, I don't have time for this right now. You can stay tonight, but only for tonight," she said over her shoulder as she headed down the hall.

"I accept your generous hospitality," he said to her retreating back as he followed right along behind her. The way her body glided ahead of him, lean and provocative, sent a rush of heat through him. "I'll keep the home fires burning while you're gone."

She stopped. He narrowly missed bumping into her.

Her light floral scent enticed him closer as she turned to face him. She was gorgeous. Long gold hoops dangled from her ears and the deep burgundy color on her lips brought out the golden flecks in her eyes.

Uncertainty, mixed with awareness, tinged her glance. He wanted to pull Maggie Kincade into his arms and begin his tried and true love 'em and leave 'em routine. It always worked. He was used to easy women and loved being around them.

Until he'd heard about his infant son, the son he'd met for the first time only a few weeks ago.

Maggie cleared her throat. "Yes…keep the home fires…burning."

"You bet," he whispered, resisting the urge to push his eager fingers into the mass of red curls caressing her shoulders.

She swallowed, took in a sharp little breath, while her

pulse fluttered in the soft skin of her neck. "Burning…
Oh…yes."

"Yes?" He raised one brow and waited.

Snapping her head back, Maggie blinked up at him. "No.
That's final."

With his whole body turned on and ready to go, he
watched her stride into the bedroom without so much as a
peek in his direction.

He listened hopefully, but all he could hear were
shuffling sounds and then a curse. Minutes later, she came
down the hall toward him, her hair a shimmering blond bob,
her body covered in tight black pants and shirt. "Is this your
disguise?" he asked, amazed at how different she looked in
the blond wig.

She tossed him a look. "Tom Rawlins, wipe that smirk
off your face. Unlike some people I could name, I work for
a living." Her voice held a hard edge that wasn't matched by
the look in her eyes.

He'd nearly scored. Her eyes said as much. "If you
change your mind, you know where to find me. I'll be
waiting."

Anger shot from her eyes, words hovered on her lips, but
she said nothing. Instead, she stepped around him, leaving
as much space as possible between them as she moved
down the hall.

"Think it over," he called to her as she strode away.

"In your dreams." She tossed the words over her
shoulder.

The slamming of the door echoed through the house.

# Chapter Two

Maggie gave her wig a warning yank as she stepped through the swinging doors of the bar. She had made it to work on time in spite of the last minute perils created by the soon-to-be-gone Tom Rawlins and the usual trouble with Bessie.

There had been a few minutes back on Hawthorne Street when she'd thought her old car wouldn't make it. Then the heap of scrap metal had heaved, sighed and sputtered back to life. The first few dollars she could spare were earmarked for repairs. She looked around and sighed. What she wouldn't give to drive north of town to her parents' house and see Jeremy for a few hours. She felt so guilty about leaving him there, but she had no choice for now.

Feeling out of sorts, she scanned the dimly lit restaurant area for Harry Washburn. After her maddening exchange with Tom this morning, she had business to discuss with Harry. She lifted the wooden gate that served as part of the counter of the bar and stepped through before lowering it back into place.

So Sean owed money to someone else and that someone was looking for Sean too. Good thing he didn't come here asking questions about Sean's whereabouts. No one was getting to Sean before she did. She wanted her money back, or the partnership Sean had promised.

That meant she had to act fast. She couldn't take a chance on Tom charming Harry into telling him where Sean was—and Tom getting whatever money Sean still had. Before that could happen, her number one job was to convince Harry to tell *her* where Sean had gone.

If she'd had more business experience and had been less trusting, she'd have made Sean give her the paperwork that proved she was part owner of his steakhouse. But she had trusted him and his charm.

She'd learned that lesson too late. But if her father found out about her poor business deal, one made with a gambler, he'd be shocked and disappointed with her, yet again. There wasn't much she could do about her mistake except do damage control and keep this a secret until she caught up with Sean.

The last thing she needed was another lecture on the lack of direction in her life, how she was wasting her time and not providing properly for Jeremy. Her father, a big name realtor around town, already thought her judgment was flawed when she insisted on raising Jeremy alone. But she'd had no choice about that. She wasn't about to marry again simply to give Jeremy a father. Besides, she and Jeremy had been doing just fine—until she'd lent her money to Sean. Still, it hurt that her father didn't think much of her parenting skills. But then he was hardly the poster parent for good parenting. She was proof of that.

Why did it matter so much to her that she prove herself to her father? Maybe she should have agreed to the cry-and-spew sessions with that high-priced child psychologist her parents had unearthed to deal with Maggie when she was a teenager. She hadn't, and for better or worse, her father and she were stuck with each other's behavior.

As for Harry, she believed he had to have some inkling where Sean had gone. After all, Harry claimed they were partners in this place… Maggie eyed the huge 'W' branded into the wood behind the bar. It was supposed to stand for Washburn, but it more likely stood for women—Harry's constant preoccupation. She reached for the coffee pot, for one quick swig before she tackled Harry.

Emmaline Barrett, wearing black pants stretched to the breaking point from far too many plates of home fries with gravy, came though the gate behind Maggie. "Where's Harry? I have to talk to him about somethin'."

Maggie tapped the counter as she scanned the bar area. "So do I."

"Talk to me about what?" Harry, his cowboy boots clomping over the floorboards of the restaurant area, plunked his clipboard on the wooden counter and swept both of them with a suspicious squint.

Emmaline tucked her frizzy, dyed-blond tresses behind her ears and grasped the draught beer dispenser for support. "My Ernie says I can't work here no more. He says I need more time with him. Him being on the road with his big rig an' all. He misses me. He says I don't get off on time."

Harry let loose a rattling sound from his throat that sounded like hail on a tin roof, and touched his nicotine-stained fingers to his gray sideburns. "Well, he sure knows how to pop back the beers while he waits for ya."

Emmaline's cheeks quivered. "I didn't come here for you to talk about my Ernie that way. I came here to tell you I'm through. I want the money you owe me."

Maggie rolled her eyes and rendered a silent groan. She knew what was coming. Harry turned his pinched-lipped look on her and said, "Maggie, honey, would you work until closing for me? Just for this evening, until I hire someone?"

Maggie let her glance slide to the fireplace where the old wagon wheel hung, and where a set of moose antlers festooned with threads of dust stuck out from the darkened brick.

Whatever had possessed her to think she wanted to own

a part of this sideshow that masqueraded as a business? "I've worked double shifts twice in the last five days. I don't think I can spare the time."

"Time?" Harry huffed. "When I hired you it was because you were looking for a job to *fill* your time. Waiting for lover boy." Harry got an odd gleam in his eye.

"Has something changed?"

Maggie bit her lip and changed her tack. "No, nothing like that. I—"

"Look, if it's more money, I'll see what I can do. Anyway, with you working alone and me on the bar, the whole tip thing is yours."

Maggie wasn't fooled by Harry. Monday's were always slow. Besides, all she wanted to do was to get her swollen feet home and soak them until they puckered. "I don't know, Harry. Emmaline and I both think you need to hire someone to—"

"You're so right, Maggie. Why, if we had someone to help us…" Emmaline opened the beer fridge and helped herself to a cola. "We'd have more time to hustle more beer." The fridge slapped closed behind her, accompanied by the cracking snap of the pop can lid. "After all, Harry, that's what you always told me you wanted."

Her cuddly tone reminded Maggie of the steamy stories the cook told about Harry and Emmaline and their lovemaking gymnastics in Harry's office. The thought of Harry in a steamy embrace, complete with bald spot and side burns, topped off by the ever-present cowboy boots…

Maggie shivered in revulsion.

Then the thought struck her. If she offered to do the shift, she might have a bargaining chip with Harry. Maybe she'd be able to convince him how important it was for her to find Sean. "Harry, I'll do the extra hours, on one condition."

Harry swiveled on the barstool and the few remaining hairs on the top of his head snapped to attention. "And that would be?"

"I need to talk to you about Sean."

"Agreed." Without missing a beat, Harry swiveled back to Emmaline. "You'll have the wages I owe you this afternoon." He glanced around the restaurant area, where the first lunch customers were threading their way through the tables to their favorite spots. "In the meantime, let's get moving."

Emmaline smiled smugly.

Maggie was more than a little distracted by two things: her pocketbook worries and the handsome stranger waiting back at Sean's house. But she knew Harry's tricks. If she didn't stop him, he'd clomp out to his office and lock the door. Things would get busy and his agreement to talk to her about Sean would be forgotten. "Just a minute, I'm not done."

"Hey, honey, what's the trouble?" Harry ducked under the gate and came into the back of the bar. "Are you still worried about Sean?" He gave her his patented lady-killer smile and the gold cap on his incisor winked.

"I want what I've always wanted, since the day I came here. I want to know where Sean is and when he's coming back."

Harry moved closer, and for a fraction of a second, she imagined him touching her phony blond wig and trying for a quick feel. She backed off and crossed her arms over her chest.

"I'd tell you if I knew. Believe me."

His cigarette breath quickened her desire to leap the bar and be gone. Leaping the bar was out of the question with the tight pants she had to wear to meet Harry's so-called dress code. Maggie moved back a little more, her legs bumping against a case of empties.

"Harry, you owe me one. I've stayed here and worked for the past few days as if my life depended on it."

"You must have it bad for old Sean." Harry grimaced and cocked one brow.

She had no intention of telling Harry why she needed to

talk to Sean. It was none of Harry's business. "I don't have anything for Sean, except what he's got coming to him when I find him."

Harry eyes widened; he looked her up and down. "Don't tell me… You're not in love with him are you?" Harry's expression softened. "Sean's broken a lot of hearts."

"For heaven's sake! Of course not!" Maggie's stare of disbelief bounced right off his shiny dome. "Just tell me where he is."

Harry sucked in his sagging stomach. "I don't know where Sean is. I'm sure he's gambling somewhere, and honey that's not good news. Sean's been on a losing streak lately and he's hooked on trying to end it." He gave the room a quick once-over. "Just be thankful that the partnership agreement I have with him doesn't allow him to sell his half without my permission, or we'd probably be staring at new owners, not one another."

Maggie saw the glint of sincerity in Harry's eyes. So he had a partnership agreement with Sean, and Harry hadn't heard from him, or heard about Sean's deal with Maggie. But if Sean wanted more gambling money, and saw Harry's Place as a source of funds, he'd have to come back. It would seem the only hope she had of finding Sean was sticking close to Harry. In the meantime, helping Harry might mean a little advanced warning when Sean finally returned. She'd needed to get to Sean first, which meant she needed Harry to tell her when he heard from Sean. "All right," she sighed. "I'll do your evening shift, but you have to promise to tell me as soon as you hear from him."

"Agreed."

An hour later, Tom surveyed the exterior of Harry's Place, Sean's steakhouse. Edna Cotter was right. The place had seen better days. Red shutters clung to weathered gray cedar shingles. The aged cedar roof had dark stains around the huge brick chimney. Old wagon wheels, bent and discolored, linked to form a walkway to the main entrance.

Sean hadn't put money into the exterior of the building, but Tom knew that didn't mean the business was in financial trouble.

Tom had been around a lot of businesses like this one. He knew the best way to learn about the profitability of the business, was to go in the back way and look around. Easing his Harley over to a small alcove formed by the dumpster and the back door, he turned off the engine.

He had promised himself a life away from places like this, a life that included a chance to get to know the baby he'd fathered, and to start a motorcycle business. He'd never considered children as part of his life, and his upbringing held little to recommend fatherhood. Yet, the day he'd met his infant son for the first time, his life had changed. From that moment on, he'd made his plan to be involved in his son's life and to help raise him.

When Sean had skipped out without paying him his money it had caused a delay in his plans. But he might make up for it, depending on how profitable Sean's business was. If it could pay Tom what was owed him, he'd wait around. If not, he'd cut his losses and try to borrow the rest of the cash he needed to start his business.

Tom eased open the back door, slid between the cartons of canned goods and moved into the hallway leading to the bar. Off to his left he could hear swearing and cursing, clear proof that the short order cook was being pushed to his limits. A busy kitchen meant a good volume of food orders, and if the cook was good at his job it meant a consistently large noontime crowd.

He stopped at the open door to the kitchen. The odor from deep fat fryers and pizza ovens wafted toward him. The order area looked clean and well organized. Near the back, he could see the beefy arms of the cook as he slid a knife through a BLT and maneuvered it onto a plate heaped with French fries. Things looked good which meant the cook took pride in his work.

Tom moved down the corridor to the saloon doors that opened into the bar. Tom walked in and settled on a bar stool to watch the activity. Any restaurant worth its salt did a brisk beer business at noontime. A paunchy man, who fit Sean's description of his partner, Harry Washburn, filled a continuous stream of beer glasses. Not bad.

Tom noted that the crowd was all in the dining area. That meant food *and* booze orders. There was hope for his loan.

Now, all he needed was a few minutes with Harry to see what the guy knew about Sean's whereabouts. Since the business seemed to be doing well, there was a chance Sean could repay the loan, which meant Tom would stick around at least for the time being. Until he figured out when Sean would be back, he planned to stay at his friend's house, whether Maggie Kincade liked it or not.

The thought of her was like a kick in the chest. He hoped she was just another pretty redhead. *That* he could handle. Yet the way she looked at him with that glimmer of uncertainty… He shook his head.

"Can I help you?" A man sporting side burns, and a paunch stood in front of him, blocking Tom's view of the restaurant area.

"Yeah, I'll have a Bud draft."

"Coming up." The man moved to cock a glass under the dispenser.

Tom got up and stood at the bar, his foot braced on the brass rail that ran around the lower perimeter. Smiling his thanks, he passed the bartender the money. "I'm looking for Harry Washburn."

"That's me," Harry said, his smile lifting his bushy side burns.

"I'm Tom Rawlins, a friend of Sean's."

"Half the world's a friend of Sean's these days." Harry

gave the counter a swipe with a damp cloth as he looked Tom over.

Tom didn't flinch. He was used to people looking him over. "Do you know where he is?"

"If I did I'd tell that one over there." Harry pointed in the general direction of a group of tables near the fireplace.

Tom scanned the area over the rim of his beer. A blond head bobbed into view behind a couple pulling on their coats. *Maggie.*

She was all business as she served a table of four men.

So this was where she worked. He was a little surprised. Given the classy way she looked and moved, he had expected to find her at a nightclub. But working here was smart thinking on her part. If she wanted to catch Sean, what better place than at his business?

And if Sean had dumped her, working here would allow Maggie to keep an eye on her investment and be close by when her man returned.

What was wrong with him? It didn't matter where Maggie worked, or whether she dated Sean. Why should he care? A relationship with her wasn't in Tom's plans.

Edna had called Harry's Place a saloon. He'd assumed it was her term for a bar, and didn't ask any more questions. After Maggie had left the house he'd gone out to get on his bike and headed over to Sean's restaurant. Edna had been drowning a cedar shrub with her hose. He'd asked her about Sean, and where he was. Lucky break that one of her cronies showed up, or he'd still be there fending off her questions about him, and his family—especially Maggie and Sean. Her questions had him scrambling to keep his story straight. He and Maggie would have to agree on what they told Edna from now on...

He glanced up at yet another wagon wheel—this one over

the fireplace—then back at the man watching him so intently. Harry obviously had a thing for wagon wheels, and most likely also had a well-tuned ear for gossip. In Tom's experience the man working the bar knew everything going on around him.

"So, Sean hasn't been around? I thought he owned the place."

"Part owner. What's your beef with Sean?" Harry rubbed his tongue over his front teeth as he glanced at Tom.

"I was just passing through and thought I'd look up my old buddy."

"Well, better luck next time." Harry fixed him with a hard stare.

Tom knew the message behind the look. Either order another beer or get lost. He ordered another beer and Harry rewarded him with a smile as he pushed the frosted glass across the counter at him. "Why don't you talk to Maggie Kincade? She's looking for Sean, too."

"Really?"

"Yeah, she's been working here for a few days now. She seems to have a thing for Sean. She asked me again today whether I've heard from him. I keep telling her to forget Sean until he tames the gambling beast, but she's determined to find him."

"Really? Do you suppose it's love or money?" Tom asked as he nonchalantly wiped the moisture off his glass.

Harry rested his arms on the bar across from Tom, a smile tucking the corners of his mouth into his cheeks. "Don't know. But the way Sean goes through women—"

"No need to explain."

"Sean attracts women like fleas to a dog," Harry continued, his gaze swinging from where Maggie stood, then back to Tom. "If this one thinks she's going to get her hooks into him in any permanent way, she'll have to take a number." Harry shook his head slowly. "Still, Maggie doesn't seem Sean's type."

Was there was a love interest mixed with a money interest where Maggie was concerned? Tom watched Maggie move with friendly ease from one table to the next. If Sean had gone after this redhead, his taste in women had improved.

"Here she comes now." Harry gave Tom a quick appraisal, his eyes sharp with interest.

A thought formed in Tom's mind, but he kept his expression neutral as he watched Maggie stride toward them.

He ducked behind the corner post and waited while she gave her order. He'd have to handle this just right, or there'd be hell to pay tonight when she got home.

Maggie strode toward the bar, a resolute look on her face. "Two Dubonnet with a twist of lemon. Four Coors draft."

As Tom listened to Maggie, he did a quick calculation. He could preserve the capital earmarked for his bike shop if he could get a job in Sean's place to pay his expenses while he was here. Taking a job here would make it possible for him to meet up with Sean when he returned. In the meantime, he'd have a chance to earn a little money and keep an eye on the competition. Not a difficult task from what he could see of her.

He strolled toward Maggie's end of the bar. Kicking his well-honed charm into high gear, he drawled, "Well, Maggie Kincade, you're a sight for sore eyes." His wide-angled smile met her look of stunned surprise.

Maggie stared up into Tom's handsome face, fighting to keep the flush from her cheeks. "You're not welcome here."

"Maggie Dearest, good to see you too."

"Whose bright idea was it to let you in here?" she demanded, her heart playing the bongo drums against her ribs.

"I'm getting to know the place."

"Well, kindly get to know some other place." She chewed the words out as she flicked a glance in Harry's direction. He was rooted to the spot, watching them.

Harry was entirely too curious about her life as it was. She didn't need him picking around her relationship with a biker, of all people. If the reading materials in the back room were any indication of Harry's sexual fantasies, he'd peg her as a member of the lash and leather club before the end of shift.

"This place looks pretty good to me," Tom drawled.

"Well, look again. This place is off limits as far as you're concerned." Tom's smart-assed smile set up a warming sensation in her chest while the scent of sizzling steak wafted down from her wig.

One of the flea brains at table six had tried to cop a feel while she was putting drinks on the table. She'd given him a clear get-lost message, but it left her wanting to even the score where womanizers were concerned. She wouldn't tolerate another male putting the moves on her.

"Nothing's off limits to me." Tom winked.

If the lecherous male, standing a few feet from her, moved so much as a finger in her direction…Tom Rawlins, with his cocksure smile and smart mouth was about to get a surprise. "So you think nothing's off limits to you? We'll see about that, won't we?" She winked right back.

There were no napkin-wrapped utensils on the counter in front of him so she knew Tom hadn't ordered anything more than beer, which was good. It meant he didn't plan to stay for lunch. Which meant that when she went after Tom the cat, Harry wouldn't lose any business.

And dammit, keeping Harry happy was important.

She moved closer to her target, her fists tight to her sides. As much as she wanted to deck him—and she could thanks to her karate lessons—she had to be careful. Drawing too much attention to herself wasn't a good idea. She planted a pleasant smile on her face and turned to Harry. "We sprayed for vermin just last week, didn't we?"

Harry snapped to attention. His gaze leapt to Tom. "You the health inspector?"

Tom moved along the bar, closer to Maggie and well within striking range. "Me? Not a chance," he said to Harry, his gaze locked on Maggie.

"I didn't think so. You don't look the type." Harry braced his hands on the counter as he spoke.

"Harry, would you excuse us for a moment? Tom and I have something to discuss."

"Not on your life. Conduct your personal business after the lunch trade is gone." Harry gave the tray an emphatic swipe and started reloading it.

"Harry's running a business, Maggie. You got to respect that. We both want Harry to succeed, don't we?"

The glint of satisfaction in Tom's eyes was almost more than Maggie could bear. The jukebox blared with Garth Brooks' *Friends in Low Places,* the rocking beat draining her patience.

"Get lost," she said as calmly as her temper would allow.

"Or what?"

She saw the challenge in his eyes and the way his gaze moved to her wig. Would he tell Harry she was wearing a wig? Or worse, would he pull it off her head? She couldn't allow Tom the opportunity to expose her red hair. As much as she wanted to get Tom off the premises, she had to control her temper or face embarrassing questions from Harry. She choked back a saucy retort that would have compared a horse's hindquarters to Tom quite well. "Why don't we talk about this tonight?" she asked, her voice sounding sickeningly sweet in her ears.

"Listen, you two. What you've got to discuss doesn't matter to me." Harry pointed his tobacco-stained finger at Tom. "You leave the poor girl alone."

He swung his gaze over to Maggie. "And you get back to your tables."

"I'm sorry, Harry. I was just trying to get this gentleman to leave. Believe me. You don't need the grief an unsavory character like this one can give you."

"By the look on your face a few minutes ago, I'd say he's pretty savory to you."

"Hardly. He's nothing but a nuisance, trust me." There were a whole lot of things she could have said on the subject of Tom Rawlins, but for now all she wanted to do was finish her damned shift and go soak her feet.

"Maybe I can help." Tom's face lacked expression as he turned to Harry, a move that planted seeds of suspicion in Maggie's mind.

Harry finished refilling Maggie's liquor order. "I'm listening."

"You look like you're pretty busy here. I have waiter experience. If you need help…"

Harry rubbed his bald spot. "As a matter of fact, I do. One of the girls just quit."

Maggie's panicked breath caught in her throat. Clutching the edge of the counter for support, she looked up into Tom's face. "A job? You don't need a job. Not here."

She saw the winning gleam in Tom's eyes and knew she had no choice but to take action. She eased closer, her body tense.

He leaned toward her. "A fella's got to eat."

She lifted her chin and aimed her words carefully. "A fella has to watch himself… If you get my drift."

"I'm shaking all over." He tossed the words at her as he leaned even closer.

If she didn't soon stop him, he'd be staring down into her cleavage—or what passed for cleavage. "You'd better be." At that instant she realized that while she was telling him to get out of town, her hormones were begging her to say something different. *Dang.*

"Maggie, you're flustered." His tone was velvet.

"I am not." Her pulse kicked up a few notches. His ever-ready sex appeal was just another reason to see his rear end swaggering out the door. "I want you out of here, not working here. That's all."

She ached to see the look on his face when his ass connected with the floor. She eased forward on to the balls of her feet.

His hand closed over hers. "All your self-defense classes are wasted on me. I know the move you're about to make."

"And what move would that be?"

His fingers caressed hers. "The one where I land on my butt." He pulled her to him, his lips moving dangerously close to hers.

A rush of heat roared through Maggie. She sucked in her breath.

His jaw angled outward and his cool determination rippled the air between them. "Don't even think about it.

You make one move to introduce my butt to the floor and I'd gladly take you down with me. And if I do, you'll be a changed woman when I let you back up."

His words tangled themselves in the fake strands of her hair. Her knees started a slow trembling dance. She wiggled her fingers free of his, placed both her hands squarely on his chest, and said, "If I wanted you on your ass—"

"Admit it. You don't want me on my ass, you want to *see* my ass." He curled her fingers into the palm of his hand and tucked them against his chest.

"Of all the—"

"Maggie, that's enough. Get back to work." Harry pushed the tray of drinks toward her. Many of the patrons stared at the two of them, mesmerized. Maggie was certain Harry would kick Tom out now.

"And you..." Harry glanced at Tom. "How soon can you start?"

"How about tomorrow?" His words dripped satisfaction as Tom gently massaged Maggie's fingers.

"Harry!" Maggie struggled, without success, to free her hands from Tom's encircling grip while she tried to understand what was going on. She had never met a man who made her feel so vulnerable, and at the same time so excited. She had to curb that excitement or Tom would get the upper hand. In desperation she aimed an icy stare at Harry, hoping he'd see reason. "You can't be serious!"

"Well, Maggie, I had a hard enough time getting you to take Emmaline's work hours this evening." Harry had a pleased expression on his face as he surveyed his new employee. "Tom here, will do nicely for tomorrow evening. Tuesday night is the beginning of the busy part of the week for me. And I've got several busloads coming through this weekend and next. Early Christmas shoppers, don't ya know?"

"I'm glad to be of service," Tom said, a mocking lilt in his voice as his gaze ran the gamut from Maggie's hair to her lips.

"And I see you're the kind of guy who will have the women drooling." Harry rubbed his hands together. "The more ladies, the merrier."

Maggie wanted to slap the smug expression off Harry's face, but first she had to pry her hands free from Tom's. When she saw the good-old-boy look that passed between Tom and Harry, her stomach rolled in protest. She knew she was fighting a losing battle but couldn't give up. Maggie pulled her fingers free of Tom's grip and reached across the bar to Harry. "Harry, you don't need him."

"Maggie, I realize you haven't been a waitress very long, but in this business you need every advantage. In my experience, sex appeal sells beer. From the looks on those women's faces, Tom has sex appeal," Harry said, his jaw doing double time on a toothpick, as he scanned a table seating six women.

She smoothed her hands over the surface of the bar and tried to dissuade him one more time. "Harry, if you want sex appeal, why not hire a beautiful woman?" *As if any beautiful woman in her right mind would work here with Harry leering at them.*

Harry tucked his chin in and gave her an all-business

glance. "What this place needs is a chick magnet. You know, the kind of man women fall for instantly. Like him."

"*Tom?* You think *he's* a chick magnet?" She heard Tom's throaty chuckle and wanted to kick him.

"I sure do. The way you snuggled up to him a moment ago convinced me. You never snuggle up to anyone here. If he can attract you, he's the man for the job."

Maggie slumped against the bar. Why didn't she see his stupid logic coming? Harry thought she was attracted to Tom. Harry was wrong. What she felt for Tom Rawlins was a lot more powerful than attraction. A lot more. She lunged straight at Tom, her fingers locking onto his shirtfront.

Tom held her wrists tightly in his hand. "I love a woman who knows what she wants."

"And of course every woman would want a chick magnet like you." She dumped as much scorn into her words as she could muster.

She was caught in his grip while his muscular chest vibrated with laughter beneath her fingers.

"And especially the lengths a woman like you would go to when she wants to get close to me," Tom taunted.

Righteous indignation evaporated. Old-fashioned lust swirled in to fill the void. More than her hands were held captive by his body. The urge to melt into his embrace had her scrambling for control. "You think I—"

"Of course you do. You're giving off all the signals. You should be thankful I'm a gentleman." He let go of her as quickly as he had grabbed her.

"A gentleman!" she sputtered. She grasped the edge of the bar for support as her mind spun through her ready retorts, looking for the one that fit a situation like this. None came to mind. Except a string of profanities that would have Harry yelling at her to go wash her mouth out. "If you don't mind, I'd like you to leave," she muttered through clenched teeth.

Moving closer, Tom placed his body squarely along the

length of Maggie's, his hip nudging hers. "Why? We're going to be working together."

Maggie fought down the urge to scream in frustration as Tom extended his hand across the bar. "If the offer's still open—"

Harry shook his hand gleefully. "Welcome to the staff of Harry's Place."

# Chapter Three

The fury in Maggie's molten glance gave him fair warning. She was definitely too hot to touch, the burning ache in his arms from holding her was proof of that. Working with Maggie would be like playing with fire on a hot summer night.

The cool taste of the beer soothed him, but did nothing to ease the electricity snapping through him. Based on Maggie's anger, things looked promising. She was extremely territorial where Sean was concerned, which meant only one thing. She expected Sean to walk through the door any day now.

Tom definitely planned to stick around, for the same reason. And if he planned to stay around, he needed a place to live. When Maggie cooled off a bit they'd come to some agreement about Sean's house. With any luck, he'd have a ringside seat to watch Maggie, and be there when Sean drifted back. In the meantime, he'd keep his ear to the ground.

Sooner or later, someone inside the walls of Harry's Place had to hear from Sean. By the look of things, the man holding out his hand would be the first person to know. Tom smiled and shook hands. "Harry, I'm glad to be here."

Harry pawed his chin. "Handsome and friendly. You're just what this place needs to liven it up."

"What this place needs?" Maggie choked.

"Run along, Maggie. You got customers to look after. Me and Tom got business to discuss."

Tom heard Maggie mutter something distinctly uncomplimentary about Harry as she moved off toward the tables carrying her tray loaded with drinks. Every rigid line of her body echoed her contempt, and seeing Maggie this way, Tom couldn't keep the smile off his face. "Quite a woman."

"You can have her. I don't see the point in fighting the likes of her to the ground when there are so many other women out there ready to appreciate a man. I remember someone pretty special…years ago…looked a little bit like Maggie." He sighed. "Maggie may be pretty, but—"

Tom pulled his gaze away from Maggie and back to Harry. "You want me here tomorrow at four, right?"

"Yeah," Harry sighed as he chewed his toothpick. "You say you've waited tables before? Can I ask where?"

Tom had no intention of divulging anything he didn't have to, but some sort of answer was necessary. "I worked at a club up in Syracuse."

"That right? A joint like this or something bigger?"

"Bigger. I've been in the business, off and on, for years."

"Well, I have to say I'm pleased to have you. Qualified help is hard to find."

Tom was only half listening as he watched the noontime crowd. All it would take was a little advertising and probably a few menu changes, and the place could be bringing in decent money. But that increase in business would take time, time he didn't have, if he wanted to get his bike shop up and running.

Tom caught Harry's questioning gaze, wondering what else could be on the man's mind.

"You work out?" Harry asked.

The question took Tom by surprise. "Yeah. I lift weights when I can."

"What we need around here is a guy who can show a little muscle to the ladies. You know. Get them excited. You game?"

Tom gritted his teeth. He hadn't left his old job and driven hundreds of miles to turn around and do the same type of work here. "I don't think so." He saw the look of suspicion in Harry's eyes and struggled to come up with a reason why he couldn't flaunt himself to the clientele. "It's against my principles."

"Principles?" Harry gaped and the toothpick dangled from his lower lip. "You a religious nut, or somethin'?"

"No, I just like to keep my clothes on."

Harry steadied the toothpick. "Didn't mean to imply anything, just wondering."

Tom never intended to tell anyone that he'd been a member of a male stripper group. That part of his life was over. "That's okay. No harm done."

Harry peered at Tom's half-finished beer. "You don't have any problem with alcohol, do ya?"

"I like the occasional beer. That's about it."

Harry blew air out between his teeth. "Whew! For a moment, I thought I'd picked the wrong guy for the job."

Tom toyed with his beer glass. If he had the money, he'd tell Harry to take a hike. But ready cash would mean he could afford to stay put and wait for Sean. "No, Harry. You got the right man for the job. I can pack the place with paying customers. You won't regret hiring me."

"Well, then I have the perfect idea. We'll dress you up in something sexy. The women will fill the till to show their appreciation of some of your finer assets." Harry gave a snort of excitement as he picked a toothpick from the jar and twisted it into the corner of his mouth. "Yes. Tight jeans, white shirt open down the front. He squinted up at Tom. "Michael Bublé." He nodded, pleased with his idea. "You'll look just like Michael Bublé."

"Who looks like Michael Bublé?" Maggie asked as she

approached the bar, not paying one iota of attention to Tom.

"Tom here. He's going to dress up all in black with a white shirt. The women will love it." Harry turned toward another customer who had just arrived at the bar.

"I'll just bet." Maggie gave Tom a sly smile. "I know a couple of regulars who've been waiting for someone just like you. One of them runs a boarding house. Maybe you can do a little barter…sort of tit for tat."

Tom didn't like the look in Maggie's eyes or what she implied. She intended to put him out of Sean's house, which made him all the more determined to stay. And splitting expenses with Maggie would be cheaper than looking elsewhere, and a hell of a lot more fun than staying in some dilapidated boarding house. "I like my living arrangements fine just as they are."

Showing only a mild interest in the barbs flying past him, Harry interjected. "Let's see. Do you have black cowboy boots?" he asked as he bent over to check the lines on the draught beer dispenser.

Maggie rested her elbows on the bar and grinned at Tom as she tapped her fingers on the glossy surface. "Sean has several pairs. I'm sure one of them will fit. I'll trade you one pair of cowboy boots for one not-so-fond farewell."

"No deal, Doll," Tom said, and watched with glee as his term of endearment had the desired effect.

"Don't 'doll' me," she fumed.

Tom smiled in spite of himself. The lady was strong willed as well as sexy. And if there was one thing in life he loved, it was a good sparring match with a beautiful woman. "I'm going to enjoy every minute of this."

"Of what?"

"Our time together. You and me." He gave her a grin designed to make her knees quiver. "You're going to enjoy living with me."

"Well, you'd better get your armor on. You're going to

need it just to survive tonight. By tomorrow, you'll be history." Maggie, a pink glow in her cheeks, touched her fingers to her wig as she stepped back from the bar.

"Like I said, I like my new living arrangements at Sean's just fine."

"You don't *have* any living arrangements there. And that's not going to change." Maggie's eyes narrowed to beady slits as she pushed the words in his direction.

Maggie looked as if she wanted to punch him. Tom moved nearer the other end of the bar. "We'll see about that."

"No we won't. I'm having the locks changed tomorrow." With that, she marched off toward her tables.

The wig squeezed her head like a vice. The smell of French fries clung to her blond wig as Maggie stomped up the steps to Sean's back door, her legs and back heavy with exhaustion. It had been a long day, but she earned enough in tips to be able to fix her old car.

The only thing that had kept her going for the last couple of hours was the notion that she would set Tom straight about a few things. First of all, working with him would be tricky, given that he knew about her wig. She'd have to convince him to keep quiet about it. No one knew she had red hair, and she had to make sure her secret remained safe. Her red hair was a Kincade trait, and the one thing about her that seemed to please her father—mostly, she suspected, because she looked like him, and his father's father, to whom he'd been devoted. Her father was well known around town, and if she hadn't worn a wig to cover her hair, someone would have recognized her and reported to him.

She'd seen a couple of her father's real estate agents having lunch today. They didn't recognize her, but she couldn't risk anyone carrying tales back to him about a familiar-looking redhead working at Harry's.

Now, on top of all her other worries, there was Tom under her roof. His plan to stay at the house had to be nipped in the bud. There was no way in the world she could tolerate him underfoot all the time. His arrogance she could handle, but the effect of his blatant sexuality on her was an entirely different problem. Made her think all the work she'd done on that area of her life had just gone down the drain.

Then there was her father and his nagging questions about the big job she pretended to have. When he learned the truth about what she was doing with her life while he and her mom kept Jeremy…

She could hear him now. From his perfectly ordered office, with his picture-perfect secretary looking on, her father would remind her about the pitfalls of investing without a proper investment counselor—meaning she should have sought his advice, of course.

Her father's disappointment, if he found out that she was waiting tables at Harry's Place, would not make things any better between them. She and her father had never gotten along, mostly because he wanted to run her life—every aspect, from who she dated to what kind of job she worked. When he had started pestering her to come to work with him in his real estate business, she knew she had to do something to establish her financial and social independence.

From the safety of her banking job in Boston, Sean O'Toole had seemed like the perfect investment partner. She hadn't bothered to check out his personal habits, mostly because, yet again, she had been attracted to a no-good bum. And fooled by what she thought she saw in him. What had looked like her ticket to financial freedom had turned into a rip off by a con man who'd used her eagerness and her money, to his advantage.

All that would change the minute she set eyes on the miserable scoundrel. And no one was going to get in the way of her being first to find Sean and get her money back, including the hunk lurking inside Sean's house. She turned the key in the back door and walked in, pulling off her wig and shaking out her curls.

The blast of a football game greeted her as she closed the door and dropped her bag on the floor. She headed toward the fridge for an iced tea. The kitchen was cluttered with unwashed dishes and Tom's leather jacket dangled over the chair near the door. Fuming, she grabbed his jacket and strode to the den, determined to set him straight before she threw him out.

Clutching his jacket like a shield, she entered the den, her head filled with arguments the lazy slob couldn't talk his way out of.

She found him lying there, nestled into the couch, his feathery black lashes dusting his cheeks in a most provocative way. His shirt lay open, exposing his smooth, tanned skin. The day-old growth of beard gave him a rakish appearance.

Asleep, his expression held a vulnerability that tempted her even more than his sexiness. Enticed by the picture before her, she tiptoed into the room and stood over him.

Should she wake him? Having him disoriented from sleep would give her an advantage she hadn't expected. After all, who could argue effectively when awakened from a dead sleep? And the man sprawled on the couch was definitely asleep. Edging the remote from his fingers, she shut off the TV.

Welcome silence surrounded them as Maggie crouched beside Tom and waited for him to stir. The warm maleness of him drifted over her like a silken scarf. His arm was stretched out over the edge of the sofa, inviting her closer.

Attraction warred with practicality. Should she shake him awake and say what she'd come to say? Or should she…

He shifted on the sofa, his arm touching her shoulder. She jumped back. What was she thinking? The man lying so sweetly asleep was an interloper, one who could interfere with her plans. "Wake up," she hissed in his ear.

"What?" he demanded as his eyes sprung open. In a panicked state he gripped her shoulders and sat up, pulling her against him.

"Hey! Take it easy," she said. She saw the anxiety in his sleepy expression turn to appreciation, then humor as he held her captive.

"You missed me so much you're hugging my jacket?" His attentive smile bathed her in a warm glow that spread awareness through her. She couldn't resist looking into his eyes, eyes that seemed to reach deep inside her, making her want him in a way that confused her. He was so close, so touchable and so damned sexy.

Suddenly, everything was more complicated.

She struggled to make light of the moment. Better that, than to expose the attraction bubbling through her. "You're a messy house guest." She heard the shakiness in her voice, but was powerless to do anything about it.

"I plan to rectify that..." he said. "The messy part at least."

"See that you do," she said, putting all the disdain she could command into her voice.

He moved his hands up into her hair, pulling a red strand forward. "I love red hair," he whispered, his voice low, suggestive.

"Just keep your hands off mine." Searching for a safe place for her gaze, Maggie studied his shoulder and tried to shift away.

"How Maggie? How do I keep my hands off your glorious hair?" His lips were achingly close to hers as his words wrapped around her.

"By putting one hand over the other on your chest, for starters." Despite the tremor sliding through her, she enunciated her words carefully.

"Oh, Maggie," he crooned.

She waited while she imagined what his lips would taste like. His eyes searched hers, exposing her need, trapping the air in her lungs. For a few seconds his gaze hesitated before moving down her face to her lips. She could feel the heat of his skin as he inched closer.

"I've wanted to do this since the first moment I saw you through the patio doors," he whispered. Then his lips touched hers, lightly, coaxing her for more.

Her mind swung in a beautiful, whirling kaleidoscope as she gave in to the delight of his kiss. His tongue slid over her lips, inviting her. Lost in the moment, she strained closer, wanting more of him. More of the man who could use his sexual power to create havoc in her life—if she let him. He'd already forced her to do things she didn't normally do, made her wish she didn't have so many responsibilities.

Then the thought of her son, living at her parents' house while she risked everything by being near Tom, snapped her out of her reverie.

She gasped; raw panic rose in her throat. What was she doing, kissing the enemy? And liking it, like a silly schoolgirl! "What do you think you're doing?" She pulled her lips from his.

"Not creating a Hallmark moment if your reaction is any measure," he said, releasing her.

She rubbed her lips with the back of her hand and moved to get out of the reach of this impossible man. "What were you trying to do?"

He shrugged as he sat up and made room for her on the sofa. "You startled me and I ran on impulse."

Her cheeks burned as she pointed an accusing finger. "Or maybe you intentionally tried to seduce me to get me to let you stay here."

He grabbed the hand that supported the wagging finger and gently pulled. "I did no such thing. I was fast asleep when you threw yourself at me."

"In your over-sexed imagination!" She yanked her hand away.

The corners of his lips tipped up into an engaging smile. "Confession time, Maggie. You liked it as much as I did."

"I did not!" She fought down the drumming in her chest as she stepped out of his reach. "I came in here to talk to you and found you sleeping."

"And what did you want to talk about?"

"We need an agreement between us, if we're going to work together."

"That should be easy," he drawled. "We're both professionals. Besides Harry's given me the evening shift. And you work mostly days, don't you?"

"Yes."

"Then, that's solved. Anytime you're faced with an evening shift, you can trade with one of the other girls. Will that work until Sean returns and we speak with him?"

Would Tom make a valuable ally at work? He might, if Harry went through with what he was talking about for the waitresses, especially the skimpy outfits he'd been hinting at. Tom seemed to be able to handle Harry—a valuable quality she might need to call upon. "If you agree to support me where Harry's concerned."

"You don't have to worry about Harry. He likes you. I think you remind him of someone Maggie…"

"I can't imagine who. Besides, Harry likes his wallet more than anything."

"Let's not worry about Harry, for the time being. What's important is that we work out a way for us to share Sean's house."

Maggie clenched her fists to her sides. "There's no living in Sean's house for you. Nothing's changed. I want you out of here tomorrow."

"We don't always get what we want, Maggie." His smile slid over her like a soft breeze on a summer day.

How could he seem so arrogant one minute, and so appealing the next? Was he playing her? If she wasn't careful she could end up making a fool of herself. Heaven knew she'd had lots of experience in that department. To ease the jackhammer at work in her chest, Maggie took a deep breath. "In this case, I will. I'll have what I want, when I want it."

"Okay, let me say my piece and then we can fight. I need a place to stay until Sean comes back. I'm willing to share expenses with you. I'll stay out of your way as much as I can." He ran his hands through his black hair, concern turning down the corners of his lips as he glanced up at her. "It would make life easier for both of us."

Living with someone who could turn her on at the flick of an eyelash could never be described as easy. Especially when they both wanted the same thing where Sean was concerned. Maggie needed to be repaid and was first in line, yet Tom seemed to believe he should stand alongside her in that line. Lessen her chances.

Maggie took another deep breath to steady her nerves. The whole idea of sharing space with him was fraught with difficulties, but if something could be worked out, it would ease her financial responsibilities. That would mean more money for Jeremy's Christmas presents.

She would certainly have to find a way to avoid any contact with Tom, given the way she'd behaved tonight. "I might consider it. But only for that reason. What did you have in mind?"

"We both do housework—"

"Not if what I saw in the kitchen is your idea of housework."

"No, it's not. Normally I'm not a slob, but tonight I plead exhaustion. I'm willing to do my share of the work around here, and pay half of the expenses."

"Do you cook?" She was softening to the idea.

"Like a dream," he said as he rose from the sofa, bringing his well-muscled torso within easy reach of her zealous fingers.

Working on a sarcastic response, she eyed him, her

resistance slipping away like the falling tide. How would she survive living in the same space as this man? He was devastatingly attractive. She didn't need a relationship at the moment. And he wasn't offering one anyway. Her life had too many niggling complications, starting with the dear little four-year-old at her parents' house. Maybe… No, Tom Rawlins would win every argument because of his appeal.

"This won't work."

"Why not?" He turned the full force of his searching gaze on her.

She fought to control the tremor of excitement rising through her body from that look. "Because you and I need separate spaces."

He glanced around the room. "What about this? You and I will have separate bedrooms and share the bathroom. You have the sunroom. I have this den. We will be working different shifts, so we won't bump into one another around here."

If she could survive his half-naked body passing her bedroom on the way to the bathroom, without jumping him, it might work.

What was she thinking? Of course she could resist temptation…if she tried. Besides, she had three of the best reasons in the world to make it work—her son, the money Sean owed her, and the fridge standing nearly empty in the kitchen. "What can I say? You win. And now, if you don't mind, I'm going to take a long soak in the tub while you put the kitchen back the way you found it."

He gave her a quick salute and a lopsided grin. "I'll go clean up the dishes."

She watched him move with catlike grace toward the kitchen and wondered just how long she'd be able to resist him, knowing that something as flimsy as a wall would be the only thing separating them.

Yet, what was even more dangerous was the way he made her feel special, and his willingness to help around the house was more than appealing. She'd never known a man who helped out around the house. Sure, Tom had reason to ingratiate himself with her, but something she couldn't identify suggested that he might turn out to be a friend. If she gave him a chance. Should she let her guard down just a little bit and see what happens?

But then again, she'd learned from her ex, Mac Evans, that men like Mac and Tom enjoyed chasing women. They loved the chase but lived in fear of being caught by a clingy female. She wasn't a clingy female, but she needed to keep her options open where Tom was concerned. After all, Mac hadn't played fair, Sean hadn't played fair, and a little housework on Tom's part didn't prove that he'd play fair either.

She had a lot to think about, but it wouldn't hurt to consider making a plan that she could use to get Tom out of her life, her insurance against his charming ways, should she need it.

Whatever she decided to do, it was essential that she keep her plan a secret. Tom, with his overgrown ego, would expect her to find his charm irresistible, and that expectation could form the basis of her plan.

What if Tom were faced with living under the same roof with a clingy woman looking for a permanent relationship? She rubbed her hands together, her mind turning over the possibilities.

With just a little effort on her part, Tom Rawlins might not be staying with her while he waited for Sean's return.

# Chapter Four

—⟶ ◇ ⟵—

Early the next morning, the cool fall air rushing over Maggie made her shiver as she climbed out of her rust heap and scurried toward Harry's. She had the early morning shift today. A lack of sleep fouled her mind as she ducked in the back door and moved along the corridor toward the bar. As she passed the kitchen, the aroma of frying bacon and fresh muffins made her stomach growl.

She plucked the coffee pot from the burner and poured a full cup. Closing her eyes, she let the memory of last night have its way. Without even trying she could still feel Tom's lips on hers, the tug of his hand as he pulled her toward the sofa.

This morning her number one priority was keeping away from Tom until she had her plan in place. She'd worked on it last night during her long soak in the tub. And one issue stood out. The only way her plan would work was if she could maintain control of her emotions and her hormones during any contact she had with the man. Another thing was clear. She'd have to juggle her search for Sean with her need to avoid Tom. Meanwhile, she'd work on possible scenarios that involved using Tom's belief that he was irresistible to her advantage.

Relieved to be at Harry's Place and away from Tom's

charms, Maggie glanced around the empty restaurant. The early breakfast crowd would be streaming in any minute. Maggie wanted to be ready. Keeping busy would keep her mind off Jeremy and how lonely she felt waking up in the morning without her son.

She grabbed a package of napkins and proceeded to refill the napkin holders at each table. They had changed the red-checkered tablecloths last evening so refilling the salt and pepper mills was the last task she needed to do before opening. Maggie moved from table to table anxious to be ready for the patrons. For once, she welcomed the bustle and noise that would fill the restaurant when Harry's Place opened.

She finished up and went back to the bar for a second cup of brew and to check her makeup. She gave her face a careful glance in the tiny mirror at the back of the bar. As she was about to powder the band of freckles on her nose, she heard Harry come into the bar.

"Well, good morning," he said, his gold capped teeth twinkling in the low light of the bar area. "It's been quite a day already and it's not over yet," he said, smiling gleefully.

Maggie had learned from experience that when Harry was happy it was time to get out the worry beads. Her scalp began to sweat under the glossy wig. What was Harry up to that made him so pleased with life this early in the day? She turned and gave him the once-over. Everything seemed normal, or as normal as they could be with Harry. "Is that so?" Maggie asked.

Harry hit the switch that lit the Bud Light sign over the bar. "That's so." Harry began to hum Rudolph the Red-Nosed Reindeer.

Maggie heard the gate lift on the bar.

"Hi folks," Emmaline squeaked.

"What are you doing here?" Maggie asked, afraid she already knew the answer.

"I'm back at work," Emmaline whimpered, as giant tears

tracked down her cheeks. "Ernie took off in the rig with some snotty bitch. They've left town for good." Emmaline leaned her arms on the bar, her lower lip trembling like a hyperactive volcano.

Trying to offer comfort, Maggie patted her shoulder. "You'll be all right. I'm sure." Maggie couldn't think of much else to say. As far as she was concerned Ernie had been a dud from the beginning, but there was no explanation for some women's taste in men.

"You don't understand. No one understands what I'm going through."

"There, there." She soothed Emmaline with as much sympathy as she could drum up so early in the morning.

Emmaline straightened. "It's so good of you to be so understanding an' all. I thought you might be upset."

"Upset? About what?"

Emmaline wiped her cheeks and sniffed. "Harry gave me my old job back, didn't you Harry?" Emmaline smiled as she glanced past Maggie.

Suspicion snaked up Maggie's spine along with foreboding. Maggie smoothed her fake locks and peered at Harry. "That was very good of you, Harry. Exactly which job did you give her?"

Harry eyed the breakfast plate the cook had just delivered to him, heaped with home fries, bacon and eggs. He fiddled with his fork and knife as he spoke into the plate. "Yeah, Emmaline will be working days because I've decided to put you on evenings."

Maggie's stomach plummeted. "Evenings? With Tom Rawlins?"

"Yeah," he gave her a watery smile. "You two look good together. And since you know one another, I thought you might enjoy working the same shifts."

Maggie squashed the urge to yell and scream, to bang her head on the beer dispenser and backhand Harry's head into the cooler. Jail was marginally less appealing than working evenings with Tom. Working with Tom was the last thing on earth she wanted—if she hoped to maintain her sanity. She had to change Harry's simple mind…or die trying.

Searching for a way to start, she moved closer to Harry and leaned over the bar. For a few seconds she'd been tempted to show more cleavage, but nixed the idea. More cleavage she didn't have, and what she did have was already being enthusiastically promoted by her push up bra.

"That's kind of you to think of Emmaline's needs, but what about her lonely evenings, alone without Ernie?" She tried to sound helpful and caring.

Emmaline's renewed sobs, rising in the background, made Maggie feel just the tiniest bit guilty, but Emmaline's feelings were not her top priority. She had to find a way out of working the same shift with Tom.

"Don't you think it might be better if she worked with Tom? You said yourself he has a way with the women. He'd be just what Emmaline needs to get over Ernie. And we do want Emmaline to get over Ernie, don't we Harry?"

Harry stopped the fork destined for his mouth, in midair. "Tom and Emmaline?" He pitched the forkful into his mouth and chewed as he scowled at Maggie.

Pressing her advantage, Maggie murmured soothingly, "Think about it. Tom is very good with the women. He'd do Emmaline a lot of good. Lift her spirits with his sweet teasing."

Fat good Tom Rawlins would do any woman. But Tom's lover-boy ways might be the answer to Emmaline's love-lost state of mind. Truth to tell, Maggie didn't really care who Tom worked with as long as he wasn't working with her.

"Think of it this way, Harry. You'd be giving two lonely people a chance to start over."

Harry chewed slowly and stared at her, then moved his gaze to some point beyond Maggie's head.

Gosh! What was taking him so long? Was he remembering a long lost love? Had Harry ever had a long lost love? She desperately hoped so if it meant he'd see her point of view.

Harry gave his head a vigorous shake. "No. No. That wasn't what I had in mind at all. You missed the point completely. I'm not surprised, given how distracted you've been lately. I saw the chemistry between you and Tom. It's the kind of chemistry that makes money for a place like this."

"Chemistry?" Maggie shook her head right back at him. "No, Harry. I swear there's no chemistry. No. Never."

Ignoring her, Harry rubbed the end of his nose. "This Michael Bublé thing is going to pay big time. I can feel it. And it will add so much more if one of the waitresses is attracted to Tom. We could have a regular evening soap opera going on right here in the restaurant. We could even have one of those bachelor and bachelorette contests." He rubbed the end of his nose some more. "Yeah, that would really work. You can't beat sex appeal for making money. Always said that was the answer. Sean didn't believe me, but I'm going to show him."

"Well, then, let Emmaline be the one playing opposite Tom in your little soap opera." Maggie struggled to hold her voice even and perfectly reasonable when all she wanted to do was scream, tear the sweaty wig off her head and scramble out the door—never to return.

Harry pointed his fork at Maggie. "I've had time to think about the best way to package the two of you. I also have a few ideas about how we can spruce up your costume. In another couple of weeks it will be Christmas, and with Tom looking like Michael, I'd like you wearing something a little more interesting…maybe a red halter-top."

She'd wear a red halter-top when Harry's hair grew back. "Harry, we've been over this whole issue. I don't need to change what I'm wearing, and Tom and I barely know each other. We're certainly not attracted to each other." She hoped she didn't blush and expose her lie.

He rubbed his palms together, his enthusiasm bubbling over into his words. "Nonsense! With the way you two exchange heated looks you'll be a big hit."

"Heated looks, my foot! What's gotten into you, Harry? Can't you see what Tom's up to? He's not the least bit interested me, or in this place," Maggie huffed, knowing by the gleam in Harry's eye that he hadn't heard a word she'd said.

"Never mind fussing. You and Tom will make a big hit with the patrons. I may even buy some TV spots during the hockey games to advertise your act."

"TV spots! Our *act!* You're kidding!" Her father never missed a televised hockey game. If he recognized her...

"No, I'm not. Now, hear me out. We can pack 'em in if we can get the sports crowd coming here during weeknights, instead of heading downtown."

"What is going on with you, Harry?" Maggie asked, exasperated by the new turn of events. Her chance to save her investment and keep her deal with Sean a secret was out the window if her father found out about her life.

Harry waved her to be quiet. "All you have to do is loosen up a bit. Play up to Tom. After all, Michael Bublé has women falling all over him. It's only right that my Michael look-a-like should have women falling all over him."

"Your look-a-like is a low life of the worst kind. A complete cad—"

Harry sucked on his toothpick, making a thoroughly disgusting sound. "Now, Maggie. I realize you have a few hang-ups where men and sex are concerned."

"*What?*"

"You know what I'm talking about here. You never have a date. You rebuff any man who's interested. I've had to explain your behavior to several of our better clients, and God knows I struggle to come up with an answer, other than that obvious one."

"And that would be?"

"That you're one of those." He wiggled his eyebrows and sniffed.

"One of those what?" Seeing the look in Harry's eyes, Maggie knew exactly what he was getting at. "Harry, this is the twenty-first century. Time you changed your attitude."

"What do you say, Maggie? Are you game to be Tom's partner on the evening shift?" he asked as if he hadn't heard her.

Scowling, she stared at the Budweiser sign as she reviewed her options. The news wasn't good. Somehow, sometime soon, Maggie had to get a grip on things. Until then, a smart woman would play along until she saw a chance to get rid of Tom. Opportunity was her only ally at the moment.

Maggie managed to finish her day shift, then faced off with Tom the following evening. They worked hard and were both exhausted after their long shift. He'd recovered quickly and by the weekend, Tom was parading around Harry's Place as if he owned it. She was fed up with the whole thing, but there was little she could do about it.

"Ain't he somethin'?" Harry asked, a gleeful grin wreathing his bony features.

'Something' hardly described the way Tom was behaving. Even so, she had to admit that he was a good worker, and his tables were filled all the time…mostly with giggling females.

Maggie picked up her tray of drinks from the bar without answering Harry. To work with Tom was stressful, but she didn't have a choice.

Emmaline's return had guaranteed that there were few hours available on the day shift, and Maggie needed all the hours she could get. She wanted to confront Harry about not being fair to her, about not understanding her situation, but she couldn't. No one must know that she had a son waiting for her at her parents' house because any explanation would only lead to more questions about her life and why she'd chosen to work at Harry's Place. But that didn't stop her from wishing she could toss the job and go home to Jeremy.

Maggie's mother, Rowena, had called to inquire how her waitress job was going. Her mother had promised not to tell her father where Maggie was working, but there was always the chance that her mother would let it slip over dinner.

During the last couple of phone calls to check on

Jeremy, Rowena had begun to pressure Maggie to leave the steakhouse and come live with them, and take the job her father had offered. Her mother had never had to concern herself with earning a living, and so explaining Maggie's circumstances and her dreams to her mother was a constant uphill battle.

She could not do much about her circumstances for now. Therefore learning to cope with Tom was part and parcel of her life…until Sean returned—which had better be soon.

Loaded down with the tray full of beer glasses, Maggie made her way to the table near the fireplace.

"Thanks, Doll," said one of her regular patrons. "Say, what are you doing after you finish here?"

She ignored him as she placed the glasses around the table.

"Cat got your tongue?" the man asked.

The man and his buddies had been swilling beer since the supper crowd left. Without meeting his bleary grin, Maggie straightened and tucked the empty tray under her arm. "Will there be anything else?"

"Yeah." The man leered at her. "*You.*"

"Afraid not," Tom said as he moved closer to Maggie. "House rules."

Maggie jumped at the sound of Tom's voice. She stepped

back from the table, her toes curling in her shoes at the feelings rushing through her. She hadn't expected him to come to her defense. "What are you doing here?" she hissed.

"Saving you from further bad behavior," he hissed back. "These good ole boys should be tossed out before they make trouble. That's the fourth tray of beer you've brought to this table."

Maggie shot him a glance and saw the hard glint in his eyes. "Are you keeping tabs on me?"

"On your tables. And your best interests," he said, without taking his gaze off the rowdy group.

Tom stood with his feet slightly spread, and his body tense, as if ready to handle whatever the band of noisemakers threw at them.

For just a second, Maggie wanted to relent and tell Tom how much she appreciated him coming to her defense, but she couldn't do it. There was no way she could dredge up the words that would let her tell him that she'd needed him, words that would leave her vulnerable to him. Her pride wouldn't let her.

Maggie started to walk away, to avoid the picture Tom made as he stood there—his body muscled and tanned, his shoulders broad and inviting. Despite his physical charms, she'd just discovered that his even more endearing quality was his willingness to be there for her. The men she'd been attracted to in her life weren't like Tom. And that made him more appealing than she could ever admit to anyone—even herself.

Tom followed her, his body brushing hers as she slowed to let a patron pass. "You seem to have experience around that particular kind of clientele," she offered as she tried to maintain a little distance between them.

"You could say that."

Tom didn't offer more, and Maggie didn't ask. She did, however, file his answer away for future reference. Tom had shown a real knack with all aspects of the business, but particularly the client part of it. Those weren't skills easily gained in just any setting, more likely he'd already worked in some sort of fancy drinking establishment...

She glanced over toward the corner of the bar where three women were waving excitedly at Tom. Maggie recognized them as regulars who now made it their business to sit in Tom's area. "I see your cheering section is back, and in fine form."

He flashed the threesome a smile, followed by a wink, and they giggled like schoolgirls. "They pay the rent. Good tippers, one and all."

Maggie was getting just a little tired of the Tom Rawlins Fan Club. She couldn't say she was really jealous, but their continued admiration did declare that Tom was a good waiter, and that particular trait of his posed a serious problem.

Twice, in the past couple shifts, Harry had mentioned how well Tom was doing, and each time he'd stared at Maggie as if she were somehow not keeping up her end of some imaginary bargain.

"And you enjoy flirting with them." Maggie flipped the words at him.

"What can I say? The women like me. And I do what I can to line Harry's pockets."

"Not to mention your own," she said as they approached the bar where the women yelped in glee. Maggie wanted to cover her ears, but she settled for a cool stare directed at the women.

"What a night! *Wow! Wee!*" Harry crowed as he rubbed his hands together. "This is the best weekend I've had in ages and I owe it all to Tom. Look at the women, so many of them, all trying to get his attention." He waved his arms around. "The word's out about our version of Michael Bublé. What a chick magnet! I just knew this would pay off."

"Really?" Maggie said, waiting for her next tray of drinks.

Harry ignored the surly look she threw him. "I don't know.

I might have to rethink the evening staffing arrangement. One more hunk like Tom, and I could retire."

*"What?"* Maggie leaned closer to get a better look at Harry's face. *Was he serious?* If Harry added another male waiter her working hours could suffer. Who knew what Harry would plan next?

"You heard me. If Tom can pull in this many women, another one like him, and I could fill this place with panting females."

"And cut one from the herd for yourself," Maggie muttered under her breath.

What would she do if her hours were reduced? She had to wait for Sean if she wanted to get her money back. Without this job, she wouldn't have enough cash to live on. And when Sean did show up, she was afraid Tom would get to him first if she wasn't around.

If Sean returned with money in his pockets, she might not see a penny of it. Even worse, the longer he gambled and lost, the less money he'd have.

She couldn't lose her shifts. She had to think of something. Almost anything would do, until she had a chance to put a working plan together.

Then, it occurred to her. *Where are your brains?*

"You don't want to get the likes of Bert and Bubba angry at you," she said as she nodded at the table she'd just left.

Harry glanced over her shoulder and back at her. "How would that happen?"

"Well, I doubt men like those two come here to be waited on by a man."

Heaven help her. How did she end up defending those two and their pawing and panting rights? "Another male would not sit well with the men in the crowd, and then there'd be all the lost liquor sales. Women don't drink as much as men do."

"Where did you learn so much about running a restaurant?" Harry asked, his brows lifted in surprise.

"It's simply good business to please as many of your clients as you can."

"Do you have other suggestions?" he asked.

She'd thought about this before… If Maggie owned this restaurant, she'd refurbish it, change the menu to offer choices to a wider clientele, and she'd get rid of the wagon wheels out front. There were lots of other changes she'd make, but she was certain Harry wouldn't go for them. "No. No other suggestions."

Harry gave her his patented babe-bait grin. Chewing faster on his toothpick, he sized Maggie up. "Most of the time I go where the money is," Harry quipped, wiping the counter vigorously.

"And what if Bubba and the boys decide to take their business elsewhere? Where will you be then?"

Harry stopped chewing his toothpick long enough to stare at Maggie. "You worried about me? No one has worried about me in a very long time. That's sweet," he said, patting her hand before she could yank it out of his reach.

Maggie wanted to correct his crazy notion that she was worried about him, but thought better of it. If she could get on the good side of Harry—assuming there was one—she might be able to get off the evening shift and away from Tom.

That way Tom and Harry could spend their hours attracting all the women they wanted, and she'd be free to earn enough money to cover expenses and plan how she would approach Sean when he returned.

"Harry, I wouldn't want you to make a mistake that could cost you big bucks. Adding another man, even if he does look like Michael Bublé, might not be the answer. So just think about it before you do anything," she said, doing her best to sound totally committed to Harry's needs.

Helping Harry had to be the final act of a desperate woman.

Harry eyed her. "You got a point. Thanks for reminding me, Maggie. No new Michael…for now. You and Tom and lots of chemistry will do just fine. That way, I keep all my patrons and more. Wait and see," Harry said, smoothing a few gelled strands sideways over his bald spot.

Later that evening, Maggie and Tom were cleaning up the last of the tables when Harry appeared with Harry's Place's resident barfly on his arm.

"Remember to lock up when you leave," he said, a foolish grin on his face.

"We will," Tom said, gathering the stray glasses resting along the mantel of the fireplace.

The evening crowd in the bar had laughed and cheered and guzzled beer as they watched a football match on TV. Tom knew just what to do to have every female patron eating out of his hand, even the table of seniors that had come in after a bus trip to Boston. A couple of times Maggie had seen him pocketing wads of tip money.

Instead of raking in the tips, she had to endure the tables of couples with children, and several tables of Bubba's buddies. Maggie had struggled to keep her spirits up, but it wasn't easy. Regardless of how she felt about Tom, there was no way she could kick him out of Sean's house because she didn't know how much longer she'd have to wait for Sean to get back, and she was out of money—except what she made at Harry's Place. But if Sean didn't get back soon, she'd have to face the fact that her investment was probably gone. Then she'd have no choice but to admit her mistake to her father.

There were already enough staff on evenings, and with Emmaline coming back to work days, Maggie could very well find herself working fewer shifts. She hated the fact that, given Tom's skills and appeal, he'd be able to keep his job—all because of his popularity with the female clients. Where had he learned to do that so well? Sure, he might have been born with some of it, but the rest of it had to be honed someplace where there were lots of women to practice on…

What rankled her even more was that Tom and Sean

were already friends. Harry was big on that and would be more likely to share information with Tom. If Tom found a way to contact Sean, or knew his favorite gambling hangout, Tom might find Sean before she did. If that happened she could kiss her money good-bye. And she couldn't let that happen…not ever. Having Tom at the house, while keeping her job at Harry's Place, gave her a way to afford groceries and gas money to visit her son, and it provided the best opportunity to catch up with Sean.

Using her fake tresses as a cover, Maggie peeked at Tom. He seemed to be completely oblivious to her as he straightened chairs and turned out the lights. He moved with his usual sensual grace and watching him made her mouth water. The way his shoulders defined themselves against the cotton of his black shirt, the way his thighs strained against the fabric of his black jeans as he strolled toward her…

*Stop! Look away! Make the sign of the cross! Think about your sore feet!*

"I guess that's it," she said, loading the last of the glasses into the dishwasher. When she pushed the button, the soft swoosh of water entering the washer helped distract her from all those swirling Tom thoughts.

"Do you need a drive home?" Tom asked as he lifted the gate on the bar and came into the small space. Tom's body heat had its own force field, setting up a humming rhythm in her. Maggie backed up against the beer coolers.

"No, I have my car, such as it is," she said, glancing at Tom.

The smile he gave her was open, almost endearing, and it made her want to stand there in the muted light of the bar area and preen.

Heaven help her!

*Have I gone soft in the head?*

In her defense, there was something so damned appealing about him, something so smooth about the way he approached women, including her. There was no way any red-blooded woman could resist his silken come-on. She'd seen it a dozen times in the past few evenings.

Tom Rawlins was one smooth operator.

"Okay, then let's get out of here," Tom said, lifting the gate and motioning her to leave ahead of him. They walked out together to the parking lot at the rear of the building where the large sentinel light created shortened shadows as they walked to the back corner of the lot.

"Pretty late to be out alone," Tom said, as he walked her to her car.

No one had walked her to her car in a very long time, and it felt so odd, almost uncomfortable. Of course, there hadn't been many opportunities for a man to walk her anywhere. The men she had dated lately—and they were few and far between—hadn't seen the need, or more likely, actually celebrated that gallantry was dead. Then again, walking with Tom could hardly meet the qualifications for a date. "I'm fine," she said, as she pulled her keys out.

"Here, let me," Tom said, as he took the keys from her startled fingers and bent to open the door.

Tom's sudden thoughtfulness knocked her breath clean out of her lungs. *How could he be so sweet? What was he doing to her?*

No one who worked with her in Boston had cared what she did, or where she went. If he kept it up, she'd be getting teary-eyed… "Please, this isn't necessary."

"I'm not doing it because it's necessary. I'm doing it because I like you."

*Whoa!* She blamed the sudden trembling of her body on the cool night air, but that wasn't true. She couldn't stop the bubbly sensation that started in her tummy at the idea that someone was willing to help her just because they liked her. All the times she'd juggled Jeremy's diaper bag and toys when she took him to daycare. All the times she struggled with bags of groceries while she opened her car door. Not one person had offered to help.

Not in her wildest dreams had she ever imagined this, or how off balance his helpful gesture and explanation would make her feel. "You really don't have to do that, but thank you," she mumbled as she wondered what it would be like to be treated this way every day.

"You're welcome," Tom said, pulling the door open and holding it for her.

At a loss for words, she slid into the seat and reached for the door handle. "I'll see you back at the house."

Tom blocked her move and handed her the keys. "Try the engine."

"You're taking the white knight thing a little too seriously, aren't you?"

"Did you get to the garage, yet?"

She shook her head.

"Why am I not surprised?"

"Look, I'm not a wallflower. I can start my car and make my way home." She fluttered her hand at him. "I'll see you back at the house," she said again.

He shrugged his shoulders in a careless, Daniel Craig, fashion. "I may not go straight home, My Sweet. So, don't wait up for me," Tom said, zipping his leather jacket.

"I'll be asleep before you get home," Maggie said cheerily, pulling the door shut and staring out the windshield.

She wasn't the least bit concerned with how he spent his off time. In fact, the less time he spent at the house the better, as far as she was concerned. Watching him in her rearview mirror as he walked to where his bike was parked, his pants hugging his butt, his swagger making her bite her bottom lip, she tried not to let her mind wander to where he might be going tonight.

The next thing she heard was the rumble of his Harley as he roared past her out onto the street. She was alone. The parking lot lights gave a ghoulish glow to Maggie's hands where they rested on the steering wheel, reminding her that she hadn't painted her nails in weeks. Painted nails belonged to another life where there was time for such niceties.

A sudden snapping sound near the trees edging the lot had Maggie glancing anxiously over her shoulder. "Probably raccoons," she offered to her semi-dark car. Not wanting to linger in the vacant lot at one in the morning, Maggie clicked the lock and then turned the key.

*Nothing. Nada.* Just a wheezing noise that didn't resemble any engine she'd ever heard.

She tried again. *Nothing.*

"Damn!" she muttered to the empty car, and this time she floored the gas pedal. The car fired, rumbled, rocked for a moment, and with one all-over shudder, settled back into silence.

Maggie glanced around the empty parking lot, hoping to spot someone, anyone who hadn't left. For one flashing moment, she wished that one of the regulars were sitting in his half ton truck, listening to the country and western station. At least, she wouldn't be completely alone and they might offer to help.

She didn't have a cell phone. Her budget didn't stretch that far. She didn't have keys to the steakhouse to use the phone. And the handiest phone booth she remembered seeing was four blocks away.

The night air nipped at her cheeks as she crossed the parking lot and headed down the darkened road. Street lights were few and far between, and the night sounds consisted mostly of the faraway bark of a disgruntled dog and the occasional whine of a siren somewhere off in the distance.

She shivered, pulled up the collar of her polyester rain jacket, hooked her purse strap over her shoulder and jammed her hands into the pockets for warmth. Her feet ached and her back felt like it was about to break. She trudged along the uneven sidewalk, skirting the rougher areas, sometimes abandoning the sidewalk altogether in favor of the street as she picked her way along.

Ignoring the amber light at the intersection, Maggie strode across the street, checking the area for a phone booth. Out of the corner of her eye, she spotted a taxi pulling away from a house just a bit further ahead of her.

"Hey!" she yelled, running toward the car, waving her arms frantically in the air at the retreating taillights.

She tripped on a piece of jagged sidewalk, and pitched forward, landing hard, banging her knees on the concrete. Pain shot like a hot knife through her knees and up into her chest, forcing her to cry out in pain and tipping her wig forward on her forehead.

She sighed in disgust, pulled her legs around and eased her bottom onto the curb. Her pants were torn at the knee, and blood oozed from a cut. Thankful that her purse hadn't spilled its contents all over the street, Maggie fished around her jacket pocket for a tissue and dabbed her sore knee.

What she wouldn't give, at that moment, for her very comfy job back at the bank in Boston. She had friends there, and an easy life compared to this one. And there was certainly no night work involved. But it just didn't excite her... She still couldn't say why she gave it up, other than her pride.

Her damned pride had gotten her into this, into the challenge to show her father that she was a capable businesswoman, that she didn't need him or his money to succeed. Why didn't she simply give up, and do what her father wanted? Life would be so much easier.

What she wouldn't give to have her father drive by now in his Mercedes with his vanity plates and his cell phone. She knew she'd have to endure a lecture from him—that couldn't hurt more than her knee did right now.

What she wouldn't give to have anyone drive by...

Easing forward off the curb, Maggie stood up and tested her banged up knee. Nothing seemed to be broken, but it hurt like hell. She moved gingerly along the sidewalk, feeling the blood slide down her leg in a warm trickle. She only had one and a half more blocks to go, and if there was anything wrong with that pay phone…

A sudden squealing of tires heralded the arrival of some sort of vehicle. She turned in time to see a car careening up the street. Western music blared through its open windows and as it drew closer, loud catcalls greeted her.

"What's you doing out there, honey?" someone in the car yelled at her.

"You working this street alone?" someone else yelled from the backseat of the car as it slowed to a stop near her.

Her fear made her forgot her pain. Maggie began walking as fast as her banged up knee would allow. Cursing herself for her stupidity for not listening to Tom,

Maggie did a quick mental inventory of the contents of her purse. She didn't have anything, not even a nail file to fend off an attack. She glanced at the houses on either side, but there wasn't a light on anywhere.

"Hey, little lady." A man's voice wafted toward her as the car cruised slowly beside her along the narrow street. "What're you walking in the cold for when you could ride with us?"

Maggie ignored the voice and kept on walking. Her breath came in short gasps, and her unsteady legs trembled from the fall.

"Come on, now. Be reasonable," the voice coaxed as the music level in the car dropped a few decibels.

"What are we wasting our time for? Girls like her are a dime a dozen," the other voice offered.

Maggie held her breath as an argument broke out among of the men in the car about the merits of various hookers they'd known.

The argument escalated, drowning out the music. Maggie risked a quick look. They weren't watching her. Maybe they'd lost interest. Seeing her opportunity, she slipped behind a large oak tree scarred with graffiti. As she moved to get out of sight, she banged her bad knee against the trunk of the tree. She blocked a yelp of pain as she hid and waited for the car to move on down the street.

The slamming of brakes told her that they'd realized she wasn't beside them any longer. The car swung into an alleyway, backed out, and reversed direction on the street. As they approached her hiding spot her heart pummeled her throat.

"Where the hell is she?" one of them asked.

"Who knows? Who the hell cares? Let's get out of here."

To Maggie's complete relief she heard the engine rev and the tires squeal as they roared away. A few moments later, and as quickly as she could, Maggie reached the corner and looked up and down the street.

She was nearly to the phone booth next to a convenience store when she heard it—the sound of a motorcycle coming down the street behind her. No one was out at this hour of the night unless they were looking for trouble. And she'd had enough. She hurried along, slipping into the doorway of the store, where she pressed back into the shadows while the roaring of the engine neared her hiding place.

The bike slowed and moved up on the sidewalk in front of the doorway.

"Come out of there, you nitwit!" a voice called to her over the idling bike engine.

*Tom!* A wellspring of happiness washed through her.

"Come out, or I'll come in after you," Tom warned, gunning the engine of his Harley.

Maggie squared her shoulders, shook off her fear and strode out of the darkened doorway. "What are you doing here?" she demanded.

"I'll ask the questions. Now, get on the back and let's get out of here." He lifted a helmet off the back support on the rear seat and handed it to her.

Maggie opened her mouth to say something scathing, and thought better of it. All she wanted was to go home, and for some reason Tom had come along at the right time. She was grateful. Why tempt fate any further? She tried to pull the helmet on over her wig, but it stuck.

"Your face is in danger of disappearing behind all that phony hair," Tom said with a flippancy that annoyed Maggie.

Hadn't she been through enough for one night? All she wanted was to go home, go to sleep and forget the whole scary mess. She glared at him, pulled the wig off and let her red hair drop over her shoulders. She resisted the urge to scratch her scalp. She'd do that when she got home.

"Hold this, will you?" She held her wig out to him.

He didn't take it. Instead, his gaze traveled from her toes to her head. "You look like you've been in a bit of a scrap." The corners of his mouth twitched. "What happened to your knee?"

"Look, do you want to help me, or not?" she asked, holding the wig out to him.

"Say, please."

"Please," Maggie muttered, pulling on the helmet, then glancing at him.

There wasn't the usual gleam in his eyes. She wondered, briefly, where he'd been, but it really didn't matter. He was here and willing to take her back home with him. Maggie climbed on behind him, doing her best not to touch him. In her state of exhaustion, with pumping adrenaline, and grateful feelings toward him, touching Tom, no matter how innocently, was not a good plan.

"Put your arms around me," he ordered.

"Why?" she countered.

He reached back with both hands, and grabbed her wrists. "Wrap your arms around me and hang on. I don't want you falling off on the first turn."

Maggie relented and let him pull her snugly against his

back, his leather jacket forming an inviting pillow separating her from his broad shoulders. As Maggie clutched the front of his jacket, she had a foolish urge to lay her cheek against the broad expanse of his back and snuggle in.

There was something so solid, and at the same time so dangerous, about Tom. She sighed—a mixture of relief and contentment mingled with a heightened awareness of the man whose sex appeal had been keeping her awake at night.

"I hope that sigh was over me," Tom said, his voice an intimate whisper coming from somewhere inside the helmet.

She jumped in surprise. "What sigh?"

"Don't try to pretend with me, Maggie. I saw the fear in your eyes. Why didn't you go home? What were you doing out walking the streets here at this hour of the night?" he asked. His voice through the helmet headphone was intoxicating in its power.

"My car didn't start."

"I know," he said slowly as if talking to a child.

"How did you know?"

"I went back, and your car was still there. At first, I thought you'd planned to go out on a date without telling me."

Just the tiniest bit delighted that Tom had been concerned over her, Maggie quipped, "Now I have to tell *you* what I'm doing on my time off?"

"No, but I'm willing to bet you're damned glad I came back." Tom gunned the motor and they pulled out onto the empty street. Maggie had to grip him tightly so as not to be pulled sideways by the force of the movement.

She clung to Tom, her thighs hugging his, the warmth of the contact sending erotic thoughts racing through her as he roared down the empty streets.

Sitting like this, with a man pressed to her crotch was different, definitely different, but the whole scenario was so much more interesting than the way she'd have thought things would go tonight. The bike leaned hard into a turn. Maggie gritted her teeth as the sidewalk swerved closer to her. Clinging to Tom with all the strength she could muster, she called out, "Do you always drive like this?"

"No. Only when I have a beautiful woman's legs wrapped around me," Tom said, his voice a warm caress though the helmet speaker as the tires squealed and the seat on the bike seemed to slip out from under her butt.

It didn't matter how many maniacal turns this man took on his sex machine she was not going to let him see just how scared and excited she was by his wild driving.

But enjoying the moment ended with the reminder of her stranded vehicle. "I need to get back to the parking lot. I need my car. I have to have it for tomorrow."

"Not tonight," he said as he executed a swooping turn of the Harley onto the main street.

"Look, don't go all macho on me. I need my car to go to work tomorrow," Maggie protested, doing her best to separate her body from his.

He tightened his elbows against her arms. "We'll pick it up tomorrow morning, and if I can get it started, I'll follow you to the garage. You need a car you can rely on."

Surprise cut off Maggie's first response. Tom's willingness to help her was unexpected, almost as unexpected as her willingness to let him make a decision for her. "What's with the sudden show of concern?"

The bike swung low around the next corner, forcing Maggie to cling tighter to Tom's leather-clad body. "Just being friendly. And face it, who else would bother to come and get you out of trouble at this hour of the morning?"

"You have a point. But don't get carried away. You're not the only fish in the sea."

"You're lucky that you didn't get picked up by a couple of barracudas tonight. This is their time of night."

She wouldn't tell him about her earlier encounter. Tom would probably just replay his lecture about women out alone and how lucky she was that he came along when he did. "Thanks for the advice."

"You're welcome."

The low, seductive quality of Tom's voice sent Maggie's pulse into overdrive again, and she didn't like the feelings that came with it. He was too sexy by far, too damned cute and cuddly…and kind.

There should be a law against men like him.

# Chapter Five

The oil mixed with the smell of a dank concrete floor assailed Maggie's nostrils as she entered the local garage early the next afternoon. Her knee hurt, and now she had a headache that wouldn't go away.

It was obvious Tom had enjoyed his white knight role because he had driven her to start her car and even followed her to the garage. With a promise to check back with her, he'd roared out into the traffic to the admiration of several women who waited on the sidewalk for the light to change.

Tom's never-ending fan club was beginning to get on her nerves. It seemed that no matter where they were, or what was going on, Tom had women fawning over him. After the way he'd treated her last night, she understood why women would fawn over him…

He'd driven her home, and made her a peanut butter sandwich. She'd eaten the sandwich under his watchful gaze. Once she finished, Maggie put a bandage on her sore knee. She had been too tired to do anything but fall into bed after that. But sleep was a long time coming.

A thick syrup of guilt flowed around Maggie's heart. A little over a week ago, she'd left Jeremy at her parents' house, thinking that she'd only have to spend a couple of hours with Sean, during which they'd go over the details of her coming into the business as a partner. That idea had quickly gone south when she found out Sean had left town. The daily calls to talk with her son did nothing to ease her longing for him.

She missed Jeremy so much, and she wanted to get her financial life settled so they could find an apartment. She wanted to get her son into a good kindergarten program, and enjoy her life with him again.

When her ex, Mac Evans, walked out, leaving her with Jeremy to raise on her own, she'd lost her romantic notions about finding love, and along with that, notions of someone to truly care about her and her son. She'd been very angry with Mac for leaving her alone to raise Jeremy, but she'd learned one very valuable lesson. She needed to make her own decisions, and not rely on someone who didn't have hers or Jeremy's best interests at heart.

Years ago, when Mac had come along with his easy smile and smooth talk, Maggie had been captivated. But behind Mac's easy going style lurked a man who did not want the responsibilities of raising a child, or having a wife.

'Big Mac' as his beer-drinking, card-playing friends called him, loved to lie in bed and order Maggie around. In the world according to Mac, love had a lot in common with another four-letter word.

Checking her wig—she'd shampooed it this morning to remove the street debris sticking out of it—Maggie proceeded toward the work desk in the garage.

"Good morning," she said to the young man sucking on a bottle of Gatorade.

"Morning," he said, as he angled his body to see past her to the TV screen and the rerun of a boxing match on the local cable network.

Maggie moved to block his view. "I'd like someone to take a look at my car."

"You got an appointment?" the kid asked, casting a

glance in her direction before moving to a better vantage point to see the TV.

"No!" Maggie answered impatiently, annoyed at the spike-haired kid.

"Well, we're pretty busy—"

The drained Gatorade bottle did a basketball styled arc from the kid's hands to the metal waste can at the back of the tiny, grime-covered office.

"Look, it's probably an inconvenience for you, but I would like to get my car fixed, preferably sometime today."

Maggie gritted her teeth as the kid stared at her. She was beginning to believe that her father had a point buried somewhere in his usual tirade about most kids today.

"How can I help you?" A male voice asked, accompanied by the swishing of the connecting door closing between the office and the garage bays.

She knew that voice from Harry's Place. A voice accompanied by the smell of cigarette smoke wafting around her.

"I need someone to look at my car. I've been having trouble getting it started," she said, turning to face the man.

"Well, if it isn't one of my favorite waitresses," Burt Coleman, a regular from Harry's Place bellowed, as if everyone within earshot were deaf.

Maggie wanted to tap the scarred wood counter in frustration, but she was afraid she'd pick up some horrible disease. If there were the faintest chance her car would start and carry her out of here... "I need someone to look at my car."

"That heap parked in the disabled parking spot?" Burt asked, coming around the counter. He gave the kid a 'get lost' flick of his head as he moved to stand across the counter from Maggie.

"There weren't any disabled markings," Maggie muttered, keeping her gaze away from Burt's wolfish stare.

"Not to worry," Burt said, searching the counter for a

work order, his greasy fingers smudging everything they came in contact with. "I'll take care of it for you. After the great service I get at the steakhouse, I owe ya," he said, fixing a leer on his face.

"See you're dressed to go to work," he said, his glance bouncing over Maggie.

She squared her shoulders and glared at him. "Yes, I have to be to work in about an hour."

"Well," Burt said, leaning across the counter, "I'll run you over to work and then come back and fix your car. I'll bring the car over to the steakhouse this evening when I get off, and maybe we can talk cars," he said with an exaggerated wink.

"Cars?" she asked, ignoring his innuendo.

"Yeah, it's time you traded in that hunk of junk."

This little bit of repartee was going nowhere, which was exactly where it belonged, but in honor of getting her day back on track, she tried to be pleasant. "It takes money to trade vehicles."

"Money's no problem. My partner and I have a couple of hot numbers in the back lot. You and me could strike a deal," he said, his gaze riveted on her breasts.

Needing to get out of there, Maggie beat back a nasty retort. "I doubt that very much," she said with as much politeness as she could muster.

"Look, I'm only talking a date, maybe some night after your shift?"

"A date?" Big, bad Burt had only one thing in mind, and Maggie didn't need an interpreter on that front.

"Sorry, but Maggie already has a date for any night she wants." Tom's voice came from somewhere over her shoulder.

Maggie whirled to face him. "I have—"

Remembering who was listening, she bit her tongue on the denial she'd nearly given. With Tom standing there, she knew she was trapped between two undesirables, but one was more undesirable than the other. "Yes, I have a…date whenever I want… Sort of."

"Well, if there's anything I like, it's a challenge," Burt said, rubbing his grease-stained palms together. "It ain't over, 'til it's over, buddy." Burt's gaze slid past Maggie and connected with Tom's.

Maggie saw what passed between the two men and didn't like it one little bit. "Can we stop this? I need to get my car fixed." She turned her attention back to Burt. "Can you fix my car, or not?"

"Sure, Honey Buns. We'll look after it. You can count on me."

"She's not your 'honey buns,'" Tom said, scowling at Burt. "And in case they didn't cover it in mechanic school, I want you to check the filters on the manifold intake."

"Sure, sure," scoffed Burt. "And the next time I'm in the steakhouse, I'll tell you how to clean tables."

Without taking his gaze off Burt, Tom touched Maggie's arm. "Come on. Let's get out of here."

Maggie followed Tom out until they stood under the gas island canopy. She felt an odd mix of relief and indignation. "What was that about you and I having a date?"

"So, not even a tiny 'thank you'?" Tom asked.

"*Thank you?* For what? I should thank you for telling that nut bar that you and I have a date—which we don't?" She fired a disbelieving glance at him.

"For putting a stop to the hulk's plans for your nubile body." Tom gave a snorting laugh.

There was something harsh, almost cruel in his eyes and Maggie took a step away from him. "There's no way the likes of Burt would ever get his hands on me."

"Don't be too sure about that," he warned.

"What do you mean?"

He shrugged. "Never mind."

More questions clung to her lips, but the look in Tom's eyes held her back. For what seemed like hours, they stood staring at one another. Finally she said, "Tom, you're not responsible for me. I'm used to looking after myself."

His eyes warmed; a smile edged the corners of his mouth. "I thought you were in need of a little rescuing. It was the best I could do on short notice," Tom said, turning away and starting across the parking lot.

"Well, the next time, let *me* look after me, will you?" she said to his back as she strode behind him. But she didn't really mean it. Tom, taking her side was so nice, and she really did appreciate his concern. The trouble was she wasn't very good at expressing her gratitude.

Not many men would have bothered to come back and check on her last night. Certainly not the men she'd known…except for her father. And he would have had a field day pressing his I-told-you-so button if he learned about her escapade and her car.

Later that evening, the noise level in the bar all but drowned out the thoughts whistling through Tom's head. He hadn't intended to think about Maggie. He hadn't intended to let Maggie, or the thought of her, get anywhere near him.

So much for grand intentions.

When he wasn't answering some female patron's question about where he came from, or what he thought of this or that, or what he'd recommend from the menu, he remembered the feel of Maggie's arms around him on the bike, the way she looked at him back at the garage. Not exactly an obvious look of interest, but the look said she was definitely aware of him.

Most women he knew, took one look at him and his body parts and began to work out plans to jump his bones. Not that he objected—most of the time. Hell, most of the time they were simply responding to his well-planned strategy of innuendo and attentiveness.

But Maggie…? Maggie was different, somehow. She was feisty, funny and she showed an awareness of him that seemed special. He liked that she genuinely displayed these traits.

Then there had been those few moments after he'd brought her home last night on his bike. He'd watched her eat the peanut butter sandwich, and saw the anxiety she displayed as she surreptitiously glanced his way when she thought he wasn't looking. Maggie Kincade might be brash and tough, but underneath all that bravado was a woman who was wary of men.

Tom had seen it before and knew all the signs.

Maggie always changed the subject when he tried to do some serious flirting with her. She was uncomfortable when men made a fuss over her. And last, but not least, Maggie always walked away, leaving the man to think he'd done or said something that had offended her.

For Tom, his work—if you could call it that—had taught him to stay out of the grasping reach of sex-starved women. So it was kind of refreshing to be spending time with a woman who gave him his space, let him lead a little in the relationship. But he also knew Maggie Kincade would give him a quick jab in the ribs if he ever referred to what they had as a relationship.

He grinned to himself. Getting their 'relationship' to the physical level—where he wanted it—would be fun with someone like Maggie.

Tom placed steaming bowls of chili before two women who stopped their giggling chatter, and turned their interest toward him. "Can we have hot chilis?" the woman who'd been doing all the talking, asked.

"Certainly," Tom answered, turning to the tray he'd placed on the waiter's stand. Handing the hot peppers to the woman, he glanced at the other woman who sat quietly, toying with the edge of the table with her fingers.

"Is there anything else?" He addressed his question to her.

"No, thank you," she said politely.

Tom went back to the bar. His mind was once again on Maggie—a dangerous direction, in his estimation, but unavoidable all the same. "Harry, can I have two white wines, a Bud, and a Coors?"

"Coming right up," Harry said followed by the slap of the fridge door. Tom watched as Harry poured the wine, and placed the two beers on a tray.

"Things are really moving tonight," Harry said, rubbing his palms together as he glanced at Tom.

"Yeah, they are at that," Tom replied.

"You and Maggie are working out great. You really are. We need to do something more with your costumes, though."

Tom didn't want to hear this, not tonight. He was tired and his mind was still stuck on Maggie. She'd hopped off his bike as if the seat were on fire, and rushed into the restaurant without so much as a thank you to him for giving her a ride to work.

He hadn't expected her to persist in sticking so closely to the rules they'd set up when she agreed to let him stay at Sean's. Most women would have been easily wooed into bending those rules. Not Maggie.

"You listening?" Harry's voice rose above the din coming from farther down the bar where a blond, muscle-bound bartender kept the beer flowing and the laughs coming.

"Yeah, sure," Tom muttered. He glanced around the restaurant for Maggie. He spotted her over by the fireplace, a look of fierce concentration on her face as she took the orders at a table of four.

Maggie looked different tonight, and had been acting strangely, seemed distracted by something, ever since she'd come out of the staff room an hour ago. And he'd noticed. He seemed to notice everything about her now... He watched the sway of her hips as she maneuvered around a table on her way back toward the bar. The way her shirt hugged her breasts had the power to keep him awake at night. *Not good.* Still he couldn't look away.

She turned, touched the edge of her wig as if to check that it was okay and headed his way. "How's it going?" he called out to her, as she approached the bar.

"Fine," she said, after giving Harry her order. Then she stretched her back and gave him a cursory glance.

"Are you okay?" he asked, wondering why her answer should matter to him when she'd been so aloof.

He didn't have any real reason for taking an interest in Maggie. He had so many unanswered questions in his own life at the moment, and adding the likes of Maggie to his list made no sense at all.

"I'm tired, that's all. I can't wait for this shift to be over. Thanks for asking," she said as she gathered her next tray of drinks and wove her way through the tables.

"Better get a move on," Harry said, chewing vigorously on a toothpick.

"Yeah," Tom said, taking his tray and following Maggie.

He delivered his beer and checked on the four men dressed in preppy Ralph Lauren pants and sweaters at a table near the back. From the corner of his eye he caught Maggie heading toward the kitchen. He angled through the tables and caught up with her. "Did I do something wrong?"

"No." She looked up at him, but tonight the sparkle was gone from her eyes.

"Did something happen?" he urged.

"Look, we share a house, not our lives. Right?"

"True. But you don't look like your life is going all that great at the moment."

Anxiety tightened Maggie's lips. "What would you know about my life?"

"Enough to see that something's bothering you," he said over the muffled din from the kitchen.

Maggie stared at him, her eyes filled with indecision. For

one fleeting moment, Tom was sure she was about to tell him something very personal. He waited, surprised at just how much he wanted her to confide in him. "I'm famous for my broad shoulders, and I come complete with crying towel," he offered, his heart doing an unfamiliar dance.

Maggie stared at his chest.

Tom could see the beginning of tears.

She took a deep breath. "There's nothing going on."

"You're sure?" he pressed, even though he wasn't sure how he'd feel if she did open up. Some women took an offer to help as license to cling.

"Look, I don't need you trying to help me. I have enough on my mind. What I need can't be found in this place," she said, her voice filled with derogatory inflection.

Relief stirred in him as he watched Maggie blink rapidly and turn away.

But feeling just a little bit rejected by the way she seemed to dismiss his concern, he kept his tone light as he murmured into the phony locks covering her ear, "See you at closing."

Maggie waited impatiently at the bar for Tom to finish cleaning up his section. Her head ached almost as much as her back. Worry over her son, Jeremy, clouded her thoughts.

Her mother had called earlier to say that Jeremy didn't feel well, and she wanted Maggie to come home. But leaving her shift short would raise all kinds of questions from Harry that she didn't want to answer. Tom had offered her a lift to Sean's house. She decided to accept and take a cab from there to her parents' house on the outskirts of town.

She could ask Tom for a lift there, but she didn't want him to find out about her son, or where he was because he'd want an explanation. Tom was getting a bit too close for Maggie's emotional comfort.

It wasn't that she didn't appreciate his kindness. She just knew from experience she couldn't afford the emotional price tag of getting to know someone like Tom—handsome, charming, careless and self-absorbed. A lothario of the worst kind.

He was just the kind of man she'd sworn off when Mac had left her stranded with a child three years ago. And the old, familiar tug of attraction—stronger than ever before—had raised its head far too many times over the brief period she'd known Tom. That was warning enough.

"Will you hurry up?" she called across the room to him.

"Sure. In a minute," he said, not turning to look at her.

Exhaustion was closing in rapidly, and she needed to get to her son. She'd wait until Tom was parked in front of the TV and then she'd grab a cab and go home to Jeremy. She realized now that she should never have left her son at her parents' house, but it seemed like she had no choice at the time.

If only she could have kept Jeremy with her while she waited for Sean. She called every day after her father had left for work, but it didn't ease the ache for him. She'd had such plans and dreams for the two of them when she'd left Boston and her life there. The money she'd invested in Sean's business had been her ticket to financial independence, to her dream of owning her own business and raising her son independent of her family.

Her mother had been delighted to take care of Jeremy, and had eventually agreed to keep her father off Maggie's back for a few weeks while Maggie straightened out her problems with Sean.

But if Jeremy was ill… Visions of Jeremy in his flannel pajamas with his stuffed lamb tucked under his arm and his thumb in his mouth flashed across her mind—knifing her heart.

"You ready?" Tom asked.

"You go without me." She'd just realized that if she used

her tip money and took a cab from the bar, she could be with Jeremy in a matter of a few minutes.

"Leaving you here is not an option," Tom said, his gaze on her, his tone stern. "Remember the other night?"

"Forget the other night. I'll be fine."

"How do you know that? It's one o'clock in the morning."

"I have something—"

Tom gripped her shoulders. "You don't fool me. Look at me," he ordered.

Feeling the warm pressure of his fingers against her skin sent a shiver down her spine. Holding her breath, she glanced at him. "I'm looking."

"What's going on? You've been acting weird all evening, and now you want me to leave you here without any way of getting home," he said, his sharp tone softening, giving way to gentle concern.

Tom being sweet was the last thing she needed right now. "I have a problem. I need to go home," she said, breathing in his scent, his closeness beginning to cloud her judgment.

"Home?"

"Jeremy needs me. He's sick."

"Who's Jeremy?"

She hadn't planned to tell anyone at Harry's Place about Jeremy, because she didn't want people involved in her personal life, or to start offering advice on how she should raise him. Her father had that covered. Most of all she felt guilty about leaving Jeremy for so long, and didn't need to be reminded about her actions. But Tom had been kind, and surely he wouldn't divulge her secret. He hadn't said anything about her wig. "My son. He needs me and I want to see him."

Tom swore under his breath. "Why didn't you say so?" He wrapped his arms around her, pulling her into his comforting embrace.

Maggie gulped back the tears clogging her throat as she

leaned into him. His maleness and the lingering scent of his cologne wrapped her in a cocoon of desire so strong it made her head light. If she weren't desperate to see her son the desire she felt would have led her into trouble…

"Let's go," he said, tucking her against him as they headed out the back way.

"I told you. I can't. I'm taking a cab to my parents'."

"Not by yourself, you're not," Tom said, snagging his leather jacket from the coat rack and opening the back door of the restaurant. "I'll take you."

"You don't need to do that," she protested even though she knew her protest was weak, and growing weaker with every minute.

"Look, I'll run you out tonight, and come back for you after lunch tomorrow. That way, you can visit your son, and make it back to work in time for tomorrow's shift…after you change your clothes, that is."

"I'm a mess thanks to a bottle of ketchup," she glanced ruefully at her outfit.

"We'll go to Sean's so you can get a change of clothes and pick up your overnight things, and then I'll drive you to see your son. How's that?"

If her father saw her waitress outfit, he'd ask a million questions, none of which she wanted to answer. How nice it would be to let someone look after the details for her. And Tom was offering to do just that. "Why would you be willing to go out of your way for me?"

"I'm not doing it just for you. Kids deserve the best love and care they can get. I put a mother's love at the top of a kid's list of needs."

"You do?"

"Does that surprise you?" He frowned. His glance penetrated her mind with knifelike accuracy.

"No. And I guess it doesn't surprise me that you'd want to meddle in my life," she said, not really meaning the part about meddling.

"Then let's go."

She trailed along beside him, planning how she'd get into the house and upstairs without her father hearing her. It shouldn't be much of a problem. She'd done it a thousand times before. "You can't tell my father what I do for a living, or where I live."

She caught the look of surprise on his face.

"Maggie, we're going to arrive there in the dark of night. I'm not likely to see your father, but if I do, your secret is safe with me."

"Thanks," she said, grateful to him for the second time that evening.

"Don't thank me yet. My silence comes with a price. Why don't you want me to tell your father what you do for a living?"

What could she tell him without going into the whole long history of what went wrong between her and her dad? "My father has a penchant for running the lives of others."

"And you're at the top of his interference list?"

"You could say that."

"Leading the list might not be all bad…and from what I see at the moment, in your case it might be good."

"What does that mean?" She scowled, sensing a shift in Tom's attitude.

"Have you considered the possibility that your father wants to help ensure a good future for his grandson?"

"You might consider minding your own business," she said, anger tightening her chest. She was so damned tired of people who thought they knew what was best for her and her son.

"I'm willing to excuse your grouchiness for tonight." Tom gave her a glance that did nothing to remove Maggie's worry. "I'll take you home so you can change, and then we'll get you to Jeremy."

"Why are you so willing to do this?" Maggie asked again, feeling less worried for the first time since her mother's call.

"Just doing a friend a favor."

In Maggie's experience, men like Tom Rawlins didn't do favors, and if they did, it was with strings attached. "You're ducking the question," Maggie said, searching his face for a hint of the real reason for his generosity.

"I have my motives," Tom said, his expression unreadable under the harsh glare of the sentinel lights outside the restaurant.

Back at Sean's house Maggie pulled her wig off and switched on the kitchen light. She had to admit that things looked pretty neat and tidy. Tom had kept his word about doing his share around the house, and Maggie appreciated his efforts. She pulled off her shoes, and took them with her as she made her way down the hall toward the bedrooms.

"I'll only be a couple of minutes," she called, switching on her bedroom light as she tossed her shoes in the closet and slid out of the waitress uniform.

Donning jeans and a sweatshirt, Maggie pulled a brush through her hair and dabbed a little lipstick on her pale lips. The face in the mirror was tense, drawn, and the usual shadows under her eyes had deepened. The strain of keeping secrets was taking its toll. But she had no choice if she wanted even the ghost of a chance to prove her abilities to her father.

The only down side to going home in the evening was that her father would be there, asking questions and generally making her feel guilty and stupid. But all that would be worth it in the end, once she was reassured about Jeremy.

She shifted her thoughts from her father to Tom. Why had he offered to take her home, and what did he mean about his motives? The more she learned about Tom, the less he seemed like the playboy type she'd first taken him for. But looks could be deceiving. She knew that better than anyone, thanks to Mac.

Not that she ever regretted having Jeremy—not even for a fraction of a second. He'd given her a whole new reason to live, a whole new perspective on what really mattered.

Her heart tightened at the memory of his birth. Maggie had been alone in the delivery room—at the last minute Mac had claimed to be sick at their apartment. She had faced the nurses and doctors, and their determined efficiency without the support of her husband, and she had never felt so lonely in her life. Then she'd heard the cry of her son, and felt the weight of his tiny body on her chest as he settled in to nurse. The loneliness was forgotten in the thrill of holding her baby for the first time.

Tears stung her eyes and she fought them back. The past was over, totally over, and now she had a son she loved, and soon she'd have a career of her choosing. Not a bank job, or one in real estate, compliments of her father's interference.

She'd prove to him, and the world, that Maggie Kincade was one smart lady. She would get the paperwork completed, making her a partner at Harry's Place. After that, she'd expand the business; maybe even turn it into a franchise business. The restaurant might not look like much at the moment, but she had plans to change it into a pleasant eatery if she got the opportunity. Taking a deep breath, she squared her shoulders and started back out to Sean's kitchen where Tom waited.

Whatever Tom's reasons for doing what he was doing, she was grateful to him. "I'm all set," she said cheerfully, scooping her purse off the counter and sliding her arms into her jacket.

Though preoccupied about seeing her little boy, she gave Tom clear directions to her parents' house and the trip took no time. As they drew up to the gates she was relieved to see that only a kitchen light was on at the back of the house. With hurried thanks, she scrambled off the bike, and into the house. Her mother was waiting with a worried expression that added to Maggie's concern for her son.

"He's in bed, dear. I gave him something for the fever and he seems to be resting quietly for the moment."

She hugged her mother. "Thanks," she whispered, her fear finding a resting place in her voice. "I'm going to go upstairs and see him."

"You do that. If you need anything, let me know."

"I will." Maggie peeled her jacket off as she rushed up the stairs then ran along the hall to where Jeremy was sleeping. Careful not to wake him, she slid down beside him, and pulled him to her. His forehead was cool and his breathing even. She settled in next to him, her heartbeat slowing in relief that her little boy was okay. Her heart flooded with love as she listened to his breathing in the quiet room. As her lids grew heavy with exhaustion and the comforting warmth of Jeremy's little body eased her anxiety, she vowed that she would find Sean in the next couple of days. She would find him, get her partnership agreement straightened out, and start her new life with her little boy.

# Chapter Six

The next morning dawned bright and sunny. Nudged awake by the light, Maggie stirred, sat up and looked across the bed to where her son lay sleeping. His tiny hands were clutching Lambie and his face, pressed into the pillow, was a picture of sweet innocence. A pain started deep in her chest as she listened to the soft breathing of her child.

Just then his eyes opened. His sleepy gaze roved the room until it came to rest on her. "Mommy!" he squealed, scrambling up and wrapping his arms around her neck. "I missed you."

Her heart contracting in her chest, she hugged him back. "Hi Sweetie," she whispered, her lips brushing his tiny forehead. "Did you have a good sleep?" she asked, struggling to keep the tears back. How she wished she could stay right here with her son instead of going back to Harry's Place or Sean's house.

"Yes." He snuggled closer. "Can you stay with me?"

"Yes," she breathed as she settled down with him once again. Sleep was out of the question for her, but Jeremy needed more rest after having a restless night. As she listened to his breathing, and felt his body relax against her, she glanced around the room.

Jeremy's room, in the immaculately maintained Georgian

styled house where Maggie's parents lived, was a large guest room with an adjoining bathroom.

Maggie knew her father and mother would be up now. Rowena would have a breakfast of bacon, eggs, whole wheat toast and ginger marmalade ready for

Jonathan when he came downstairs in his flannel robe. He would expect his breakfast to be served in the dining room after which he would go back upstairs for his morning ritual of showering and shaving. He would then don an immaculate three-piece suit with coordinating tie and go into his office downtown.

Once her father was out of the house, she expected her mother would want to tell her all about Jeremy's sudden illness, and find out how things were going at the steakhouse. Feeling pangs of hunger, she waited until Jeremy was once again asleep before tiptoeing out of the room and down the back stairs to the kitchen.

"Hi, Mom," Maggie said, hugging her mother. "Jeremy's sleeping like an angel. I was awake a couple of times to check on him, but did stir all night."

Maggie kissed her mother and inhaled the Chanel N°5 perfume her mom always wore.

"Good morning, honey." Her mother smiled at Maggie as she poured coffee into a porcelain cup, spooned in two sugars and stirred in cream.

"I see Dad hasn't made any concessions to his health," Maggie said. She wiped the sleep out of her eyes as she hunted in the cupboard for her favorite Pooh Bear mug.

"You're not going to fight with your father over breakfast, are you?" Rowena said, worry and reproach knitting the skin between her brows.

Maggie didn't want to fight with her father over breakfast or any other meal, for that matter. She'd come here to see her son, and it was better to leave it at that. "No, Mom, I'm not going to fight with Dad."

"You realize what's really wrong here? You and your father are too much alike."

Maggie had heard this comment before, and knew just how wrong that was. The only thing she had in common with her father was her hair color and her temper. Beyond that, they were from different ends of the planet.

"Mom, I don't want to argue about Dad. Jeremy is my real concern."

"I'll take your father's coffee in to him, and I'll be right back." Rowena patted her arm affectionately as she bustled off to the dining room.

Maggie sipped her coffee, a special blend prepared for her father, and waited for her mother to return.

"Jeremy had a cold, but when he got sick to his stomach, I decided to call you," Rowena said as she came back into the kitchen. "He seemed to settle okay last evening, but your father and I worry about him."

"Thanks, Mom. I'm taking Jeremy to the medical clinic this morning as soon as he wakes up. I want to be sure he's okay. He's had ear infections that started like this—a bit of fever and not feeling well."

"Have you got an appointment?"

"Cookie will get me in."

"Have you talked to Cookie since you got home?"

"No. I haven't talked to friends because I don't want Dad to find out where I work," she said, lowering her voice as she glanced toward the door to the dining room. "Cookie won't tell anyone."

"Probably not. She's got her own problems. Leo left her for his secretary."

*"You're kidding!"* Cookie had fallen in love with her high school sweetheart find married him right after graduation. Maggie had always believed Cookie's marriage was one of the good ones—so much for that notion.

"I wish I was kidding, for the twins' sakes. Those sweet little girls…" Her mother shook her head.

Cookie Carmichael had been one of her classmates who had always seemed to have her life on track for success. Something must have drastically changed in her marriage.

"As soon as Jeremy wakes up, I'm going to get him dressed and take him. Can I borrow your car? I got a friend to drive me out here last night. My car's in the shop."

"Don't leave without seeing your father," her mother cautioned.

"Thanks Mom, but I can't do that. Dad and I would just end up fighting."

Rowena grimaced. "Go and say hello to your father. He and I were talking about you the other night."

"Heaven help me! What rule did I break now?" Maggie said, exasperated with her mother for constantly trying to push her to settle her differences with her father.

"He's nearly finished the *New York Times*, and I know he wants to see you."

"What about?"

Rowena took a deep breath and cleared her throat while she twisted a pearl button on her cashmere sweater set. "Your father wants to hear what your plans are. I told him you were housesitting while you worked as a manager trainee."

"He didn't ask where, did he?"

"No, but he's beginning to question the story. And frankly, I'm not comfortable telling him something that isn't true. You have to be prepared that he will check your story out before too long." Rowena tucked a strand of Maggie's hair behind her ear, her touch gentle. "Honey, you need to get things resolved."

"Mom, I'm sorry for putting you in this situation, but I need a little more time. Sean hasn't come back."

"But, you're in his house. Where did you get the key? How well do you know this man? Oh, Maggie, how can you stay there alone? Aren't you afraid?"

Maggie wasn't about to tell her mother that she'd picked Sean's lock… Or how she came to have a key now. Or that she wasn't alone there. That information would give her another reason to doubt Maggie's ability to get her life in order.

"Mom, I have a little old lady living next to me. She's alone."

Maggie didn't bother to explain to her mother that no sane person would attempt to burglarize Edna's house. Unless they wanted to be missing a few vital parts south of their belts, or they had a fondness for lead shot embedded in their butts.

"I'm sure there are people there who are fine upstanding citizens, but it's hardly your kind of neighborhood."

There was a scolding tone to Rowena's voice that really annoyed Maggie. Why was it that every time she darkened the door of her parents' house, she felt like a recalcitrant kid all over again? Of course it didn't help that she'd had a well-deserved reputation as a troublemaker when she was in school.

And of course, there was that whole issue of the Hong Kong playboy she'd hooked up with her first summer after graduation. His not-to-be missed body and his British accent were his only claim to a pedigree, and Maggie hadn't even attempted to resist him. She cringed when she thought back to those days.

It was a good thing she'd asked Tom to let her off down at the gatehouse. Otherwise, the roar of his bike would have had her mother asking a lot more questions, and her father would have been disgusted over what he continually saw as her irresponsible behavior.

"Mom, it's a perfectly good neighborhood, but things are in a little bit of a mess right now."

"What kind of a mess?" her father said, from the door to the dining room.

Maggie nearly jumped out of her skin at the sound of his voice. "Nothing," she muttered, wondering how much of the conversation her father had heard.

"Why don't you come in and sit at the table? Your mother will get you whatever you want for breakfast."

"Mom's not my servant, Dad. I'll get something later." She slid into one of the chairs at the kitchen table, knowing that her father never ate there.

"We need to talk," her father said, sliding into a chair across from her.

Maggie nearly choked in surprise. She glanced at her mother, but she was busily putting an English muffin in the toaster oven.

"What did you want to talk about?" Maggie asked, a heavy sense of foreboding settling in her chest. She'd been so careful to disguise herself at work. Only Edna knew that her hair was red, and for some strange reason Edna had remained silent on the subject.

Her father clasped his hands in front of him on the glass top table. "Let's start with what you're doing with your time. Your mother's enjoying having Jeremy, but our grandson is lonesome for his mother."

Maggie wanted to ask her father how he'd know that, given how little time he spent in the house, but she didn't need another confrontation with him. "I'm trying to get my new job going well so that I can have Jeremy with me."

"If you'd let me contact them, there are dozens of businesses that would take you as a trainee."

"You helped me in Boston. You got me a job there; that's enough."

"I got you a job because that useless cretin you married couldn't provide for you," her father said, his voice low, controlled.

"You're never going to let me forget that, are you?" Maggie said, her voice rising, the old anxiety writhing in her stomach. Why was she letting him get to her?

"We all have to learn from our mistakes. You seem to think that you can do whatever you want without worrying about the consequences," her father said, his voice edged with annoyance.

Maggie knew her father was referring to Jeremy, and the fact that her son had been born within weeks of her marriage—a marriage that never would have taken place, if her father and mother hadn't pressured her. If they hadn't interfered.

"And, of course, Dad, you've never made a mistake.

Never wished you could change what you'd done.

Except maybe having me…"

Maggie heard her mother's gasp and saw her father's face blanch. Why had she said that? How could she be so cruel? "I'm sorry. I'm really sorry," she mumbled, glancing at her mother.

"For the record, we have never regretted having you, not for one single moment. We love you." His words cut through Maggie, filling her with shame.

Despite her differences with her father, she knew how supportive he had always been of her mother and what Rowena had been through in trying to carry a child to term. "I owe you both an apology. I didn't mean to say that."

Her father looked at her, his face white and drawn. "Don't you see how lucky you are? Your mother and I wanted children, tried so hard, while you had a baby with so little trouble."

Maggie heard bone deep regret in her father's voice, and realized for the first time how difficult it must have been for both of them. Feeling like a dolt, she murmured, "You're right. I'm so lucky to have Jeremy."

"Yes, you are," he said, his gaze on his wife as she came to the table with her coffee. The look he gave Rowena was filled with meaning, with shared memories and suddenly Maggie felt like a voyeur in an exchange she wasn't supposed to witness—and like a stranger in the house she'd grown up in.

It was time she left before she made another major blunder. "I'd better get dressed and get a move on."

"Don't go," her father said, and she could see that he meant it.

Maggie saw the hint of white in his dark red hair, noticed the way his skin wrinkled along his throat. Her father was getting older. The man who had dominated her entire life was showing signs of age. Maggie felt the tug of war between her love for her father and her pride.

"I have to go. I'm taking Jeremy to see the doctor to have him checked out." Before her father could glimpse her tears, Maggie stood and went upstairs.

Nothing about the McNamara Medical Clinic had changed in the five years she'd been away in Boston. Except Cookie Carmichael. She looked so much older…and so tired.

As Maggie approached the reception desk, Cookie glanced her way, her distracted expression shifting to a wide grin. "Maggie!" she squealed. "When did you get back? Are you home for a visit? Where's Jeremy?" Cookie pummeled her with questions as she came around the desk. "God, I've missed you! There's no fun in my life." Cookie wrapped her arms around Maggie, hugging her tight, her long earrings digging into Maggie's neck. But Maggie didn't mind. Cookie hugged like she needed the connection.

And besides, she needed her friend's enthusiastic reception. Enthusiasm was in short supply in her life at the moment. "I'm here to see you, and to ask if you might squeeze Jeremy in for an appointment with one of the doctors."

"Absolutely." Cookie returned to her desk and checked the schedule. "Dr. Hayes has an opening in about ten minutes. He's great with kids. What's wrong with Jeremy?" Cookie asked, smiling at Jeremy who was hugging Maggie's leg.

Picking her son up in her arms, Maggie explained about the fever, and her concern that he might have an ear infection.

"Come with me," Cookie led them to an exam room. "You make yourself comfortable and I'll tell the doctor you're here. By the way, this new doctor is gorgeous, and he's single, and he's really sweet..." Cookie's voice trailed off.

Where was her friend's indomitable enthusiasm? "It's been so long since you and I have had a chance to spend any time together," Maggie said, suddenly overwhelmed with the memories of their years in high school when they were inseparable.

"And I've missed you so much. What I wouldn't give to spend an evening just hanging out and talking." Cookie sighed.

"I've missed you too." Maggie checked her friend out. She'd lost a lot of weight. Her clothes were hanging on her five-foot-eleven frame and her expression was tense. "Are you okay?"

"No." A smile trembled on Cookie's lips. "But I can't go into it right now," she said, tidying an already neat exam table while Jeremy kept his arms wrapped around Maggie's neck.

"Mommy, I'm thirsty."

Maggie pulled a bottle of apple juice out of her bag. "Cookie, are you and Leo having problems?"

"Not anymore. He took his honey, got a tattoo across the cheeks of his butt and is out finding himself."

Maggie opened the bottle and passed it to Jeremy as she settled him on the exam table. "He left? Just like that?"

She nodded, cocking her hands on her bony hips. "But believe me. When I'm through with him, he's going to wish he could wiggle his nose and disappear."

Leo had been the handsomest guy in their class, and he and Cookie had been the cool couple. When they announced they were expecting twin girls, the old gang had gotten together and thrown a huge double baby shower. Cookie and Leo were the poster couple for happy ever after. "What's gotten into Leo?"

"Fear of middle age, as far as I can figure out. But I no longer care. All the years I spent looking after that man, and he rewards me by running off with a woman barely out of her teens. It just goes to show, you can't trust a man. Any man."

"I can relate to that," Maggie said, nodding.

"After what I've been through with Leo, I'm here to tell you, Maggie. If a man looks too good to be true, he probably is."

"Amen to that," Maggie said, meaning it. They talked for a few minutes until another woman arrived in the room, looking for Cookie.

"Are you at your parents' house?" Cookie asked.

Maggie shook her head. "It's a long story."

"Sounds like you and I have a lot of catching up to do. Write your number on this, give it to me on your way out, and I'll call you. We girls got to stick together," Cookie said, before heading out of the room.

As it turned out, Jeremy was fine. Dr. Hayes gave him a thorough check up and Maggie was relieved. All the way back to her parents' house, Jeremy talked about ponies. Jeremy wanted a pony, and had been delighted to discover that his grandparents had horses.

Rowena was at the door when Maggie eased her mother's Mercedes into the garage.

"How's Jeremy?" her mother asked, reaching for her grandson.

"He's fine," Maggie offered, feeling sorry again for her earlier behavior.

"Can you stay for lunch?"

"I'd love to but I have to get to work."

Rowena stroked her grandson's head. "Jeremy and I are going to the library today after lunch."

"That's a wonderful idea," Maggie said, forcing back a flood of regret that she couldn't be the one to take her son, or go with them. One way or the other, she had to find Sean.

"How are you getting to work?" her mother asked as Maggie took Jeremy from her and hugged him close for a few minutes more.

"Mommy, please stay," Jeremy pleaded.

Her arms trembling, her voice thick with remorse, she said, "A friend is picking me up. I called him from the clinic, and he said he'd be here in a few minutes."

"A *male* friend?" her mother asked, surprise evident in her voice.

Her mother had reason to be surprised. She'd told her mother she'd sworn off men until she had her business plans completed. Her promise to stay out of a relationship until her life was more stable had been part of the reason her mother had agreed to keep Jeremy without telling her father what Maggie was doing. "Mom, he's someone I work with, nothing more."

Her mother gave her a disbelieving look.

She hugged Jeremy and kissed his cheek. "You be good for grandma, and I'll see you in a couple of days," she said, wishing so much that she didn't have to leave. Hoping what she said was true.

"Mommy, don't go," Jeremy squeezed her cheeks between his chubby little hands.

Maggie forced the tears back as she hugged her son one more time. "I have to go, but I'll be back real soon. And I'll call tonight."

"You have a good day, honey," Rowena said, taking Jeremy from her and going in the back door.

Awash in guilt, Maggie walked down the drive toward

the gatehouse where she'd told Tom to pick her up. She was pacing back and forth, trying to think of ways to find Sean, when Tom roared up the drive.

He cut the engine, smiling at Maggie as he did so, and pulled his helmet off. "Beautiful country estate. I got a better look this morning. Nice morning for a bike ride," he said.

"I hadn't noticed," she said, grumpily.

"So, what's wrong with Princess Maggie this lovely morning?" Tom asked, his black hair glistening in the sun, and his eyes twinkling as they gave Maggie the once-over.

"Nothing. Just the usual stuff."

"Meaning?"

"You don't want to know."

"Ah! But I do. Anything that affects my princess, affects me," he teased her.

"You wouldn't want me to ruin your day as well."

Tom booted the kickstand in place, and got off the bike. "What's wrong? Is it Jeremy?"

"No, I took him to the doctor this morning and he's fine."

"Then?"

"I had another face-off with my father. Let's just say that visiting my parents has its downside."

"How so?" Tom asked, a concerned expression on his face.

"I'm supposed to go into the business with him. Take over so he can retire."

Tom nodded as he took in the beautifully manicured lawns sweeping up toward the Georgian-styled house, the tennis courts and the green house. "Looks like this business doesn't pay very much," he said.

"It isn't *always* about money, you know."

"And we don't *always* have the luxury of choice when there are children involved," Tom replied, his gaze locked on hers, his hands coming to rest on her shoulders.

"What's that supposed to mean?" Maggie asked, glaring up at him.

"I mean that sometimes we have to make sacrifices for our children."

*Our children?* Did Tom have a child? Maggie was too exhausted from the stress of the past few days—not to mention the stress of leaving Jeremy—to question him on it. "If you have something to say, why don't you just come out and say it?"

Tom looked at her, his gaze searching hers in a way that made Maggie's heart pound. "It's none of my business, but if I had parents who had this kind of money." He glanced around for emphasis. "I would let them help me, especially when the welfare of my child was at stake."

"They are helping me!" Maggie said, shooting an angry glance in his direction as she plucked his hands off her shoulders. One then the other.

"Don't be so touchy."

"Don't involve yourself in something you don't understand," she shot back.

"I understand a lot more than you realize," Tom said, his eyes darkening as he stepped away from Maggie. "You're a spoiled brat who never grew up. And that's fine. But with a child involved, you need to put his interests first."

"Like you'd know," she fired at him, angry that Tom was taking her father's side in this argument. "And, just for the record, I'm not a spoiled brat. Since I finished school, I've worked for everything I've gotten in life. And in the future, I'd like to suggest that you keep your opinions to yourself."

An angry set to his shoulders, he fired back. "What makes you think you have the whole working-for-a-living thing cornered?" He looked like he was about to say more, but decided against it.

"In case you haven't noticed, I don't pass judgment on your lifestyle," she said. That wasn't completely true, but he didn't make any comment.

"Do you want a drive back, or not?" Tom pulled on his helmet and swung his leg over the bike.

"We're not finished," she said.

"We are, as far as I'm concerned," Tom said, fastening his helmet.

He started his bike, and raised the kickstand. "Coming?" he yelled over the rumble of the engine.

Maggie glared at Tom as she climbed on behind him and fastened her helmet. "You owe me an apology," she said into the mike enclosed in the helmet.

"Maggie, I'm shutting off the mike. You'll have to wait until we get back to the house."

"Hold it! I'm not done!" she yelled into the dead mike.

Annoyed with Tom for assuming he knew enough to interfere, and angry with herself once more for getting involved with Sean, Maggie reluctantly clung to Tom as he pulled out onto the highway and started back toward town. She wanted to explain to Tom just how difficult things were between her and her father.

She understood that Tom thought she was putting being independent and earning her own money ahead of the welfare of her son, but that wasn't how she saw it. When she realized that Mac wouldn't help her, she'd vowed to make a life for her and Jeremy. Once she realized that her job in Boston barely covered expenses, she had to do something. When Sean offered her a chance to be a partner in his business, she'd jumped at it. She'd taken the inheritance her grandmother had left her, and put it all into Sean's business without telling her parents. Maybe it was selfish of her to want to succeed on her own merits, but deep down she wanted to make her father proud of her. And being successful in business was the only criteria her father accepted. Tom had to understand why she was doing what she felt she had to do.

Wait a minute. Why should she defend her behavior to a stranger in her life, someone who would be gone when he got his money?

It had to be the whole stress thing.

Instinctively, she huddled closer to Tom's back as they rounded a sharp turn onto the highway. The solid feel of him, the way he handled his bike, the remembered touch of his hands back at her place, all these things drew her to him in a way she couldn't explain.

Tom Rawlins wasn't her type. Anymore. He was everything she didn't want now, and couldn't handle in her life. But as she rode behind him on his bike, she had trouble calling to mind his faults that supported her belief.

He was a bit of a rogue. He had too many women after him. Harry liked him—not a good sign. The cook liked him—not sure how good that was. Those were all pretty solid faults, weren't they? The body of the man on the front of the bike was pretty solid too, and when she breathed in the musky scent of him mixed with biker leather, it caused all kinds of jumbled feelings.

"Stop the fantasizing!" she muttered to herself, as she tried to pull her arms back.

Tom pressed her arms tighter against his muscled body, sending spikes of yearning cascading through her. She gulped air and fought the delicious drowning sensation created by Tom's closeness. Heedless of the consequences, Maggie let the wayward feelings rush her. A longing to be closer to him, so strong it snatched the breath from her lips, bubbled up in her. When she closed her eyes, the feeling took full rein. If only this sense of oneness could last.

If only…

"We're here, Princess. You can unlock your arms," Tom said into the mike, sending Maggie's heart ricocheting along her ribs and the color rising on her cheeks.

*What had she said out loud while the mike was on?*

"I thought you said the mike was turned off," she muttered, yanking her arms away.

"Driver's prerogative, Princess," Tom said, his voice low and sexy.

"Don't call me Princess," she said, unsnapping the

helmet as she got off the bike. She needed distance from this man, a chance to collect her thoughts and untangle her emotions that seemed to be more and more involved with Tom.

"Fine by me. We need to talk. We have a few issues we need to work on, you and me," Tom said, hooking his helmet on the handlebars of his bike. "Oh, and before I forget. Whatever you do, don't attract Edna's attention. She's looking for me."

"After your body, no doubt," Maggie said, derisively as she followed Tom through the garage into the house.

Tom opened the door to the house, pulling Maggie against him as he walked into the kitchen. "She's not the only one after my body." Tom tossed the challenge, his lips coming down on hers as his arms locked around her.

The kiss was hot, demanding—the kiss of her dreams. All the pent up emotion of the past weeks joined forces with her loneliness, lowering Maggie's resistance and raising her libido. With a groan, she wrapped her arms around Tom's neck and kissed him back, her tongue seeking his, her body arching into his.

He sucked gently on her lips as his hands slid down her back to the cleft between the cheeks of her bottom. "All those miles on the bike…your legs around me." He lifted her until her feet were off the floor, his mouth devouring hers.

Trapped in his embrace and loving every second, she returned his kiss, her body arching into his as she wrapped her legs around him. He lowered her to the floor, his lips never leaving hers, his breathing rapid.

"I've always wanted to have sex on the kitchen floor with a beautiful woman," he murmured against the heated skin of her neck. He pressed his erection into her pelvis, eliciting a soft moan.

Hard, cold tile pressed into her body while hot need filled the space where his pelvis made contact with hers. A purposeful grind of his hips had Maggie gasping for air as she stared up at his face.

"So what are you waiting for?" she asked as she pressed her body upward into his erection and reached to remove his leather jacket.

His dark eyes scanned her face as he held her in his powerful grip. "Is that a dare?" In one easy motion, he tilted her head back and began to lick the hollow of her throat, his tongue creating circles of fire that quickly spread to the rest of her body.

She clasped his head in her hands and angled her lips toward his. His mouth was wet, his breath hot as his tongue swept past her lips.

Alive with need, Maggie moved her body against his erection. Wet with anticipation, she moved her hands toward the zipper of his jeans…

With a groan, he once again took full possession of her mouth.

Maggie tore at the buttons of his shirt as she returned his kisses, her body teetering on the edge of surrender. She groaned as the palms of her hands slid over the muscles of his bare chest. His body heat blended with hers, his breath hot along her lips.

Abruptly, Tom ended the kiss.

Maggie's fingers stilled. "What is it?" she whispered along the warm maleness of his throat.

He rolled off her, and gazed at the ceiling. "Can't do this," he said, breathing hard.

Her lips burning, and her body in overdrive, Maggie searched his face. "What do you mean?" she managed to ask over the roar of her heart.

"We have a deal, or have you forgotten?"

"A deal?" Her mind slowly tipped back to reality. How could she have nearly made another mistake? Forgetting Cookie's words of warning, and her own bad experiences, she'd nearly become another notch in this man's belt.

"Yes, I remember," she fibbed, "but I didn't think you did."

"Right," he snorted. "Sure."

"Does that mean you don't want lunch?" she asked, trying her best to sound smart and cool—the two things she didn't feel at the moment.

Hell. What was wrong with him? He'd given up the opportunity he'd been waiting for since the first moment he'd met her. He'd blown it. She was ready to have the kind of sex he wanted—the hot casual kind. He wanted to give her the full benefit of his routine, the one where he had sex with her a few times, then walked—leaving her with all his preplanned excuses on why they couldn't see each other again.

Yet the sight of her lying beneath him, her body arching toward his, had him wanting to run away like some inexperienced teenager. What was happening to him? Why did he feel that somehow this woman was different? That he was about to do something he'd regret? And now she was watching him, but he couldn't meet her eyes. He couldn't let her see that he felt…uncertain…afraid that he wouldn't be able to leave her the way he had other women. And that was too risky because his plans didn't include a relationship…except that of being father to his new son.

Not good. Not good at all. This couldn't be happening to him. He didn't want a relationship, and certainly not with Maggie, a woman who excited, frustrated and exasperated him all at the same time. He forced his lips into smile. "Lunch?" He scrambled up off the floor, buttoning his shirt and zippering his pants. "If you want food, go right ahead. Hope you find something in the fridge to satisfy you."

Faking bravado he didn't feel, he forced his body to

move forward. "I'm going out. See you later," he said, as he sauntered toward the back door.

He forced himself not to look back because if she had tears on her face...

If he had hurt her, he was sorry, but he couldn't let himself care. He couldn't. Maggie would be part of his life until Sean returned. Nothing more.

He reached the door, turned the knob, his need to escape burning in his head. He didn't need Maggie in his life. He...did...not.

He slammed the door behind him.

# Chapter Seven

——— ＞ ◇ ＜———

Hours later, Tom plunked his keys on the kitchen table and shook his arms out of his leather jacket. He'd gone for a drive to get a grip. And he needed to get a grip. He'd come too close to messing around with Maggie. In his experience, a woman raising a child alone was always looking for a husband.

Despite that, it had been a long time since a woman got under his skin the way Maggie Kincade had this morning.

Maggie's life and her circumstances were none of his business, and that's the way it had to stay. She'd said as much. His plans didn't include getting involved with a strong-willed redhead, not in any permanent way. But that hadn't stopped him from doing a little research on his own earlier in the day. Before he'd picked Maggie up, he'd gone to her father's offices to see for himself. Call it nosiness, or call it minding someone else's business, but he was curious to find out why Maggie was so desperate to recover the money Sean owed her.

After seeing the house her parents lived in, and getting a look at the real estate office her father owned, Tom concluded that Maggie didn't really need to chase after Sean for money.

So, that left only two possibilities. Either Maggie had the

hots for Sean, or she had major issues with her parents. The more he thought about it the more Tom doubted that Maggie would have kept her thoughts about Sean to herself if there'd been a failed relationship. Women usually snatched every opportunity to tell all, if they'd been wronged. In Maggie's case, Tom suspected her pride was what was driving her, not some sexual fantasy over Sean.

Or was that wishful thinking on his part?

Maggie had obviously believed she was a partner in Harry's Place, and found out she wasn't. Maggie wanted to prove herself to her father. Tom also suspected that for Maggie to prove herself to a man like Jonathan Kincade would mean she had to become her own financial success.

But what about her son? Why leave him at her parents' house, and move in here? What was she hiding from? How long did she plan to leave her son with her parents?

Hearing Maggie enter the kitchen, he turned to face her. Tom could see the strong resemblance between Maggie and her father. He'd nearly bumped into Jonathan Kincade in the lobby of his building when he went to check out the place. Maggie and her father had the same jawline and the same hazel eyes and the same red hair—which explained why Maggie wore a wig. He figured she didn't want anyone to recognize her as her father's daughter.

"After this morning, I'm not sure what you want from me. So, why don't you tell me?" Maggie asked, her fists planted on her hips, her feet spread wide apart on the ceramic tiles of the kitchen floor.

Tom could see she was a little pissed, and maybe a little embarrassed… "I want to talk about your son, Jeremy."

"Jeremy? What has Jeremy got to do with us?" Maggie said, her eyes squinting dangerously.

He didn't want a major argument with Maggie, and he had no reason to get involved in how she raised Jeremy. Like Maggie, he'd come here to find Sean. Why not leave it at that? "Forget I said anything," he muttered, reaching for the fridge door. He didn't need to be facing her to be aware of the hole her gaze was boring into his back. "Let's change topics."

Tom fished a soda out of the fridge, and let the door slide closed as he snapped the can open. He wanted a beer, but he had to work this evening, and it would seem he had to respond to Maggie.

"No, by all means, continue," she said as she planted herself alongside the counter, so close to Tom that he had to ease away.

Her hair curled around her shoulders in luxuriant waves of coppery red. Her eyes had taken on a golden hue, and her lips were open slightly. Her stance told him that if he intended to have anything more to say, he had better go slowly. "Maggie, how did your visit go with your parents?"

"Are we talking about that now?" Maggie crossed her arms causing her breasts to strain against the cotton of her shirt.

What was it about this woman? He'd been with lots of women, and not one could make him hot the way Maggie could. Tom stifled a groan and went to the kitchen table, choosing to sit on the chair on the far side of the table—his best chance of hiding the erection threatening to embarrass him. "I was wondering how your son feels about being left with his grandparents."

The silence in the kitchen made the clock sound like a loud gong as it chimed out the hour. Twelve o'clock. They were expected at work in four hours' time.

"What does my son's welfare have to do with you?" Maggie asked through clenched teeth.

He had a choice. He could let the subject drop, apologize and leave. Or he could continue. In a flash of insight, he realized how easily he could understand Jeremy's feelings of abandonment because when he was young his mother had left him to go to work. After all these years, he still felt a quiet sense of desperation when he remembered his life with his mother.

A little boy wouldn't be able to grasp the idea that the separation was temporary. "I'm concerned."

"Leave Jeremy to me," Maggie challenged him, her eyes bright, her face flushed, as she propelled herself away from the counter and stomped past him.

"Wait!" he said, grabbing her arm as she strode by him.

"Take your hands off me. I've had enough for one day. First my parents, now you. Everybody wants to run my life…and tell me what to do when it comes to Jeremy. But it's my life, and he's my son, so butt out!"

"Maggie, if he was my son—"

"Well, he's not. Besides, who are you to tell me what to do when it comes to Jeremy?" Maggie moved to stand in front of the window.

She was right. He'd fathered a child, and never known about it until a few months ago. As to how he felt, he hadn't a clue, except he knew that possibly a child's happiness hung in the balance.

He reached Maggie in two strides, and cupped her shoulders with his hands. "I'd like to help."

Maggie's eyes stung with tears. The man who had nearly made love to her on this very floor had demanded answers to questions he had no right to ask. And said things that hurt her, without one tiny bit of care. And then he offered his help…

"Please let go of me," she whispered, desperate to escape him before her voice broke. She'd had enough to worry about and what Tom Rawlins thought didn't matter a twit to her.

Tom let his hands fall to his sides, his eyes dark, and for a few moments Maggie thought she saw signs of regret in his eyes. But Tom Rawlins didn't have anything to regret. He'd had exactly what he wanted out of life. Men like Tom always did.

"Maggie, I'm sorry. I didn't mean to hurt you."

She didn't want to believe him. To believe him was to admit that his opinion mattered to her. "No, you were trying to run my life. And if I needed someone to do that, my father would be first in line."

"I just think that you do far too much worrying about money, and not enough worrying about what your son needs."

"Well, you're entitled to your opinion," Maggie muttered, exhausted, and afraid that there might be a tiny grain of truth to what Tom said.

"Maggie, you're right. I'm not trying to raise a son alone, but that's part of why I'm here."

What did he mean? "I don't understand." Maggie saw a look of vulnerability in Tom's eyes, and her heart did double time. Vulnerable was not a word Maggie would ever have used to describe Tom Rawlins. Tough, maybe. Self-confident, certainly…but never vulnerable.

The Tom Rawlins of this world took what they wanted, and left the rest.

"Sit down," Tom said, his voice a low growl, but Maggie was sure she heard a pleading note in it.

Curious, Maggie slid into the chair across from him, and placed her hands, palms down on the table. Tom could still be kidding her, in fact, he probably was. "Do you have a son?"

Tom rubbed his jaw, his eyes not meeting hers. "Maggie, I want to tell you something. My mother was absent from my life, even when she was around. My dad died when I was eight. As I see it, you're very lucky. Your parents just want what's best for you. They have money and influence, and they're willing to help you any way they can."

The air rushed from Maggie's lungs as she stared at Tom. His life hadn't been as easy as she suspected. "I'm sorry. I had no idea."

"No reason you should. And there's no reason to feel

sorry for me. I've learned to cope," he said, his eyes locked on hers, his smile rueful.

Maggie reached across the table and tucked her fingers into his hands, and felt an answering squeeze. Tom Rawlins hadn't said one word about himself or his background until now. And Maggie had never asked. "But it couldn't have been easy for you," she murmured.

Tom played with her fingers, his hands rubbing hers, again sending heat rushing through her body. "You get over it, or you let it run your life. I chose to get over it."

His life hadn't been easy, but he persevered and she admired him for that.

"Jeremy's a very lucky boy. You're a very lucky mother to have him. All the money in the world can't replace what you have."

"You're right," Maggie said with a level of regret.

"Of course I am." Tom gave her a cheeky grin, leaned across the table, took her chin in his hands, and kissed her.

A warm flush made her whole body glow. There were so many little things about Tom that annoyed and infuriated her, but he had one quality that made the rest seem irrelevant at the moment. He made her feel utterly desirable.

Yes, at that moment, and beyond any doubt, Tom Rawlins was the single most dangerous threat to her world.

She'd almost made a huge mistake earlier. She had to regain control of this situation, get the conversation back to Tom and his earlier remark. "You didn't answer my question. Do you have a son?"

"Like you said, Maggie, I have no business meddling in your life, which means you have no business meddling in mine."

Did Tom have a son and regret not being part of his life? Was that why the man kept harping at her about Jeremy? It made sense.

She watched as he left the kitchen and went into the den. She heard the television come on, and then a sports announcer's excited description of a football play. She touched her lips, remembering those few lethal seconds when he'd kissed her… Yeah, he was definitely dangerous.

Living with Tom would prove her undoing. But it was the look in his eyes when he talked about Jeremy. He really wanted her to do the best she could where Jeremy was concerned, and he didn't even know her son. He showed more caring for her child in the past few moments than Mac Evans ever had.

Fighting the memories of those few days after Jeremy was born and before Mac left, Maggie clutched the edge of the table. She couldn't let Tom get to her like this. This was not the Tom Rawlins she knew, and she had to believe that his caring was a ploy to get closer to her. Hadn't she nearly had sex with him right here on the kitchen floor?

She'd promised herself that she'd never, ever again become involved with someone like Tom—someone smart, sexy and self-absorbed. What she needed was to get her plan organized—the plan to get Tom out of her life and out of the picture.

In her confusion around how nice Tom seemed to be, she'd let him get too close. She touched her heated cheeks. She had to put a stop to this before she did something really stupid. And the way she was feeling right now, doing something stupid wasn't that far off.

Maggie disappeared into her room and Tom took the opportunity to get something to eat. Hiding out like this was hardly a man's answer to a dilemma with a woman, but for now it was the best he could do.

Hell! He'd nearly told her about his baby boy, and he had no intention of telling Maggie Kincade something so personal. He'd managed to distract her for the time being, but he was pretty sure Maggie wouldn't let the subject drop. He'd learned a long time ago that you couldn't trust women when it came to really personal stuff, because they either wanted to become involved, or they ended up using it to be hurtful.

He'd have to be careful from now on. Maggie couldn't be allowed to learn anything more about him.

Tom whistled tunelessly as he dabbed mayo and mustard on rye bread, and slapped several slices of smoked turkey onto one side of the sandwich. Maggie was more of a problem than he'd thought at first. It wasn't just her physical charms, although those were plenty powerful enough…but it was also the way she had argued her case, and defended her right to be a parent with a life of her own. He might not agree with her, but he was impressed by her determination.

Didn't he feel the same way when it came to his infant son?

He cut his sandwich in half and pulled a pop from the fridge. He was about to enjoy his lunch when he heard Maggie coming full speed down the hall from her bedroom. Intrigued, he waited to see what would happen. She rounded the corner and came into the kitchen, her face flushed, her eyes squeezed into nervous slits.

"What's up?" he asked, piling Doritos on his plate.

"I do need to talk to you," she said, swinging her gorgeous body around and coming to rest against the counter within touching distance of his fingers.

"Anything serious?" Tom asked, recognizing the set of her jaw and her dark expression for what it was. Maggie Kincade was on the warpath. He placed his lunch on the table as he sat down and waited for the inevitable.

Maggie slid into the chair across from him and knit her fingers together nervously. "I don't think this arrangement is working out very well."

"That's odd. I was just thinking how pleasant life was. A good lunch." He eyed his sandwich, then moved his glance to her. "A job, and a roommate who keeps me on the straight and narrow."

"That's part of the problem. I mean…you and I spend too much time together…getting on each other's nerves."

"I don't think it's your nerves you're worried about. I'm thinking it's another part of your anatomy," he said, waiting for her hot denial.

"Think what you'd like," Maggie said, a rosy tint staining her cheeks. "But I'm serious. You and I, living here, will not work."

Tom frowned in disbelief. "Hey, wait a minute. First, you tell me not to run your life, and then you prance in here and start trying to run mine."

"Well, you're the one who told me I shouldn't put money ahead of my son. What if I told you I wanted to bring Jeremy here to live with me?"

"I'd say you're not thinking straight. Your mother would be upset, and your father would be on the doorstep of this house, wanting to know where his grandson was. And besides, with shift work, how would you take care of him?"

She squeezed her fingers tighter. "I'll worry about my father," she muttered.

"And if Jeremy's going to live here, you'd better start worrying about who will babysit while you're at work. You haven't thought this through, Maggie."

Her startled glance told him he'd caught her in a lie…that she had no intention of bringing Jeremy into this house. "What's really going on?"

"I want you out of here."

"You mean you want me out of your life." Tom chomped on his sandwich as he glared at Maggie. He was unable to believe that a short while ago he'd been entertaining the idea of making love to her.

Now, he was sitting across from the ice princess. An ice princess with an agenda. "So you want me out of your life? What have I done?"

Maggie's jaw clenched while her eyes shot sparks of green. "I'll tell you what you've done. You've come here, bullied your way into my life, and taken my hours at work, work I need to pay my bills until Sean returns. And if that isn't enough, you've decided to be my conscience where Jeremy is concerned."

For one millisecond Tom considered telling Maggie about his son, but telling Maggie would make him vulnerable and perhaps strengthen the tie between them. And there was no way in hell Tom wanted any more reason to feel tied to this particular firebrand. "I was only pointing out that money isn't all your son needs."

"Look, you said as much before. I didn't abandon him. I've left him with his grandparents for a few days. I visit him every chance I get. I call him twice a day."

"You're missing the point. Your father could buy Sean's lousy pub any day of the week, and he'd probably do it for you, just to see you happy."

Maggie scowled. "This has gone far enough. Either you agree to leave—"

"Or what?" Tom saw anger flare in her eyes, and knew he'd hit a nerve. "Face it, Maggie. You and I have a pact that neither can break without a lot of explaining. I'm not leaving here until Sean comes through that door." He nodded in the general direction of the back entryway.

Anger scorched his thoughts as he debated what to do, how to respond that would make this woman understand that he was serious. The only choice that had a chance of working, in his opinion, was to clear a few things up between them. "Then, there's the little issue of you and me working together. I'm staying put at Harry's Place. Like you, I want to be around when Sean comes back, whether it's here or at the steakhouse. You and I will just have to learn to accept our arrangement. As for your loss of hours, you can always ask your mother for a loan. Your father doesn't have to know, and you can keep your little secret and your precious pride."

"I won't ask Mom for a loan," she said stubbornly.

"Then, you'll just have to sleep in the bed you've already made, won't you?" he asked, taking a deep breath to cool his temper.

He liked his life simple and uncomplicated. And he had no intention of changing anything, especially not for the spoiled, coddled woman sitting across from him…a woman who looked for all the world like a redheaded Barbie doll.

# Chapter Eight

———>—◇—<———

What was she going to do now? Maggie pulled the keys from the ignition of her old car, and headed toward the back entrance of Harry's Place. Tom had twisted her thoughts, made light of her concerns and had accused her of being a spoiled brat. Was there a grain of truth in what he said? Was that how other people saw her? She sincerely hoped not.

As Maggie strode into the bar, her thoughts turned to Tom and his to-die-for body. But Emmaline stood there, instead of Tom. Maggie rested her arms on the bar and tried for a smile. "Hi Emmaline, I'm looking for my check. Is Harry in?"

Emmaline turned to her, a look of righteous indignation on her rounded features. "How should I know? You're the lady of the hour. You're the one working the evening shift with all the big tippers," Emmaline mumbled, pulling at her skirt where it hugged her hips.

Maggie brightened. "You wanted to work evenings? Would you like to trade?"

"Maybe…" Emmaline twisted a curl on her forehead as she stared at her coffee cup, half-empty on the bar.

Had Maggie found an ally in Emmaline? If the two of them could convince Harry to switch their shifts, half of

Maggie's problem would be solved. *If* they could convince Harry…

"I'm more than willing to trade with you, but we have to get Harry on our side," Maggie said, anxious to escape having to work evenings.

Emmaline turned her stare on Maggie, her expression sullen. "It won't work. Harry will never agree to a change like that, not for me, anyway," she said, flatly.

"Why not? You're the perfect one to work with Tom, and you're willing to work evenings. I told Harry that when he first juggled the shifts. If we both go to him, he'll listen to reason," Maggie said, hope lifting in her heart at the prospect of escaping the long nights working next to Tom. If she had her evenings free, she could be with Jeremy to tuck him into bed at night.

Emmaline toyed with the handle to her cup, moving it back and forth in a narrow arc on the bar surface. Maggie wondered how long it would take before the coffee spilled onto the bar.

"What's up, ladies?" Harry inquired, rounding the corner of the bar, a toothpick protruding from his teeth, and a coffee cup in his hand.

"Emmaline and I have a proposal for you. Something that would make both of us happy."

"I'm all for keeping the women in my life happy." Harry peered at one and then the other as his jaw worked on the beleaguered toothpick.

Maggie spread a weak smile in Harry's direction. "Emmaline and I want to trade shifts."

Harry stopped chewing and stared at Maggie as if she were a bug climbing up the window. "You want to trade shifts? I see how you and Tom look at each other. The sparks flying between you light up the room. I'd better have a little man-to-man chat with Tom about keeping you happy."

Maggie wanted to tell him what he could do with his job,

his chats and his dirty insinuations. But she needed an answer. "Come on, Harry. We're not asking for much. Just a change of shifts. You don't lose anything."

"Not so. I told you before. I have plans for you and Tom."

"Great! Someone else meddling in my life," Maggie muttered, mostly to herself.

"What did you say?" Harry scowled at her, his toothpick halted on his lip.

"Nothing. It would be so much easier for me if I worked days, that's all."

"Why would you say that to the man who's been so good to you?"

What was wrong with her head? Talking with Harry was as bad as talking with Tom, but for a different reason. But now that she'd brought the topic up, she had to follow through, or lose the chance to get something going right in her life. "I could work the day shift, and if things were a little slow, I could work in the office. I have bookkeeping experience. I could do the bank reconciliation, or something like that," she offered.

Harry's beady glance slithered snake-like over Maggie. "You just might have a point, there..."

Harry chewed, and chewed some more on his toothpick, while Maggie tried to imagine which would be worse, all day with Harry, or all evening with Tom. Neither option appealed, but unless Sean walked through the door in the next few minutes, she had to keep trying.

Harry burped, and moved his toothpick to the other side of his mouth. "You're doing this because you think I don't value you as an employee, aren't you?"

"What!" Maggie's eyebrows shot up in surprise. "Value me?"

"Yeah, you've been a good worker, taking the extra shifts. I put you on with Tom, and he's a real good waiter. Maybe you feel he's showing you up a little bit... Maybe you're jealous of his tips. Is that it?"

Maggie shook her head. "No, I don't feel anything where Tom's concerned. I'm quite happy to leave him." *In more ways than one.*

"Maggie, Honey, I see where I went wrong, here. I shoulda made my changes sooner. But there's still time. I'll talk to Tom, and get back to you on this."

"Get back to me about what?" Maggie's voice squeaked.

"You need to feel appreciated," Harry said, giving her hand a fatherly pat. "I'll make it up to you, I promise."

Maggie jerked her hand back. When Harry Washburn showed any feeling, any that even vaguely resembled benevolence, it was time to regroup.

And two days later, she had even more reason to worry. She and Tom had ended up on a day off together. She'd spent the morning at her parents' house with Jeremy before coming back to do her wash and clean her room. The trouble started when she arrived in the yard to find Tom working on his bike. His bare, muscle-hardened shoulders were on full display as he twisted the wrench. Then there was the way his jeans hugged his butt when he leaned over.

She'd said a quick hello and disappeared into the house, out of the way of temptation. Hiding in her room, she sorted her dirty clothes, changed her bed and generally tried not to listen for any sound of Tom. Thankfully, he'd taken off in the late afternoon, but he returned looking rumpled and sweaty.

It was all Maggie could do to put the salad together while he barbecued the pork chops. She couldn't stop licking her lips—all because of the way Tom's hair clung to his neck in cute little curls. His jeans looked as though they'd been finger painted on his body.

She was never so thankful in all her life as when he announced his intention to watch TV in the den.

She'd escaped to her bedroom, listening to the muted roar of some sports event, and waiting to see if Tom made any effort to come toward her end of the house. She couldn't erase the smell of him, or forget the way his lashes dusted his cheeks, his open smile when he walked into a room.

When she closed her eyes, she saw him spread-eagled on the sofa in the den, the smooth skin of his chest inviting her to touch, the fine line of hair from his flat abdomen leading down toward the his pants, and the way his jeans stretched over his...

*Agony!* As she lay across her newly made bed, she still felt the warmth of his body between her thighs as they roared along on his bike. Her body insisted on clinging to the memory, creating heat that roamed through her like a wild animal on patrol.

Then there was that time when they'd nearly made love on the kitchen floor... She rubbed her thighs. What if she went out into the den? What if she let him know just how horny she was?

She rolled on her side, stared at the closed door and tried to cool her thoughts. Men like Tom Rawlins saw women as sex objects, nothing more. Something to be toyed with... Her pulse did a dance against her ribs at the mere thought of how a man like Tom might toy with her. She ran her fingers over the hot flesh of her tummy, skirting the coiled red hair nestled in the V of her thighs. "Think of something, anything but his damned body," she muttered to the ceiling.

Edgy, she got up and tiptoed to the door. Should she go out there? Have her way with him? After all, she was a liberated female...definitely female.

*No!* A man like Tom would expect her to succumb to his charms. She didn't want to be predictable.

"Then, what are you going to do?" she asked her wide-eyed image in the mirror over her dresser. She peered at herself, tucking her hair neatly behind her ears.

What was that tense line around her mouth? When had her pupils ever been as big as they were tonight? *If you haven't the nerve to go out there and get what you want…*

She returned to her bed. There were other choices, she mused. A long walk, followed by a really cold shower should do the trick.

After the late walk and a restless night filled with dreams of Tom Rawlins in all his naked glory, Maggie had spent the morning with Jeremy. Spending time with Jeremy made her world right again. Balanced her.

Jeremy had wanted to go to the stables out back and Maggie had indulged him. They helped clean the horse stalls, with Jeremy squealing in excitement every time a horse lowered its head toward him. Jeremy's grin of happiness wreathed his face when she lifted him up so he could pat her father's favorite Appaloosa.

Back at the house, she skirted the den where she knew her father would be reading the paper. Jeremy settled in front of *Sponge Bob* after his lunch so Maggie kissed her mom good-bye and managed to make it out of the house without talking to her father.

Later that day, when Maggie called the house to check on Jeremy, her mother sounded upset and worried that if it took much longer, Maggie's father might learn the truth. Maggie tried to calm her with a promise to speak to Harry about Sean's whereabouts again, but Maggie knew the prospect of finding Sean was pretty hopeless.

Added to that, was the problem of Tom.

He'd managed to insinuate himself into every part of her life, and she had to put a stop to that. And if he continued to do as well at work as he had in the past week, Maggie wasn't even sure if Harry would keep her on as a waitress.

Who cared if she didn't have Tom's abilities when it

came to playing the crowd? Tom had the advantage. Over half the crowd were women on the make. Tom's natural habitat.

Tom was very accomplished when it came to working a room. He moved among the tables, laughing, talking, joking, and women lapped it up. Even when he'd been a little insulting, the women laughed, loving any kind of attention from him.

But the one positive trait that Maggie had seen in all of Tom's flirtations was that he never followed through with them. And the harder a drooling female tried to catch him, the more adept he was at avoiding her advances. He always let them down in the nicest of ways, and often with a little self-deprecating humor thrown in.

A couple of times, even Maggie laughed at what he said. Tom's humor was infectious, and Maggie had to admit, she was attracted to him.

Here she was again, attracted to another man on his way out of town. Only this time she'd seen him coming and tried to avoid him. What she felt for Tom wasn't the romantic, foolish attraction she'd felt for Mac. In this instance it was lust, pure and simple. And lust she could handle. *Couldn't she?*

Hadn't Tom said he didn't want to be tied down? If he prized his freedom, wouldn't that mean that as soon as he got his money, he'd be gone? No strings or women attached? Perhaps there was a way she could use Tom's aversion to commitment to her advantage...

Yes. She'd thought about this before. Aversion to commitment was the key to getting Tom out of her life.

Her idea had merit. She'd been distracted by his charms and hadn't followed through on her plan, but there was still time to send him packing.

She could tell him about what a great stepfather he would make, how nice it would be to settle down with someone like him. She could even pretend to make plans to spend the money they both hoped to get back from Sean. He'd see how serious she was over him when she showed how willing she was to pool the money. A tiny lie, but one with huge potential to change her situation.

Money and parenthood—two key ingredients that would see Tom headed out of town on his Harley.

Yes, a few little nesting touches; pretty place mats, vanity towels in the bathroom, a few candlelit dinners. Lots of eye batting, simpering expressions. She could fake an attraction for Tom. Truth was she didn't need to fake it—she'd have to keep it under control.

Her ace in the hole was Tom's fear of commitment. If she started making plans for the two of them together—talk a little wedding talk—he would have no choice but to move out of the house. That was one walk a man like Tom would never take—a walk down the aisle. The idea had wonderful possibilities, and a huge potential to exact revenge.

She did a little dance around her bedroom, swooping the duvet off the floor and whirling it around cape-style over her shoulders. The plan was perfect! It would work! All she had to do was cling to him, wait on his every word, insist that he spend more time with her… Tom would be gone in days.

Once he was out of the house, she could manage the rest. Surely Sean had to be about ready to come back to claim his house and his business.

What she needed was to come up with a few good moves, no-fail ones that would absolutely get the message across that she was available, that he was part of her long-term nesting plans.

She pranced in front of the mirror experimenting with a few Bambi moves. She widened her eyes, opened her lips just so and did her best to look blank and lusty. It needed work, but she would practice every possible move that would convince Tom she was a woman with plans to tie him down.

Tossing the duvet on the bed, she rooted around her

cosmetic bag and dug out lipstick and mascara. Humming to herself, she plumped up her eyelashes, brushed her eyelids with dark color and smeared on the eyeliner. She inspected her handiwork in the mirror. Not bad if you liked the hooker look.

It might work, and then again, it might not. She'd have to watch herself, stay in control, keep her emotions removed and remember why she was doing this—especially if Tom took her change of heart seriously.

And if he did? What would she do? A sudden warming sensation rushed through her as she remembered Tom's kisses.

Her own lust, her pure unadulterated lust, could become her enemy in this scheme. But surely Maggie could handle lust… Deep in thought, she made her way to the kitchen.

Maggie heard the rumble of Tom's bike. Fighting off the butterflies warring in her tummy, she went to the sliding glass doors of the den and peeked out.

Tom was coming across the yard, his arms loaded with grocery bags, his black hair flattened to his head from the helmet. There was a raw, physical quality to Tom that made Maggie want to lick her lips. Instead, she took a deep breath, forced all carnal thoughts from her mind, and opened the door. "I thought you'd never get here," she gushed.

"Why, what's wrong? Is Jeremy sick again?" Tom asked, concern knitting his eyebrows together.

"No. I have a bottle of Chianti. I thought you might like a drink of wine with a late lunch," she murmured, letting the insinuation float between them like a light breeze through an open window.

Tom stopped halfway in the door. "Are you all right? You don't look so good." Tom peered at her as if he expected to see measles pop out, or the beginning of horns on her forehead.

Oh, this was going beautifully. She'd only suggested a drink together and already he was trying to change the subject. "That's hardly fair. I've spent the past hour in the tub, moisturizing my entire body. A girl has to take care of her skin." She let the lie slip though her lips and waited for his reaction.

Tom hesitated, looking her up and down. "Here, take this," he said, passing her one of the paper bags filled with groceries.

"Sure," Maggie murmured. It was working. Tom was definitely on edge.

Maggie felt the chill of the milk container against her breasts as she followed him to the kitchen. The cool sensation on her skin dampened her enthusiasm. If there was one thing she knew about Tom, he was very experienced with women. Which meant she probably sounded like an amateur.

They unpacked the groceries, working together like an old married couple, and for one foolish moment, Maggie wondered what being in a relationship with Tom would be like. Tearing her thoughts away from such silliness, Maggie poured two glasses of wine and passed one to him.

"To us," she said, standing closer to him than there was any need to be.

"To us," Tom repeated the words, holding the wine glass to his lips as his gaze roamed over her, taking in every part of her, and making Maggie feel sexy, and desirable.

Her blood warmed under his careful scrutiny. "What are you thinking?" she asked, hoping she sounded exciting and eager.

"Thoughts about you, Maggie," he said, his voice steady.

"Little old me?" She batted her mascara-drenched eyelashes, and was dismayed to feel tiny flecks of the black stuff hit her cheekbones. With her luck, her lipstick was history as well.

She couldn't let a minor miscalculation on the war paint front distract her from her plan. "Why don't we go sit down in the den? I want to hear all about your day. I've missed you so much."

"Maggie. I went for the groceries, not on safari."

"I know, but I've grown accustomed to you being here. You know. Close to me." She thought about giving her eyelashes another workout then remembered the black droppings on her cheeks.

Tom touched her forehead and peered into her eyes. "Have you seen a doctor recently?"

She clutched his arm and let her lips hover over the skin on the inside of his wrist. "A doctor is not what I need," she purred.

Tom pulled his arm back and a very peculiar expression came over his face. "Maggie, sit down."

"Whatever you say," Maggie said, triumphant in the knowledge that Tom was worried. "How about the den, like I suggested?"

"The den is *my* territory," he said, enunciating his syllables as if Maggie were deaf.

"It's such a lovely spot this time of day," she said, trying for a husky tone.

"Yes, but we agreed to split the house, or have you forgotten?"

"How could I forget something like that? I want you in the den," she murmured, watching his face to see his response. She was going to invade more than his space if she had to.

"Just reminding you, that's all," Tom said, taking the bottle of wine from the counter.

"Oh, Tom, I'm willing to cross any territory, especially yours, if it means we get closer," she murmured over the edge of her glass.

"Whatever," he said, a baffled expression on his face.

As she led Tom toward the den, Maggie wiggled her hips just enough to send what she hoped he'd see as a come-on. A little bump and grind would get the message across. Besides, Tom had a way of looking at a woman that made wiggling a necessary activity of daily living. "Why don't we sit together on the sofa?" she offered in the most sultry voice her vocal chords could produce.

As much as behaving like a clinging female went against everything she prided in herself, Maggie was willing to make the sacrifice. She sank into the sofa, tucked one leg under her and gave a long, exaggerated sigh. Sipping her wine, she glanced coyly at Tom as he sat down next to her, his hand brushing her knee as he settled back.

"This is nice, isn't it? Just the two of us, a bottle of wine and no distractions," Maggie whispered, licking her lips and giving him what she hoped was a wide-eyed Bambi look.

Tom put his arm over the back of the sofa, just inches from her shoulders, providing her with the perfect opportunity. She eased closer into the comfy spot his arm created.

A long sigh of contentment escaped her lips. *Steady girl. Remember the plan. You're the sex kitten. He's the old tom cat.*

Maggie lay her head on his shoulder, all in the name of duty of course.

In the space of a breath, his arm tightened around her. She couldn't resist snuggling closer, the warmth of his body and the muscled hardness of his chest wrapping her in a beautiful feeling. What it was she wasn't sure, but certainly something she'd never experienced before.

Of course, even if the feeling was real for the moment, it wouldn't last. She knew that better than anyone. But all this heat and shortness of breath was working. She ran her fingers lightly over his chest and was delighted to hear Tom's quick intake of breath.

"To what do I owe the honor?" he asked, moving away from her to top up his glass and hers before putting the bottle back on the coffee table.

"Honor?" Maggie tried the Bambi look again, but wasn't sure if she'd gotten it right.

"Yeah, you've never struck me as the vamp type."

*Was he onto her so easily?* "Maybe you don't know the real me," she cooed, taking a gulp of her wine to hide her unease, and to give herself more time to regroup. This role was harder than she'd expected. Being close to Tom was like being close to a red hot, mind-blowing, sexual fantasy.

Her instinct was to cut and run. But her plan didn't allow for any form of cowardice. She'd just have to endure the hailstorm of feelings aroused by his closeness and soldier on. "You think I'm not capable of being attracted to someone like you?"

"Maggie, face it, you *are* attracted to me. We've both known that since the moment we met."

She wanted to get up and leave this hulking egomaniac behind, but there were bigger things at stake. "Meaning?"

"What happened to make this woman—the one who wouldn't give me a second glance a few days ago… Why does she suddenly find me so irresistible?"

"Oh, that," she said, feigning disinterest, which was a bit of a struggle, probably due to the wine weaseling through her system. "I have my bad days, like anybody else."

She smiled sweetly at him, meeting his skeptical glance as she did so. The whole thing wasn't going so well, and most of the problem was hers. She was no good at seduction, no good at all. And it showed. What had made her believe such an idea could work? He was very close to seeing right through her efforts. Which meant that she was scant minutes from being exposed for the fool she was. Maggie wanted to fade into the sofa, out of the reach of Tom, and away from her stupid scheme.

"I understand. I have my bad days too," Tom said, settling back beside her, his thigh brushing hers as he put his arm around her.

"You do? I find it really hard to work for Harry," Maggie said, grabbing the first topic that came to mind. Running a nervous hand through her hair, she watched Tom sip his wine, intrigued with the way his throat moved when he swallowed. He seemed to believe her explanation and her performance.

What would a true seductress do next? Would she touch him? She would most certainly be making wooing sounds. She cleared her throat in preparation, and then changed her mind. Wooing sounds would only make him more suspicious.

Where would she start, if she intended to seduce Tom? Maggie had to admit he had a very masculine profile, and his eyelashes were so thick, and black. And his body…a piece of erotic art.

Tom moved closer. His dark eyes sent awareness rocketing through her.

"I've never known you to stare at me quite so intently," he said, his voice husky.

His thousand-watt sex appeal surrounded her.

She gave him a shaky smile as she struggled to gain control of the ache starting low in her body. "Tom, I don't know…I mean I want you to know that I really feel—"

"You feel what? Come on, Maggie, you can tell me." Putting his wine glass down, he took hers and placed it beside his. Slowly, he leaned closer, his fingers playing with her hair.

He was so close she could feel his breath on her cheek. She had a wild urge to wrap her arms around his neck and kiss him. A real vamp would do that…and it would be so easy.

And the whole clingy thing? She had to convince him that she was clingy, heard wedding bells in their future…all that other stuff that would drive him away. "Have you ever really wanted someone? Someone in your life, for good?" She swallowed over the pounding of her heart. "Someone to spend the rest of your life with?"

"No, I haven't. But things change, don't they Maggie?" He didn't pull away from her. He wasn't acting as if the whole subject scared him.

"I guess so. I always thought I'd get married," she said, aghast at the tremor she heard in her voice.

"And you did."

"Yeah, but it didn't work out." Why was she telling him this? She needed to focus on the plan. She struggled to put her Bambi look back in place.

"But I'm not giving up on getting married. Are you?" she asked with as much sweetness as she could muster.

"Haven't thought about it in a long time," he mused, a smile hovering at the corners of his mouth.

"What kind of woman would make you want to settle down?" Maggie let her fingers trail over his jaw as she snuggled closer.

Tom gave her a look that reached right down to her toes. "Are you applying for the position, Maggie?" he asked in a hoarse whisper, his gaze raking over her face, sliding toward her lips.

*When the polar ice caps melt.* "I could be. You're a man with a plan for his life, someone who would be a good provider, someone who cares about children, someone who knows how to please a woman," she said in her best silky, breathless tone. She licked her lips in what she hoped was a come-get-me-big-guy way.

Tom shifted on the sofa. A small crease deepened between his eyes. "Is that how you see *this*?"

Was there a touch of coolness in his tone? Was she about to be rewarded for her efforts? "Sure…I mean, I want to know where you stand."

"Where I stand? Maggie, we've barely kissed," he said, his voice laced with caution.

It was working. She wanted to jump up and down with glee, but the celebration would come after he'd headed out the door. "That's my fault. I want you to make love to me," she whispered, stroking his chin.

"Maggie Kincade, you're not the kind of woman who's looking for a relationship. Neither am I."

He had that right, but Tom Rawlins was in for a surprise. "What makes you think I'm not looking for a relationship?"

His gaze warmed, his eyes searched her face. "I don't know for sure, I guess," he said, easing his fingers into her hair, gently rubbing her scalp, making her head tingle.

His scent surrounded her, his body's warmth melded with hers as he held her head ever so gently in his powerful hands. "Why don't we just let things happen on their own?" he whispered.

*Steady girl. It was now, or never.*

She had to come on to him in a way that would make him see she was playing for keeps. "The way you make me feel, I know what will happen," she murmured as she wrapped her arms around his neck and pulled him to her.

"Kiss me, Maggie, and we'll see," Tom said, his hands sliding down to her shoulders as he angled his mouth to hers.

The man thought he was in charge—which was great. He wouldn't realize he wasn't until it was too late. Maggie leaned into him, her lips seeking his. She opened her mouth, her tongue meeting his, the heat of her lips blending with his heat.

He didn't move when she kissed him, but she heard his raw intake of breath. He tasted so good…his lips so soft, yet firm. Her body tingled all the way down to the space between her legs.

His mouth began a slow, sensuous path over her neck. His hands cupped her breasts, wiping away her self-control. Hungry for the feel of him, for his touch, for all the things she hadn't had for so long, Maggie arched her back in pleasure. Her body hummed to his touch as his hands worked their way over her skin, touching, igniting, burning through to her core.

With a rasping intake of breath, Tom pulled her up the length of him as he settled into the sofa. He kissed her hard, taking her breath as his hands cruised up her spine, and into the hair at the nape of her neck. "We were here once before, do you remember?"

She resisted the urge to move her pelvis against the erection pushing against her tummy as she tried to figure out what Tom was talking about. Maybe her ability to understand English when aroused was affected. She hadn't read about that happening, but now thought anything was possible.

She gave in to the urge to do a tiny little grind against his pelvis. "I don't remember. I'm sorry."

His hands locked over her backside as he held her against his arousal. "I mean this room. Remember you came in here one night and tried to get in bed with me?" he whispered against her lips.

Maggie entwined her fingers in his lush hair as she kissed him. "Not true," she said as a gasp of pleasure escaped her lips.

"We were nearly in this exact position. Until you got all worked up about my housekeeping skills."

She couldn't listen over the roar of blood through her body and the overwhelming need to kiss him again. And then there was the whole business of the way he was easing his body against hers, her legs sliding apart...

"This was going to happen, sooner or later. You know that, don't you?" he asked as he kissed the soft skin between her breasts.

"Yeah..." *Me coming home to see your rear end going out the door. No muss, no fuss, just lots of lust and then au revoir.*

His lips fluttered over hers as his hands loosened her t-shirt from her pants. "The lady wants me," he murmured in her ear as he eased Maggie's shirt over her head, sending her hair cascading over his chest.

She shivered in the cool air. Her nipples budded against the lace of her bra. "Yes, the lady wants you." *Out of her life.*

His eyes glittered as his lips laid a path of heat to her nipples.

She gasped in delight. "You're good. I have to give you that."

"When it comes to you, good is easy." He pressed his erection into the space between her legs.

Her body moved against him, ready for what came next.

From the back of her mind, her plan flitted like pale vapor into her consciousness. She was supposed to be all clingy, talk about wedding bells and tuxedos. "I want to stay like this forever. I want to be with you forever," she murmured low and sexy, hoping he wouldn't notice the way her lips trembled.

She didn't mean the words. She couldn't. But surely she sounded clingy, demanding, just the kind of woman that would drive Tom away.

"Whatever you want, Sweetie," Tom whispered as his lips took hers in a demanding kiss that sent her reeling while his hands undid her pants.

This wasn't working quite the way it should, she thought desperately as she came up for air. He was supposed to get all upset when she talked about commitment, the long ever after. He was supposed to withdraw from her, glance longingly toward the door. Bracing her hands against the pillow behind his head, she moved back off his chest. "We're going too fast."

"Too fast?"

"Yes. I need to know how you feel about me."

"You want to know how I feel about you? *Now?* Does hot and horny cover it? Can't you see you're driving me nuts?"

Driving him nuts didn't go far enough. Driving him out the door was the goal. "I want you, but not this way, Tiger," she purred.

"Tiger. Nobody's called me that before."

"Get used to it...Tiger."

"Then what are we doing out here when there are two beds available?" he asked, looking downright eager.

The moment of truth. He wanted sex, and she wanted sex, but sex wasn't part of her plan. It couldn't be. "Are we ready for this next step, what this could mean to each of us?" she asked.

He gave her a disbelieving stare. "Your body says yes. My body says yes. What are you talking about?"

"I'm not sure you care enough for me. I don't want a one-night stand. I want a real relationship, a real commitment from you." She held her breath, hoping he'd get up off the sofa and head for the door.

"Well, well, well. Where did that come from? Has Maggie Kincade fallen for the enemy?" He searched her face for the one truth she wanted to keep hidden.

"We need to think about this," Maggie murmured.

"I've done my thinking."

With your friend below your belt, no doubt, she wanted to say, but held her tongue. Instead, she whispered close to his ear, "I want you to want me for more than sex. I've been thinking a lot lately about finding a father for Jeremy…and your concern for my son…"

The words dangled in the air between them. Silence stalked the room.

He lifted her off him, and sat up on the sofa. "So this is what you're really up to. I show concern for Jeremy, and I'm instant father material. So unlike you."

Maggie scrambled to sit up next to him. In keeping with the plan, she pushed her lips up into a pout. "Really?"

"Yes, really. You're teasing me, Maggie Kincade. Is this some new kind of tactic to get rid of me?"

"What? I'm not leading you on. I'm serious." She tried for a very sober expression.

"Come on, Maggie. Are you taking notes?" Tom said, good-humoredly.

"Notes?"

"For the next time. There will be a next time. I may not be the marrying kind, but I'm giving you fair warning. A beautiful woman is a beautiful challenge. Be prepared. We won't be stopping the next time. Not for any reason." He tweaked her chin, and gave her a smile that had her wanting to go away with him and put up with anything just to be with him.

"There's no end to your ego, is there?" She managed to get the words out before her voice abandoned her.

Tom's hands shook and his body pained from the agony of wanting the woman sitting next to him. And it didn't help matters that she seemed so willing, so wanting… "What was this all about, if it wasn't about us having sex?" he asked.

"I'm not a one-night stand. I'm a mother. I need security," Maggie countered, the color rising in her cheeks. This time her eyes filled with what looked like honest confusion.

"I don't get it, tell me what it is you want," he said, watching with interest as he forced his body to relax.

"When I first met you, I didn't think you were right for me. Now, I think we may have a chance."

Tom didn't know what had changed Maggie's mind, and possibly her heart, but he was suddenly looking forward to the next few days before Sean came back. The thought of long evenings working together, waking up in the same house—possibly the same bed—made him hard all over again.

"Maggie, you and I are going to have a great time together. I want you. You want me. We can take this slow, and enjoy ourselves."

A look of panic came over Maggie's face. "You mean it, don't you?"

"Why not?"

"But…but I want more than that."

He'd heard it all before and then made his escape a dozen times or more. "Let's just see where this goes."

"That won't work for me," Maggie said, her voice low and edged with tension.

His plan had worked for him ever since his first date in junior high. And once again a woman with a beautiful body and a willingness to play right into his plan had made herself available. He loved the chase, the sparring, the chance to capture the heart of a woman, especially a woman like Maggie.

Their few moments on the kitchen floor the other day had confused him, but seeing her so anxious to have sex with him removed his guilt. And he realized now that his feelings of reluctance were more about guilt than anything else. Besides, it was obvious Maggie wanted what he wanted. The commitment thing was easily managed. If she persisted, he'd simply leave.

Tom looked at relationships that way. It was two people playing a game, one he could always win. He glanced at Maggie, taking in everything about her, the pout, the body, the determination. "Maggie Kincade.

What's that song? *We've Only Just Begun*? I believe the title clarifies where we are and where we're going."

"It's not going anywhere. I'm not having a fling with you."

"Oh, yes you are." He gave her a slow smile, one he reserved for those few women in his life who had made the chase worthwhile.

# Chapter Nine

Two days later, she came face-to-face with the fact that she'd failed in her plan to get Tom out of the house. Completely and utterly failed. Now she was battling a bigger problem—an even greater attack of lust. She had to face the very real possibility that sooner, rather than later, Tom was going to…to get her into bed.

Tom didn't seem the least bit bothered by the fact that Maggie wanted to cling to him. He just seemed content to let things happen. Or he was confident in his ability to control the agenda, both before and after they had sex. Her clinginess should have Tom running for his Harley, and the fact he hadn't, told Maggie that he believed he was in control.

And dammit, maybe he was. When she'd embarked on this plan, she'd never imagined it would turn out this way. What started out as heavy flirtation and a clingy routine had changed into something much more serious. This man now invaded her thoughts while his body hinted at promises he clearly meant to keep.

For the past forty-eight long hours she had fervently wished he would take off and go somewhere, anywhere but back to the house with her. Yet, he'd followed her in, offered to fix her a hot drink, and made her feel the kind of warm fuzzies that were dangerous to her equilibrium, not to mention her life. Without being pushy, he made it abundantly clear he had the hots for her.

She'd never been pursued like this. She'd never known the agony of wanting someone who clearly wanted her. Yet, he hadn't made another move, except to make her feel like the most pampered woman on earth and it was diving her nuts.

There had to be another angle. Tom wanted something other than the sex. Yet, he seemed perfectly sincere in that claim.

Not only was her plan to get him out of the house breathing its last breath, she felt powerless to resist his overtures. She'd had so many fantasies about Tom, fantasies that blended into her waking and sleeping dreams, leaving her with a frustration that just kept growing.

Because of his special show of caring and attention around the house she'd lie awake, waiting to see if he'd make a physical move. When she heard him go past her room to the bathroom, her body glowed like the moon on a cloudless night.

If she had a sex life, this wouldn't be happening, or if the batteries hadn't gone in her vibrator…

And to add to her troubles, Sean was still missing, and Harry still insisted that he didn't have any idea where Sean had gone.

After paying a whopping bill for repairs, Maggie parked her car in the back of the steakhouse. Tom had offered to drive her again, but she refused. She had to take whatever measures she could to reduce her exposure to him. Everything about Tom had her running for cover these days. Her body, rather than support her mind, wanted him *under* the covers instead.

The whole issue of money was getting to her as well. Her

biggest fear was that Sean would come back, and he wouldn't have the money to pay her. If that happened, Maggie's efforts were moot and she could find herself on the short end of the financial stick again.

And if that weren't enough, Tom was becoming a bit of a celebrity at work. He'd proven to be an excellent waiter with people jostling to get one of his tables. Everybody liked him, from the cooks in the kitchen to the cleaning staff. Harry's Place was in danger of becoming Tom's Place.

Feeling frustrated and annoyed, Maggie trudged up the steps and through the back door of the steakhouse. The first thing she saw as she moved along the corridor past the kitchen was Albert, the cook, swearing and grunting as he hefted a pot of chili from one burner on the stove to the other. Maggie moved on down toward the swinging doors leading to the bar.

"So, there you are," Harry bellowed. Maggie cringed. Her stressed out nerves pulled tighter. "I've been waiting for you," he said.

Maggie wanted to ignore Harry and get on with her shift, but ignoring Harry was like trying to ignore a hurricane. "Hi Harry. What's up?"

Harry rounded the end of the bar, bearing down on her with more speed than she'd ever seen coming from his spindly legs. "I've got it all worked out," he boasted, "and you're gonna love it."

Maggie had this horrible sinking feeling as she stared at Harry, his bald dome glowing a sickly puce under the yellow light. "I'm going to love what, Harry?"

He wagged a nicotine-stained finger in her direction. "I told you the other day. I've come up with an idea, and it's going to make me rich."

Maggie stared into Harry's eyes, trying to decide what to do. "Harry, I'm not here to make you rich. I'm only here to find Sean."

"I know. I know." He waved his hands in dismissal.

"No, Harry, you don't get it. I need to find Sean, and you can help me."

"I'm an open book when it comes to Sean. He may be a dud when it comes to the money management department, but he sure has the women calling here. There was one beautiful broad in here at lunchtime looking for him." Harry squinted. "Looked a little like you, only the hair color was different."

"I don't care if the whole Dallas cheerleading team shows up here looking for Sean. I simply want you to tell me where he is and when he'll be back."

Harry shrugged. "Can't help you."

"Or won't help me," Maggie muttered, stepping around Harry and lifting the panel that let her step behind the bar. Tossing her purse in the musty cupboard under the bar, Maggie smoothed her fake hair.

"Here comes Tom now," Harry said, his voice filled with excitement.

Maggie's heart kicked over, bumping into her chest. She fixed her gaze on the array of draft beer taps. Without a word, Tom flipped up the bar section and came to stand next to her, ensuring his body touched hers in all the sensitive spots. Maggie shivered with awareness, quietly sucked in a lungful of air and edged away.

"Kids, I want to talk to you about my idea," Harry said, hitching one hip onto the bar stool across from them. "I have a great plan to make more money, and that could mean more money for you two as well." His smile set up a hollow feeling in Maggie's stomach.

"What plan?" Tom asked, glancing at Maggie.

"Don't encourage him," she hissed.

"Picture this," Harry said, holding his hands up as if he were taking a snap shot of the two of them. "Tom, you in a muscle shirt, tight—and I mean *tight*—black jeans, cowboy boots and a cowboy hat. Imagine Maggie in a red halter-top, a skirt, fishnet stockings, and heels."

"What!" Maggie yelped. Beside her she heard Tom swear under his breath.

"Wait a minute, Harry," Tom said, his gaze intent on Harry's smiling face. "It's nearly impossible to wait tables with a cowboy hat on."

Harry had mentioned the halter top the other day, but she thought he'd been kidding. She should have known better. "And how am I going to carry a tray of drinks wearing a halter-top and high heels?" Maggie asked.

"I suppose we could compromise a little, but the two of you dressed in more provocative outfits will have the customers lining up at the door."

"I'm not doing it. I am not wearing fishnet stockings and a red halter-top. That's all there is to it," she said.

"Is that you're final word?" Harry asked with resignation.

Between keeping her libido under control around Tom and working her feet off for Harry, she was exhausted. And now this.

If her work wasn't good enough for him, she'd find a job in another bar. Catching Sean was important, but she could make a deal with Emmaline to let her know when Sean showed up. "I will not parade around here looking like a call girl. I get enough razzing as it is." Maggie squared her shoulders.

Harry looked affronted. "Then, I guess you can give me your notice. I'm sure I can find someone interested in working the evening shift with Tom," Harry said, a smug gleam in his eyes.

Tom had met a lot of hustlers like Harry over the years, but most of them had more finesse. Maggie had been acting strange ever since they'd had their little session in the den a couple days earlier, and Tom had assumed she was upset with him. But maybe Harry had been the reason she'd been behaving so strangely. "Wait a minute, Harry. Surely, we can negotiate something here. Maggie's a good waitress, and she needs to be here until Sean comes back."

"What did you have in mind?" Harry asked, his gaze on Maggie.

Tom could see, by the way her fingers gripped the edge of the bar and the way her wig seemed to rise higher on her forehead, that Maggie was holding back one hell of a redhead explosion. "Look, Harry, I agree with Maggie. If you want to attract the better paying customers, you don't want your waitresses looking like call girls. You want them to look classy, elegant."

"In a pub? I don't think so," countered Harry as he pulled a toothpick from his shirt pocket.

"But if we spent a little time and effort, this restaurant could be a lot more than a pub. This part of town, near the highway, needs a really good restaurant," Maggie said, glancing from Harry to Tom, her hopeful expression fading. "Never mind..."

Tom touched Maggie's arm. "Just a minute," he urged.
She didn't respond.

"Harry, why don't we consider something like this? It's the beginning of the Christmas Season, why don't we replace the red and white tablecloths with red ones? If you agree, Maggie and I can decorate for you, give the place a little Christmas atmosphere."

"Don't have the money," Harry said, a glum look on his face.

"Then why not have Maggie and I wear a bright red t-shirts with our black pants?"

"Do I have a say in this?" Maggie asked, her voice dripping with sarcasm. "It's my body, and I'll decide what I wear."

"That's the whole point, Maggie dear. You are attractive, and you're pretty good at your job." Harry shrugged. "But I'll start looking for your replacement if I have to. Emmaline wants to work evenings. I'll talk to her," he said.

Until now, Tom hadn't cared who worked what, but he suddenly cared very much about working with Maggie. She'd proven to be a good worker, making the customers laugh at her corny jokes, building a rapport with many of the regulars. Without Maggie, the evenings at Harry's Place would be boring.

"Harry, give Maggie and me a chance to talk this over. How soon do you need an answer?"

"End of the shift," he said, moving his calculating gaze from Maggie to Tom.

Maggie let Tom lead her away from the bar to a table in the corner. "Whose side are you on, anyway?" she asked, forcing herself to breathe slowly to control her anger.

"Yours, in case you haven't noticed."

"Yeah, right," Maggie snorted.

"If you want to work here, you've got to go along with Harry."

Maggie hated to admit that Tom was right. She sighed with longing. What she wouldn't give to toss it all and go home to Jeremy, to forget all about Harry, Sean and the partnership he'd promised. But without the partnership, she needed her money back in order to find another investment. "Going along with Harry, as you put it, doesn't solve anything."

"It keeps you employed until Sean comes back. You're not thinking clearly today. You okay?"

"Never better," Maggie mumbled, refusing to meet his assessing glance.

"Then, show a little appreciation for my efforts."

Showing appreciation was last on her list. "Harry's nuts."

"And you're in trouble," Tom added.

Maggie looked into his face, and saw humor mixed with caring—a potent and dangerous combination where her emotional wellbeing was concerned. His hand touched her arm in a protective movement that nearly had her crying into his shoulder. "What do you suggest we do?" she muttered, forcing back the urge to give in to her need for a little nurturing, and snuggle close to Tom. Instead, she moved her glance to the dining room area, and saw Harry circling the tables like an aging Bald Eagle over a field of rabbit holes.

"Let me talk to Harry. I'll do my best to get you a less revealing outfit," he said.

*Why was Tom being so kind?* "You'll try to get Harry to agree to your suggestion?" She really couldn't believe it.

"Basically, yeah. Harry's not a difficult guy to deal with when you give him a chance," Tom offered.

"The only chance I want to give Harry is that he can quit rather than be fired when I'm a partner." she told him.

"So Sean offered you a partnership?" Tom asked.

She nodded.

"That's interesting…" Tom rubbed his jaw.

"Why?"

"Harry holds controlling interest in this establishment."

Startled, Maggie glanced at him. "How did you learn that? Have you seen their partnership agreement?"

"The cook says Harry told him." He shrugged.

Maggie toyed with her platinum blond tresses. If Tom were right, Sean would have had to talk to Harry about making her a partner. Harry's response to her so far clearly showed that he had no idea that she was to have any role in Harry's Place, except to work as a waitress while she waited for Sean. "What am I going to do? I stand to lose everything, especially if Harry has control, and Sean comes back without the money…which is looking more and more likely."

"Let me handle Harry." Tom smiled at her.

She ignored the skipping thump her heart did. "Handling Harry is a specialty of yours?" Maggie asked, to cover her burning need to grovel in appreciation.

"No, but I'm a quick study. Trust me on this." With that, Tom got up and walked back to his tables, leaving Maggie completely alone.

Exhausted and worried, Maggie worked like someone possessed until her break time. As she was about to put her own food order in to the cook, Tom came up behind her.

"Maggie, I've fixed things with Harry."

She glanced up into his face, and her heart skipped at least two beats. Tonight, Tom was even more gorgeous, with the beginnings of whiskers darkening his jaw, and moisture dampening his upper lip. She wanted to lick the sweat off his lips, and move on down from there. "How? Is Harry going to let me choose what I wear?"

"Harry agreed to let you dress like me."

"Cowboy boots, hat and a muscle shirt? You've got to be kidding!"

"No. He's agreed that because it's nearly Christmas, he wants us to wear bright red t-shirts with our black pants."

"What you suggested in the first place?" She laughed and hugged Tom's arm. "Thanks."

He put an arm around her shoulder.

"You're welcome, Princess. Just remember, you owe me one."

She didn't care what she owed him. This was huge. And allowing herself a few more moments of pure sensual bliss, she stared at his handsome face then hugged him. Getting so close to Tom was all wrong. And she'd probably live to regret letting him anywhere near her heart. But by going to bat for her, Tom had sneaked past her defenses.

She knew she'd be awhile rebuilding them too. Yet staring up into his dark eyes, after witnessing what he'd done for her, she had to face facts. No man outside her family had ever treated her with such caring, and it made her sad to think she'd never ever expected such behavior from a man.

Why was that? Why had she always assumed that a man

could treat her badly, and when he did, that it was her fault somehow?

The next man she had a relationship with would show her the kind of respect and caring she deserved.

When she and Tom parted company, and they would when Sean came back, she'd try to remember that Tom helped her understand herself a little better. As she watched him move around the restaurant, she couldn't help thinking that meeting Tom had turned out to be a good thing.

# Chapter Ten

Maggie peered out the kitchen window and watched Tom work on his bike in the driveway. It was clear by the way Tom whistled as he puttered with the bike that he loved what he was doing. After yesterday, Maggie's whole perception of Tom had taken a sharp turn into uncharted territory. He had helped her out with Harry. Of course he'd made reference to her owing him something, but she had nothing to offer him, other than sex and that was never going to happen. She'd survived being around him for days now, and yet she hadn't succumbed to his charms.

In a way, it was unnerving that Tom Rawlins had turned out to be a man of surprises. Not so shallow. Not unreliable. Not always a womanizer.

She remembered the exact moment in the middle of the night when she realized she knew more about Tom Rawlins than she had ever known about Mac Evans. And she had been married to Mac for over a year and had a child by him.

"Life is a strange event, sometimes," she muttered to herself. She was about to turn back to the grocery list she was working on when Edna Cotter came around the corner of the house, her lips set in a very purposeful way, and with Galahad bobbing along behind her.

What do you suppose she's up to? Maggie wondered as she watched the older woman's face light up at the sight of Tom. Was there no age limit on the man's sex appeal?

Edna's usual hand waving and gesturing were absent which brought Maggie to full alert. Hand waving was Edna's signature move. And Tom was nodding and smiling. "I'd better get out there," she grumbled to herself.

Opening the door, she was met by a gush of laughter from Edna.

"Hi, Edna, how are you?"

Edna turned to Maggie, her eyes bright. "I was just inviting you and Tom to dinner tonight. He says that you're both off, and that he'd like a break from doing all the cooking."

Did Tom not remember her warnings about Edna? "Really? *Where* have you been doing all the cooking, bro?"

Tom gave a nervous chuckle. "Well, sometimes I like to try other people's cooking. Edna says she's going to do oysters for us."

"You like oysters?" Edna queried, her attention directed at Maggie.

She could lie and say she was allergic, but the truth was that she had yet to find a food that she was allergic to; if she had it might mean she didn't have to diet so vigorously. "I've never had oysters before. But you don't have to go to the trouble of cooking them for us."

"Oh, you'll love them. And besides, cooking is no trouble at all," Edna said, grinning at the two of them. "I'm so happy to be able to meet more of Sean's family."

*I'll just bet.* "Well, that's very kind of you." Heaven help her, she'd used a phrase right out of her mother's book.

"That's settled then. See you around six." Edna waved and toddled off around the corner of the house with Galahad in hot pursuit.

"Tom, what moment of insanity made you accept her invitation?" Maggie asked.

"I thought it would be nice to include her in our lives.

Remember, we did promise to go to dinner at her house the first day we met. And she's alone in the world."

"Alone? Edna Cotter has a million nosy friends whose favorite form of entertainment is gossip—the juicier, the better."

"What has that got to do with us?"

"Have you forgotten? We told her we were brother and sister."

"Half-brother and sister."

"Well, in Edna's eyes that's like saying you're half-pregnant. She's going to want to hear all about our family."

"Especially yours, right?" Tom tilted his head at her. "You're afraid that she'll uncover your secret life."

"Of course, I am."

Tom wiped his hands on a greasy rag as he studied her. "Maggie, if we say we can't go tonight, she'll only keep asking. Why don't we run through our story, try to make it sound plausible?"

"And if she trips us up?"

"You can have a bad bout of menstrual cramps or a migraine."

"I have a better idea. Why don't you tell her your jock strap is too tight?" she countered.

"Ouch! You're blushing, Maggie."

She blocked her hand from reaching to touch her cheek. "Stop changing the subject. What are we going to do?"

Tom came around the bike and draped an arm over Maggie's shoulder. "You need to get out more, develop a social life. We'll go over our story, be as ready for her questions as we can be. After that, we'll just enjoy ourselves. I'm sure the food will be great, and we'll have a quiet evening out."

"You don't know Edna like I do," she warned.

Tom squeezed her shoulders in a very brotherly fashion. "Stop fretting. While we're convincing her we're related we can pretend it's our first real date."

"A date with a lunatic, you mean. I feel like getting drunk."

He tapped her nose playfully. "Another advantage of having our first date next door. If you do drink too much, you won't have far to walk...or stumble."

"You're impossible," she said, loving the way his arm felt around her shoulders, and the smell of his sweaty body. Struggling to remain aloof, she marched back to the house to regroup. As she peered out the kitchen window at Tom, she realized that despite everything, he made her feel...happy.

Maggie nervously smoothed her sage green tank top over her body as she took one last look at herself in the full-length mirror. She'd painted her nails and toenails to match her top and straightened her hair enough to take the frizz out of it. She didn't have a clue why she was going to all this trouble for a dinner with Edna and Tom.

Nerves were the most likely cause. When she first met Edna, the woman had peppered Maggie with questions about her life and where she'd grown up. When Edna had made a casual comment about Maggie's hair color and suggested a connection with the realtor, Jonathan Kincade, Maggie had denied any connection to anyone in town. Instead she had given the life story of her best friend from college. Edna seemed satisfied, but Maggie knew she had to be on her guard tonight, or Edna might discover who Maggie was. Such a discovery would be the end of Maggie's plans. Edna would be on the phone to her friends the second she and Tom returned to Sean's house.

From the sunroom, she spotted Edna's open back door. Obviously in invitation, it signaled they could come right over. Maybe she could just plead illness and stay home, but Tom might mess up their cover story, leading to more questions from Edna.

A long low wolf whistle broke the silence. "Maggie Kincade, you look good enough to kiss," Tom said.

"Don't even think that way. All we need is for you to have my lipstick on your lips when we do our brother and sister act next door."

"Good point. Maybe after dinner?" He waggled his eyebrows and smiled at her as he picked up the bottle of white wine they'd hastily bought.

"We'd better get going. You remember your lines, do you?" she asked.

"We have the same mother, but different fathers. I'm the child from her first marriage, and you're the child from the second. Oh yeah, our mother was widowed. We're here because our cousin Sean wanted us to housesit. We hadn't realized that he asked both of us, but we've had a great time catching up as we haven't seen each other for a couple of years."

"Sounds good. Remember, when all else fails, change the subject."

Out the door and across the lawn they went, and with each step Maggie's stomach banged harder against the back of her throat. How could Tom look so cool, so at ease, when she was about to hurl on the hedge? Of course, Tom had nothing at stake, no fear to match hers—that Edna might figure out the connection between her and her father, Jonathan Kincade.

So if Tom got caught in a little white lie, so what? He wouldn't be around to face the consequences. "What if Edna's done a whole lot of digging around about us?"

"What's she going to find out? You've covered your tracks. I don't have any connections here. We'll be fine," he said, nudging her up the steps and tapping on the screen door.

"Oh, you two dears. I'm so glad to see you," Edna said, opening the screen door. "Come into the living room. I'm just about ready."

"Can we help?" Tom asked as he and Maggie followed Edna to the front of the house.

"No. You just sit right down here. I'll only be a couple minutes."

Maggie glanced around the room. The walls were painted a bright yellow. Every wall was covered with breathtaking artwork, landscapes in bright colors. "These are beautiful."

"So glad you like them. Painting is a hobby of mine, and I also do the framing work on them," Edna said proudly. "I'll show you the rest of my art after dinner. In the meantime, make yourselves comfortable."

She disappeared through another door, leaving Tom and Maggie to stare at the corner of the room where the largest birdcage Maggie had ever seen sat on a table. Over it was draped a dark cloth, but occasionally something inside the cage poked at the cloth.

"Well, what do you suppose lives in there?" Tom drawled.

Maggie stuffed herself into the corner of the sofa, and as far out of range of whatever was in the cage, as she could manage. "I don't know, and I don't care."

"You don't like birds?" Tom asked as he went over and tapped the huge, cloth-covered cage.

Then she heard a frantic sound, followed by the cloth billowing outward.

"Don't do that! I don't want whatever's in there to see me."

"Good point. Knowing Edna, it could be anything from a snake to a raven."

"Here we are," Edna chortled as she rushed in with a large blue plate covered with raw oysters in the half shell. She angled the plate onto the book-covered coffee table and sat down across from them in a chair with huge claws for feet.

Tom leaned forward, a smile wrapping around his cheeks. "Fresh oysters! I haven't had these in a long while."

He picked up a half-shell, raised it to his lips and something gray slithered into his mouth and down his throat.

Maggie nearly gagged.

"Down the hatch," Edna said, following Tom's lead.

Maggie forced her gaze to the plate, trying to decide what to do. She couldn't swallow something that ugly. "I'll pass."

"What? Oysters are a delicacy and so important to your sex drive. Everyone needs oysters in their diet. Besides, if you don't eat up, I'll be forced to let Rachel out of her cage. She loves them." Edna pointed to the birdcage.

"Rachel? An oyster-eating bird?" Her natural history education was obviously in need of an update.

"No, not a bird. Rachel. She's a dear little thing. I found her going through my garbage one day. I couldn't bring myself to live trap her, and when I discovered she was injured I brought her in here. She loves living with me."

Another thump and bump sounded from the cage, and a pointed brown and black nose poked out from under the cloth.

Maggie yanked her feet up onto the sofa. "And Rachel is a—"

"A woodchuck. I built that cage to get her up out of Galahad's reach. She's almost ready to be released back into the wild." Edna gave Maggie a wistful glance that held more than a little regret.

*The woman had to be kidding.* Maggie glanced at Tom who wolfed down another oyster. Maggie wanted to leave. The thought of eating dinner with that creature a few feet from the table was scary and disgusting.

Edna turned her attention to Galahad who had appeared out of nowhere.

"You've got to help me out," she whispered to Tom.

"With what?"

Maggie pointed to the cage. "With Rachel. I can't eat with that creature lurking, and Galahad roaming around."

Tom shrugged. "She's caged. Galahad's harmless."

"Big fat help you are."

"Don't get all worked up," he said between oysters.

"You're just thinking about your stomach," she scoffed.

"And you should too. These are the best oysters I've ever tasted."

"They should be," Edna interjected as she turned her attention back to them. "I got them fresh from a friend of mine. Best aphrodisiac in the world."

"Who in this room needs an aphrodisiac?" Maggie asked.

"Not me," Tom said, wiping his mouth with one of Edna's mud-colored, environmentally friendly napkins.

"What about you, Maggie?" Edna asked.

"Me? I don't have a sex life."

"I don't believe it," Edna said. "A woman like you, in your prime. You need these oysters more than Tom or me. Eat up."

"Oh, I couldn't ruin your enjoyment," she lied over the bumping noises coming from the cage. Afraid that the creature might escape, Maggie edged out of her seat and moved to the other side of the room.

Searching for something to explain her sudden repositioning, she pointed at the painting of the nude hanging over the fireplace. "Very nice." It wasn't, but it was the best change of topic she could come up with on such short notice.

"I like it too. An old boyfriend of mine painted it. I was only twenty at the time."

"That's you?" Tom asked.

"Yeah," Edna sighed. "I had so much fun with him."

Maggie was too busy sniffing the air to care what Edna had done back before Maggie was born. "I smell something burning."

"Oh dear me," Edna hopped up.

"Can we help?" Maggie queried.

"Stay put. I'll be right back." Edna scurried off to the kitchen while Maggie remained on the far side of the room, far away from the cage.

After a few minutes, Edna appeared in the doorway again.

"Dinner's on," she announced.

With a blend of relief and foreboding, Maggie followed Tom to the dining room.

"You two sit here. I'll be right back." Edna pointed to two chairs directly across from each other at the narrow table. "Pour the wine, would you, Tom?"

"Will do," Tom said, reaching for the corkscrew and bottle resting on the corner of the table. Tom poured Maggie a glass of Chardonnay, which she promptly gulped down. Within minutes, her head responded to the call of alcohol by going all light and funny.

"Easy, there. You don't want to peak too soon," Tom said. He looked at her over the rim of his glass, his eyes dark even in the glow from the huge candelabra set at the far end of the long table.

Trying to get comfortable, Maggie stretched her legs out under the narrow table, bumping into Tom's as she did so. Instinctively, Maggie moved her legs out of the way.

She ignored the open invitation in his eyes. "Pour me another glass. I need it." She stared around at the purple walls of the dining room, checking for any other animal hiding spots. She gulped her second glass as insurance. As the wine whistled through her system, Maggie slid down in her chair, stretching her legs out further under the table.

Tom slid his legs around hers, trapping them. "What an interesting position to be in." Tom rubbed his legs along hers.

"What are you doing?" Maggie muttered, struggling to free her legs.

"I'm playing," he said. His hands slid across the table toward her, and he caught her fingers in his.

"Not with me you're not." She wiggled her fingers and legs to free them.

He tightened his grip.

"Relax, Maggie," he whispered with the most seductive tone she'd ever heard, as his thumbs massaged her palms.

"How can I relax, with you chock-a-block full of oysters and a woodchuck waiting to break loose, not to mention a crazy woman in the kitchen with her pet skunk?" But the wine had taken hold, and the caress of Tom's fingers wove a trail of sensation that made her want to squirm with pleasure instead of push away.

"Relax and let me show you."

Somehow his shoeless foot had wormed its way between her legs and was working up toward her thighs. "I don't want you—" She gasped as his toes wiggled into the space between her knees.

"Oh, Maggie. That feels so good," he whispered as his hand reached out to stroke her hair.

The gentle tug of his fingers made her want to turn her face into his hand and kiss his palm. "Edna will see us."

He leaned over the table, his lips headed straight for hers. "So what?"

"Now, what are you two up to?" Edna bustled into the dining room with a large-wheeled cart, loaded down with steaming bowls of food.

Maggie snapped her lips closed. "Nothing."

"I was helping Maggie. She had something in her eye." Tom turned his charming smile on Edna.

"You two are so kind to one another. That's so nice to see in a brother and a sister." Edna tittered while she filled plates from the cart.

"Yeah," Tom said, his gaze locked on Maggie's, holding her in its velvet grip as he pretended to study her eye.

The heat growing in Maggie's body started at her knees, swirling up into her tummy. All she could think about was pressing her lips to Tom's, tearing his shirt from his gorgeous, rock-hard body, and making love to him in the middle of Edna's dining room table. Instead she eased her trembling body back into her chair and watched in disbelief as Edna placed a huge bowl of fish chowder in front of her. "That's lovely, Edna, but I don't need—"

"Now, never you mind. You work hard, and you need to eat," she scolded as she put a bowl in front of Tom.

Meanwhile, his foot was working its way back up toward her thighs again, his gaze daring her to answer him with her body. Over the roar of desire, Maggie was vaguely aware of Edna sitting down at the head of the table. Maggie gulped more wine, and reached for her soupspoon, just as Tom's foot squeezed between her thighs.

She fired a warning glance at him.

He answered by wedging her legs apart and easing his toes up into the dark recesses of her thighs. She gasped in pleasure.

"Is the soup too hot?" Edna inquired of Maggie.

"No, it's wonderful." Maggie reached for a roll, anything to keep her hands from reaching for Tom.

"This is absolutely wonderful, Edna," Tom murmured as his toes rubbed Maggie's aching flesh, and his gaze trailed over her blushing face.

"Glad you like it. I have to confess. This chowder came from the local fish market. They do such a nice job with fish—so tender and moist—it's irresistible."

"Moist and irresistible," Tom said while his toes continued to wreak havoc below the table.

Maggie wanted to give him a look that would make him remove his toes, but it wasn't in her. All she really wanted was to writhe against their probing firmness, and to let the heat building in her take control. She should have moved her chair back, moved her body out of his reach, but she was powerless to resist the pulsing heat cascading through her.

Somehow, Maggie managed to get through the chowder

and the main course without throwing herself across the table and into Tom's arms, but it had taken every ounce of self-restraint she possessed.

"Now, tell me about yourself, Tom. Maggie told me that she and Sean are cousins."

"Sean's my cousin too, and we were waiters in the same restaurant years ago."

"Oh, where?" the older woman inquired.

"Syracuse." He winked at Maggie.

"Never been there, but I imagine it's nice, don't you think, Maggie?"

Maggie fought the urge to wiggle her bum closer to Tom's toes as she sifted through her wine-soaked mind for an appropriate answer. "I'm sure it's nice. But I've never been there."

"You haven't?" Edna asked.

It was hard to concentrate on what the woman was saying with Tom's toes continuing to massage her aching flesh. "I went to Cornell, but that's as close as I got to Syracuse." It was only partly a lie.

"That's a wonderful school. I had a niece who taught there. I don't get it. Why would you work in a saloon when you could have a much better job?"

Maggie had always had her answer ready when people started to pry into why she didn't go the country club route. "I didn't really care for college. I like to work with my hands."

"I do too," Tom said, but it sounded more like a croon to Maggie's ears.

Once the first course was finished, Edna appeared with a lamb dish prepared in a tagine. Maggie tried to concentrate on something other than Tom's under-the-table antics. She attacked her plate of food, the flavors literally melting in Maggie's mouth. Edna knew how to cook.

"Edna, you did a great job with the lamb. I'll have to get your recipe sometime," Tom said, his toes creating circles of sensation on Maggie's inner thighs.

"I'm sure I can find a copy. I type all my recipes out on the typewriter, and then photocopy them. I'll check while I'm getting dessert. Who wants coffee?"

Maggie had to stop Tom before Edna figured out what was going on under the table, or worse, in case she had the big O right there at the table. With all the self-restraint she could muster, Maggie eased her chair back just enough to feel Tom's toes slip away from her inner thighs.

The tension in her body eased. "I'll have coffee. Do you want me to help you?"

"No, you just relax and enjoy the evening. I'll be right back."

The moment Edna disappeared Tom got up and came around the table. He stood behind her, his fingers working over the skin of her neck, down along the edge of her tank top as he cupped her breasts in his powerful hands.

"Maggie, I want you," he whispered in her ear, his hot breath reducing her to Jell-O.

She turned and his lips came down on hers, hard and demanding while his fingers played with her hard nipples through the smooth fabric. "We have to get out of here. Now." Her breath bubbled up against his lips.

"We'll have to come up with an excuse," he whispered, his mouth covering hers, as he eased her up off the chair and into his arms.

She pressed herself against the length of him hungry for his touch, his warmth and the way he answered her need. Wonderful feelings of excitement made the room spin. "I'm going to faint…but I'm not the fainting kind."

"That's *it*!" he said as he kissed her again, letting his lips linger on her cheek.

"What is?"

"Here." He picked her up in his arms to the sound of her muffled whoop of surprise.

"What are you doing?"

"Taking you home. Close your eyes and pretend to be

out cold." Holding her hard against him, he went into the kitchen.

"Edna, I'm sorry, but Maggie just fainted. I'm taking her home. We'll have to take a rain check on dessert."

"Is she okay?" Edna touched Maggie's arm.

As much as Maggie wanted to see the look on Edna face, she kept her eyes shut.

"I'm sure she will be. Looks like she had a little too much wine."

Maggie did the best version of a rag doll she could manage as Tom carried her out the back door and across the yard to the house. Maggie luxuriated in the touch of his hands and his arms around her and the way the muscles of his chest pressed against her.

As he stepped inside the patio doors, he closed the curtains and lowered her to the floor. "Now Princess, it's payback time," he said as he took her face in his hands and kissed the breath from her lips.

Tom let his fingers slide through her hair, across her shoulders and along her neck as he deepened the kiss. Feeling the pressure of her body as her arms moved up around his neck told him all he needed to know. "I'd invite you to my room, but it's a mess. Is yours any better?"

Maggie's dreamy expression softened her features, making her even more beautiful. "Not much, but the bed's made," she whispered.

Tom scooped her up and carried her down the hall, remembering the first day he'd followed her down the same hall, and what his expectations had been then.

"I know what you're thinking," she said, toying with the chain at his neck as he carried her.

"You do? I'm thinking your hair is one of the most beautiful things about you." He put her on the bed as gently as possible and fanned her hair out around her head.

"Oh really? I thought you were remembering the day we met."

"And maybe you can read my mind." He ran his fingers along her brow and down along her cheek, drawing out the movement until he saw her eyes darken. His fingers reached her mouth.

"Maybe," she said, the tremor in her voice telling him the effect his touch was having on her.

"Can you read my mind now?" he asked, easing his fingers along the super sensitive line of her lips.

She edged her hips over, creating room for him on the bed beside her, a soft smile suffusing her face. "Like a book," she murmured, eagerly pulling at her tank top.

"Not yet. I want to undress you. I want to see you become naked." He reached for the zipper on her pants, trying to move slowly despite the pressure building in him. Maggie lifted her hips and Tom slid her free of her clothes. Next, he started at her feet rubbing them, eliciting a mew of pleasure from her as he did so. "Want me to recite a nursery rhyme for you?" he asked, lifting her foot and sucking gently on each toe.

She raised her head, her heated gaze meeting his. "I love what you're doing to me," she whispered. Her head fell back on the pillow and her back arched in pleasure.

Having kissed and suckled each toe, his mouth moved up to the tender inside skin of her legs, while his body strained for release. She writhed against him, angling her body in line with his as soft groans slid from her lips.

Her hot hands moved over him, and with each sharp intake of breath, she freed yet another button on his jeans.

"I want you," she murmured, her words rushed as she pulled his underwear off his erection, her fingers frantically working to feel the fullness of him.

"Careful." He breathed the two syllables close to her ear as he settled in between her legs.

She lifted her pelvis to meet his, her fingers scraping his shoulders with a rasping eagerness they both understood.

"Now," he whispered, his hands moving down toward the V between her legs.

She wiggled, bringing her pelvis hard against his erection. Her hands reached to pull her top over her head.

Her breath came in short gasps as Tom undid her lace bra and her perfectly formed breasts slid toward his waiting mouth.

"I want to touch you," he murmured, easing his fingers into the heated space between her legs while he took her nipple into his mouth.

Maggie bit down on her bottom lip to keep from screaming. She had never felt this agony of pleasure before, had never known what it was like to lose herself in someone. And still his fingers moved inside her…his mouth continued to ravage her breasts. She raised her arms over her head in pleasure, pushing her pelvis closer to his demanding fingers, eliciting a groan from him as he raised his eyes to meet hers. Pinning her wrists with one hand, he angled his body over hers.

She was at his mercy and reveled in it. As he eased into her, she crested a wave of sensation so powerful she could only whimper.

# Chapter Eleven

The next morning, Maggie woke up in a mass of tangled sheets and with a headache pounding behind her eyes. She could blame the headache on the wine, but the rest...

She raised her aching head and glanced around the room. Everything pretty well looked the same as before, despite the fact that she'd had the best sex of her life last night.

She now knew Tom was very skilled at pleasuring women, because she was sure as hell pleasured. Every part of her anatomy had the memory of his fingers imprinted on it. "Tom?" she croaked, clearing her throat while she held her head steady.

Then she saw the note propped up on the overnight table. She managed to stand, and with one eye closed, she squinted at the note.

*Gone out. Back later.*

Disappointment washed through her. She'd wanted him to be here when she woke. She'd wanted to believe that she mattered to him in some small way. But he'd taken off. How silly of her to believe that she mattered to a man like Tom!

Naked, she moved as quickly toward the bathroom as her head would allow. Prying open the medicine cabinet, she gulped down a couple of pills and a glass of water to ease her pounding head. She closed the door and caught sight of herself in the mirror. Her skin was flushed from whisker burn, and there was a huge hickey on her neck.

In her experience men weren't born great lovers. They learned the skills needed to arouse a woman so completely. And Tom was a master. He had to have gained his considerable skill somewhere…

Last night she'd let herself believe that his skillful lovemaking had something to do with his caring for her. In the clear light of day, she knew that wasn't true. How could she have been so gullible? Was she destined to always be attracted to the Macs and Toms of this world? She'd kidded herself into believing that type of man was in her past. Now, the morning after, she was waiting and wondering where Tom might have gone. Disgusted, she turned on the shower and climbed in. She'd stay right there until the water washed some sense into her.

Forty minutes later, Maggie's skin was shriveled, but despite her attempt to apply logic to the situation her body still warmed at the thought of Tom. Of course, he hadn't returned, and she was left waiting. Waiting for a man… Same old story.

"Well, at least, I didn't leap out of bed and play Susie Homemaker…cooking him a big breakfast," she muttered, pulling her sweat top over her damp, frizzy hair.

The ringing doorbell made her jump. "Did Tom forget his key?" She padded barefoot down the hall to the door. "I'm coming," she called, aware of the excitement rushing through her at the thought of seeing him.

She pulled the door open to a healthy squeak from the hinges that needed oil. "Edna?"

"I thought I'd drop by and see how you're feeling. I was worried about you last night when you fainted," Edna said, holding out a basket of muffins.

The delicious aroma of spice and apple held Maggie's attention. "Thank you. I'm feeling better, a lot better."

Maggie didn't know what else to say. Edna wasn't the kind who wasted time on idle chitchat unless it was leading somewhere.

Edna peeked around her. "Tom's bike's gone. He's out, is he?"

"Yes, did you want to speak to him?"

"No, I really was hoping for a chance to chat with you, Maggie."

Maggie's breath stopped. What did Edna know? Perhaps she knew about the foreplay that went on at her place last night. Edna believed she and Tom were brother and sister. Another reason to ditch Tom. He'd made her do things at Edna's table last night she would never have done otherwise.

She'd deal with Tom later. First there was Edna. "Would you like to come in?"

"That would be lovely," Edna said.

Maggie busied herself filling the coffee pot and setting it to perk, anything to keep from facing the inevitable. She hadn't a clue as to what she would say, except the truth maybe…

"Maggie, I don't mean to pry, but you still look very familiar to me."

Maggie steadied her hands on the counter as she turned to face Edna. "I do?"

"Yeah." Edna sighed, a winsome expression on her face. "You look so much like someone I once loved a great deal."

Please don't tell me about your sex life, Maggie pleaded silently. "I do?"

"Oh yes. He was tall and handsome with the most wonderful red hair. Just like yours. You have his smile, his flash of humor, and your eyes. Oh my! I never thought I'd ever get over those eyes," Edna sighed.

"Who are you talking about?"

"Your grandfather, sweetie," Edna said, a twinkle in her eyes that made the woman look twenty years younger.

"You knew my grandfather…" Maggie lowered her head in defeat. The jig was up. Edna wouldn't waste a nanosecond running with the news to her father, and he'd be here before she could get her hair combed. What a mess!

"I knew your grandfather. I nearly married him, except he was wound too tight for my liking."

"Wound too tight?"

"Yeah. Jonathan Kincade Senior was a control freak. I loved him, but I wasn't going to live my life jumping through his hoops. He treated women like thoroughbred racehorses who couldn't quite make the winner's circle. I told him where he could stuff his attitude."

The woman was definitely different, but the more Maggie listened, the better she liked Edna. "I didn't know my grandfather very well. I was pretty young when he died."

"Well, he did a good job turning his son into someone just like him, and that's a pity."

"You're telling me! Dad has made running my life his priority. He's probably doing background checks on the country club members under forty as we speak," Maggie said, splashing coffee into two cups and bringing them to the table.

Edna's gnarled hand shot out and grabbed Maggie's wrist. "I understand about your issues with your father. I was young once like you, and my father wanted me to marry well. That was part of Jonathan's appeal. He was a nobody, and I wanted to prove something."

Could their lives be so similar? No. Edna was borderline crazy and a busybody to boot. They had nothing in common except this newfound connection to her grandfather. Maggie tried not to stare at the woman. "I have nothing to prove, I just want to make my own decisions."

"And your dad doesn't approve, right?"

"No, but that doesn't change anything."

"Maggie, don't let your argument with your father stop you from making good decisions. I'm convinced your father started out a nice little boy, but the powerful force of your grandfather's personality held sway over his life."

The look in Edna's eyes said she knew a lot more than she was saying, and Maggie had to admit to being curious. "Any advice?" Maggie asked.

"I suspect your father simply doesn't know how to deal with you on your terms. He sees life as being very black and white. He can't imagine that you wouldn't want his help, and he thinks you're just being stubborn." Edna released her wrist. "If I were you, I'd find an opportunity to have a real chat with your dad."

"Thanks for sharing this with me," Maggie said, realizing with those words how much she sounded like her mother.

"I have something else to ask you about." Edna leaned back in the chair with a satisfied gleam in her eye.

Maggie most definitely did not want to hear what came next, but for the life of her couldn't think of a way to stop Edna. "And that would be?"

"Where did you get that hickey on your neck?"

Maggie's face flushed hot as her fingers covered the spot. "I don't have—"

Edna's eyes followed Maggie's fingers. "I recognized the raw lust between you and Tom last night."

*No!* "You did?"

"I did. And it's wonderful. What would life be without lust? So much more exciting than the alternative. So, I guess your story about you and Tom being half-brother and sister was just a story, right?"

Maggie couldn't come up with an answer, so she just sat there and let the axe fall. Edna would make sure that everyone within a hundred miles knew about her and Tom. Her father and mother would have a fit when they found out.

A chuckle started deep in Edna's stomach. "You don't have to worry. I'd never give away your secret. You and Tom are wonderful together. You two have my blessing."

"Well, thank you," Maggie said, surprise lacing her words. "But we're not boyfriend and girlfriend."

"Then what are you?"

"We…we're friends who work together," she offered, her mind going over this new development. Having Edna's blessing was a treacherous arrangement. Bingo halls and a love of gossip could be a lethal combination when it came to Edna keeping a secret. Edna Cotter's need to gossip was on a timer, set to go off when the burden to keep quiet lost its appeal.

"I'm sorry to hear that," Edna said, her tone sincere.

Maggie mentally crossed her fingers and offered up a short prayer that Sean would walk through the door very soon, ready to pay her what he owed her.

Tom throttled back as he turned into Sean's driveway. Last night, he'd had the best sex of his life, all because Maggie's response to him had been genuine. There'd been no fake movements designed to prove how experienced she was, no calculated porn-styled moves to turn him on. Maggie's response to him had been real. So real he couldn't get his thoughts away from her.

The day was beautiful, and he needed more time to think, so he took a little spin though the backroads outside town. Finally, he turned back, and as he did he passed Maggie's parents' house. He hadn't gotten a good look the first time out there, but coming back into town, he got a chance to really check the place out. There was a lot of money in Maggie's world.

When he reached Sean's house there wasn't a sound when he entered. Could she still be sleeping? He scanned the dirty cups and the basket of muffins as he placed a bag of fresh croissants on the counter. She must have decided to have breakfast with someone else. A little disappointed, he headed to the den. The Cowboys were playing today, and he didn't want to miss it.

He'd just settled in when Maggie appeared at the door.

"Hi there, beautiful. Where have you been?" he asked, keeping an eye on the game.

"I could ask you the same thing. You disappeared without a trace."

"I left a note," he responded, turning and catching the tight set of her luscious lips.

"And that's all?"

"I wanted to let you sleep."

"I've had all the sleep I want. What's next on the agenda?"

Maggie was definitely sounding hostile. He hit the mute button on the remote. "I'm sorry, Maggie. Here, come and sit beside me. I didn't mean to upset you by taking off. I was just trying to be considerate."

She stayed by the door, her arms crossed firmly over her breasts. "I'm not upset. I simply need to talk to you."

He could see anger mixed with worry in her eyes, a combination that hadn't been there before. He turned off the television. "Let's go to the sunroom. It's a beautiful day."

With a shrug, she led the way. "I had a visit from Edna this morning. She knows all about us," Maggie said, dropping onto the wicker sofa.

So that was it. Maggie was worried that Edna would go to her father. "Well, it's actually better to have her know. It makes it easier for us."

"You're kidding. We can't trust Edna. Sooner or later, she'll tell someone about Jonathan Kincade's only daughter working in a saloon, as she calls it. My father will go ballistic when he finds out."

Tom sat down beside her on the sofa, and pulled her close. "Maggie, you've got to stop worrying so much about your father."

She resisted his touch, moving to push him away. "Easy for you to say."

"Maybe, but when Sean gets back and things get straightened out with him, you'll be able to deal with your father."

"So do you think Sean's on his way back here? I can't fend off my father much longer." She brushed her hair off her forehead.

Tom saw the worry in Maggie's eyes and wished he could do something. Unable to resist, he tilted her chin up and kissed her with all the gentleness he could muster, and was pleased to hear her groan of delight. She laced her fingers around his neck, her touch light on his skin.

"We're only steps away from the bedroom," he whispered as he sucked gently on her bottom lip.

"No." She gasped. "We can't do this. I don't need a man cluttering up my life."

Her words held a sting he hadn't experienced before. "I'm cluttering up your life? Well, I guess that's good to know."

"Drop the hurt routine. You and I have a living arrangement. Last night we stepped over the boundary. It's no one's fault, but it can't happen again."

"I wasn't just fooling around with you last night. If that's what you believe, I feel sorry for you."

"Don't give me that! You were taking what you wanted."

"So were you. Maggie, you and I are good together."

He didn't want to say just how good last night had been for him. And as much as he hated to admit it, he agreed with Maggie, at least about the idea that they both had things in their lives that weren't settled. And for him that started with his son.

"I mean it, Tom. We can't fool around."

As tough as she sounded, Maggie's couldn't look at him—a clear indication she felt something for him. Her behavior made him begin to wonder how he'd feel when their life together was over.

And it would be over when Sean walked through the door.

With her feelings all mixed up where Tom was concerned, Maggie made her way into work—but just barely. Her car was acting up again.

She shut off the engine and waited for her car to stop making weird burping sounds. When it sighed to silence, she pulled her keys from the ignition and headed for the back door of Harry's Place.

How many times had she hoped that Sean would be there when she walked in? And today she needed Sean to be there more than ever.

She'd left Tom at the house and headed in early to see if she could find some way to get Harry to help her connect to Sean. Harry had to have information. She strode past the kitchen and into the bar. Glancing around, she caught a glimpse of Harry talking to a couple of men at one of the tables.

Harry wasn't the kind of person that would let his partner go off without knowing how to contact him. Sean's phone number had to be somewhere in Harry's office. Checking to be sure that Harry was still busy, Maggie headed in that direction.

Every *Playboy* centerfold ever published had found its way onto Harry's office walls. Maggie moved around the desk, trying not to disturb the mess. There had to be a Rolodex of numbers somewhere in this mess. She lifted a large yellow pad with words written in a careful script. Harry seemed to be composing a letter to someone.

"You wouldn't be looking for me, would you?" Harry demanded.

Maggie jumped, sending the yellow pad sailing across the desk. "I was wondering if you had a phone number for Sean."

Harry sauntered into the room, his beady eyes locked on Maggie. "You have no right to be here without permission,

Maggie. I'm really worried about you. And you've become obsessed with finding Sean too. That's not healthy."

"I want to talk to Sean."

"I suspect you want to do more than talk. You're looking real tired these days. You seem preoccupied and worried. I'm beginning to wonder if you should be working here under the circumstances."

"What?" Maggie howled in protest.

"You heard me. You need to rest, get a grip on yourself. This isn't the place for you until you learn how to handle whatever is going on with you."

"There's nothing wrong with me that finding Sean won't fix," Maggie fumed.

"Maybe not, but all the same—"

"Oh, Harry, there you are," a female voice purred.

Harry turned. "Jolene, I didn't expect you so soon."

"You told me to come in for an interview. I'm here." Jolene's chemically enhanced lips stuck out in a gigantic pout.

Disgust took root in Maggie as she watched the way Harry's mouth went slack. The fabric in Jolene's top had to be made of ballistic nylon to hold the huge hooters that made their way into the room ahead of the woman.

"So this is why you think I need a rest?" Maggie gave Harry an icy stare.

"Maggie, I told you. I want to dress the place up. You keep fighting the changes I want to make. You can't get along with people—"

"That's not true!"

"It is. You were nasty with Emmaline. You attacked Tom when he first came to work here. You're rude with me. You walk around like you own the place. You got issues to take care of. This is the last place you should be."

If he only knew. Was he serious? Did he intend to replace her with Jolene? She couldn't think about that right now. She needed to get away from the two of them. "You can't fire me," she said, swinging around the desk and charging out the door.

Nasty words describing how she really felt about Harry and his new bimbo rushed her mind as she strode toward the bar area. She slammed into the swinging doors and ducked under the counter for her purse. She stood up and ran smack into Tom's belt buckle. "Ouch!"

"Woops. What's happening? You look like you could do serious damage to someone. Hope it's not me."

"It could be, if you're not careful," she grouched.

"Something going on you want to talk about?" Tom rested his hands lightly on her shoulders and the warmth of his hands and the look in his eyes made her wish that they had a future. Heck. Even a present.

"Harry has decided to fire me."

"*What!* You're kidding!"

She watched Tom's face for any sign of insincerity and found none. "Ask him yourself."

"I will. Where is he?"

"Interviewing my replacement."

Tom's hands tightened on her shoulders. "I get the picture. You wait here."

Words of protestation were on her lips, but she blocked them. If there were any chance that Tom could work his magic with Harry one more time…

While she waited, she filled a couple of beer orders for Emmaline, wiped the counter and checked her watch. When Tom came around the corner, there was a satisfied smile on his face. "I convinced Harry to let you stay."

"How did you do that?"

"I told him that if you left, I'd leave with you."

"You were bluffing, weren't you?"

He didn't meet her inquiring gaze. "Let's just say that Harry saw the light."

❧

Maggie hugged Tom's words to her as she worked her evening shift. Tom Rawlins never ceased to surprise her, and this nice surprise gave her spirits a lift. She caught

Tom's glance as he placed plates of food on a table next to one of hers. She hadn't thanked him properly, but she would as soon as they got back to the house. In the meantime, she had to get a rowdy bunch of regulars finished up so that she could clean the table for the next group waiting at the bar. "Here's your bill," she said, passing it to the man sitting at the end of the table.

"You in a hurry?" the man asked to the guffaws of the other men at the table.

"It's a busy night," she said, watching Tom as he moved toward the bar.

"Listen, we expect service when we come here," the man closest to her said.

"Take your concerns to management," she suggested without looking their way.

"What's eating you?" one of the men on the other side of the table asked.

"Nothing. I'm busy, that's all. If there's nothing else…" She glanced up and saw Harry waving to her. She gave him a questioning look.

"Phone," he called out to her over the din of people's voices.

Anxiety poured through her as she entered the corridor behind the bar. Only her mother knew where she was. "Hello," she said as she rescued the dangling receiver.

"Maggie, Jeremy's sick again, and I'm worried. Can you come home?" her mother asked.

If she left, there wouldn't be enough staff for the shift, but why was she worried? Harry could always call Jolene, and see if she could play waitress for a while. Her arms ached to hold her little boy, to soothe and care for him. "I'll be right there," Maggie whispered.

She stopped long enough to tell Harry that she had to go,

without explaining where. He wasn't happy, but it wouldn't hurt him to help wait tables for one night.

"This is what I mean; you need to get your life in order," he complained as he took her order book.

She didn't give a Fig Newton about Harry's opinion. Jeremy needed her and that's all that mattered. She raced for the back door. Once behind the wheel, she started the car. It gave a rumble, shook and settled back, completely silent. She tried again. Still nothing.

"Can I help?" Tom said through the closed window.

Relief spread through her at the sight of him standing there. "Yes, I can't start my car."

Tom opened the door and stared down at her. "Again? Thought you had it fixed. Where are you going?"

"Jeremy's sick. And yes, I thought it was fixed."

Tom's expression softened. "Wait here. I'll get my jacket."

"Your jacket?" she yelled to his receding back as he ran for the door.

"I'm taking you to your son," he called out as he yanked open the back door of Harry's Place and disappeared inside.

"Harry's going to be really angry now," Maggie muttered to herself as she waited in the cooling night air.

The bike hummed along the highway with Tom doing his usual ducking and diving around turns, pulling out and roaring past traffic—only this time Maggie wasn't afraid. She was more afraid for Jeremy. She should have been there...

She hugged Tom tightly as they made their way out of town. "You didn't have to do this, you know," she said.

"You need to see your son, and he needs to see his mother," Tom said, his words surrounding her, filling the moment with intimacy. Maggie couldn't remember ever feeling this cared for by a man. A bit of a cad, for sure, but still a man who never ceased to surprise her. Was this real caring or was he simply building up a little store of kind acts that he could cash in on later?

When they reached the house, Tom insisted on driving her right up to the door. She was too worried to object. "Thanks. I really appreciate all your help," she said, pulling the helmet off her head.

"I'm coming in with you."

"You don't have to. I can manage from here."

Tom got off the bike. "Stop arguing with me, and let's go."

One look in Tom's eyes told Maggie that he meant what he said. And he was right. Why argue? Tom was behaving like a friend and, right now, she needed a friend more than she ever had in her life.

"How's he doing, Mom?" Maggie asked as her mother opened the door.

Rowena grabbed her daughter and hugged her. "He's been crying for you."

"It's okay." Maggie soothed her mother as best she could then raced for the stairs, her mother right behind her. At the sight of her little boy cuddled deep in the comforter, Maggie started to cry.

"Mommy!" Jeremy whimpered.

"Jeremy, honey, I'm here," she crooned, wrapping her arms around her son, and snuggling in close to him. She felt the heat of his tiny body through the sheets and dread filled her. "How long has he been like this?"

"Dr. McNamara dropped in an hour ago. He thinks Jeremy has the flu. He told me to give Jeremy baby aspirin for his fever. He also said you could call him when you got here if you needed to speak to him."

"Thanks, Mom. I'll call him as soon as Jeremy falls asleep," she murmured, taking her son in her arms and rocking him gently.

"It's so nice to have you here, Honey. I'll be downstairs with your friend when you're ready to come down," her mother whispered as she closed the door behind her.

Maggie lay on the bed, listening to her son's breathing and the funny little snuffling sounds he made as he settled down to sleep. Later, immensely relieved to hear Jeremy's breathing calm down to an even and steady rhythm, she touched his forehead. It was cool and dry. According to the half dozen books she'd read on child rearing, a cool forehead was a good sign. And to recover from the flu, Jeremy needed a good sleep.

She eased open the door and slipped down the stairs to the kitchen. Her mother and Tom were talking in the kitchen as she reached the half-closed door. Tom was saying something about how pleasant Maggie was to work with, how she was so kind to the patrons.

Really? Did he mean that?

More likely he was buttering Rowena up about something. Women like her mother would be putty in Tom's hands. She strode into the kitchen to find Tom at the cooking island doing something with a frying pan.

Well… What was all this? Her mother never let anyone in her kitchen, especially near her stove.

Rowena turned at her approach, a smile on her lips. "How's Jeremy?"

"He's sleeping like an angel. I don't think I need to call Dr. McNamara," Maggie said, hugging her mother close. "Thanks for calling me. Thanks for everything."

"He's a darling little boy, and I love having him here." Her mother held Maggie tightly, her hands rubbing Maggie's back as she used to do when Maggie was a kid. "Honey, I wish you'd stay here with us, and explain your plans to your father. Let us help you—"

"Mom, please, let's not go there tonight. Tom and I have to get back to work as soon as possible." Maggie eased out of her mother's arms, a little ashamed and a lot annoyed that Tom was party to the usual argument about how she lived her life.

"Tom says that he'd look after things at work for you tonight, if you want to stay."

Maggie exchanged looks with Tom who shrugged his shoulders and continued whatever he was doing at the stove.

"This isn't about my work, it's about Dad. You know that. He'll be home soon from his Chamber of Commerce Meeting, and I can't listen to another lecture on my poor parenting skills."

Rowena sighed. "Maggie, I want you to talk to your father about your plans now that you've moved back to town. He can help you. He wants to help you. Besides, Jeremy needs you here with him."

Silence filled the kitchen as Maggie stared at her mother. Maggie knew her mother was right, but conversations with her father were so difficult. Deep down she realized that she was at least partly to blame. She should have been honest with her dad and told him she hated her bank job and wanted to establish a business of her own. But she thought she couldn't because he'd only try to force her into his business, and he was extremely persuasive when the stakes were high enough. And his grandson was the highest stake possible.

Besides, she was responsible for Jeremy, for creating a life for him. If she had only used better judgment where investing with Sean was concerned... Maggie turned away and concentrated on the gathering dusk outside the window.

"Ah, is anyone interested in a bit of omelet?" Tom asked, glancing from one woman to the other.

"That would be fine, Tom," Rowena said, her anxious gaze on Maggie. "I didn't eat any dinner. Too worried about Jeremy."

"What about you, Maggie?" Tom asked.

She met his eyes, his gorgeous dark eyes and felt her knees begin to wobble. "Yeah, I'll have a little."

They sat in silence while Maggie picked away at the omelet Tom had made. Although Maggie wasn't really hungry, she had to admit that she'd never tasted anything quite so good. "This is delicious."

"Glad you like it," he said, his smile warm, his eyes searching her face.

"I owe you one." Maggie had the ridiculous urge to touch him, to reassure herself that he really was there with her.

"How so?"

"You brought me out here, and now you've made dinner for Mom and me."

"My pleasure," he said.

She wanted to stay here with her mom and Tom, and to be here when Jeremy woke up, but she couldn't. Her father would be home soon, and suddenly it mattered to her what Tom thought of her. It would be so embarrassing to have Tom see how awful her relationship was with her father. "Mom, we have to get going."

"I wish you'd reconsider."

"I can't." Maggie got up from the table.

"Well, I guess that's it," Tom said. "Thank you for your hospitality, Rowena."

"Anytime, Tom. It was a pleasure having you here. And thanks again for bringing Maggie. I can't imagine what I would have done without the two of you."

*Call my father? Ask him to help with Jeremy?*

Maggie knew there was no point in voicing her thoughts. Rowena had never ever made Maggie's father share the responsibility of childcare, why should anything change when he had a grandson?

"I'll call you later, Mom," she said, giving her mother a quick hug.

Outside in the cool evening air, Maggie felt Tom's fingers on her back as he guided her away from the bike toward the wrought iron bench along the side of the garage.

"I'm going to talk, and you're going to listen," he said with a hard edge to his voice.

# Chapter Twelve

Tom fought to get his feelings under control as he faced the redheaded menace. Maggie's reaction to Rowena's earlier outpouring of concern had shown him just how selfish Maggie could be. He'd tried to convince himself it wasn't his problem, but someone had to make this woman see what she was doing to her son and her parents.

"Maggie, I want you to think about how your behavior is affecting everyone you care for."

"I've given it tons of thought. That's why I'm not living here. I can't handle the constant nagging about how I live, and what I do."

"But you have to consider how your decisions affect Jeremy."

She scowled. "What do you mean?"

"I mean waiting for Sean to come back may be a wasted effort, and waiting for him, regardless of the reason, is not worth the unhappiness you've caused your family. I've known Sean for years, and he has never been good at meeting other people's expectations."

"A whole lot like me, is that what you're saying?"

"Maggie, you're not going to get me tangled up in an argument about who's right and who's wrong where your father's concerned. But you're going to listen to what I have to say."

"If it means that we get out of here before my father comes back, I'm all for it." Maggie crossed her arms over her chest and peered at him.

"Is that a promise?"

She nodded.

"Fine. Here goes. I don't understand why you made such a dumb investment in the first place, but since you have, I suggest you let your family help with your finances."

"Let me remind you. You made the same dumb investment." Her eyebrows twitched over her snapping green eyes.

Tom did his best to ignore her combativeness. He had a point to make and the stunningly beautiful woman sitting next to him just wasn't getting it. "You should consider moving back into the house so you can be with your son. He needs you and you need him."

"Now, wouldn't my father love that!"

"It's not about your father. It's about you and your responsibility to your son."

"And you'd know about parental responsibility?" she challenged.

"As a matter of fact I do. From the receiving end."

Maggie shot him a look. "And that would be?"

"My mother couldn't manage her money. She went from one wild scheme to another with boyfriends who didn't give a damn, except to relieve her of her cash."

"I'm sorry. It must have been awful," she said with sincerity.

Tom saw the genuine concern in Maggie's eyes, but wasn't finished making his point. "It was hard. A kid needs his parents to put him first. You could be doing that if you'd accept help. You're lucky to have parents who are willing to support you through this financial crisis. Why don't you try putting your son ahead of your silly pride?"

Maggie jumped up off the bench, her face clouded with anger. "Go to hell," she muttered.

He'd hit a nerve. Maggie was feeling guilty about her behavior, as well she should. "No, Maggie Kincade. I'm not going to hell. I'm going back to work. If you want to go with me, get on the back of the bike. If you'd rather rethink your decision after what I said, stay here."

Without looking at her, he got on his bike.

He'd let her see a part of him he'd seldom exposed to anyone. If only she could learn from it. He felt the bike shift with her weight, and her hand touch his shoulder for support.

"Put on your helmet and let's get going," he said, saddened by her decision. "Put your arms around me," Tom ordered, heading the bike down the long drive.

"I don't have to."

Tom swung the bike hard around a curve, sending Maggie sideways.

"Okay, you made your point," she yelled, grabbing his waist and hanging on for dear life.

"Maggie, one way or the other, you're going to do as you're told," he said, letting his anger get the better of him.

"Or what? You'll lock me away in the dungeon?"

He steered the bike into a tight turn as he moved onto the main road, sending Maggie sideways. "Don't tempt me."

She hooked her fingers into the leather of his jacket, feeling the thrill of the air rushing past her.

Tom roared along the road without saying a word to her. She thought about what she'd just left behind, and at that moment she had to admit to herself she wanted to be with Jeremy more than anything in the world. But she didn't ask him to turn around. It was too late for that.

Tom was right. It was her pride that held her back from admitting her mistake to her parents and to him, but she had to take a stand somewhere in her life. Otherwise, she might as well head home, put on the fancy cocktail dress her mother kept in the closet for her, and hang a bride-for-sale sign around her neck.

The endless drive back left her with lots of time to evaluate her situation. What if Tom decided that he no longer wanted to help her, and that's why he wasn't talking to her? At the thought, her heart was awash in loneliness. Why did life have to be so unfair? She couldn't let this man get to her. She couldn't. Besides, he was totally wrong for her—she knew he was moving on as soon as Sean got back. He'd said as much.

The bike slowed as Tom pulled into the back lot at Harry's Place. "We're here. You can get on with your plans to be female entrepreneur of the year, Princess."

"And you can mind your business," she fired back as she climbed off the bike and ran to the back door of Harry's Place.

Two days had passed since the disagreement with Tom. He hadn't spoken to her, except when he had to. No more offers of drives except when she took her car in again. Then she'd taxied where she needed to go. Both days, he'd come home from his shift and gone to his room. After she'd gone to bed, she could hear the television on in the den. Tom was clearly not having anything to do with her. Conciliatory behavior had never been her long suit and she hadn't a clue as to how to broach the impasse between them.

Yet a part of her wanted to be close to Tom, to tease and fool around the way they'd been doing. But he hadn't acknowledged her existence since he'd brought her back from her parents' and that hurt like hell.

They'd both been called in to do a day shift, and Maggie

had high hopes that she might be able to make peace with Tom at work.

Seeing new patrons moving toward one of her tables, Maggie made her way past one of Tom's tables filled with laughing women. As she did she couldn't help but notice that Tom was doing his usual hot flirt routine with the women, and they were fawning over him. Disappointment lurked at the back of her mind. Tom hadn't exchanged glances with her, not once during their shift, yet here he was all over these women.

With dogged determination, she made her way to the foursome who were settling in and picking the menus out of the tiny metal rack in the middle of the table. Maggie, with her pen on her pad and a smile on her face, stood just to the right of one of the men who was dressed in a very expensive dark blue suit.

"What can I get for you today?"

The woman across from her spoke first. "We've never been here before, but we've heard the food is good and the service is wonderful. Isn't that right, Jonathan?"

The man next to Maggie hunched his shoulders forward, his manicured fingers tapping the menu. "Yeah."

Maggie's smile froze in place at the sound of her father's voice. She fought the urge to glance down at him. She couldn't meet his eyes, because he'd know who was hiding under the ridiculous wig she wore. Frantically, she searched her mind for a way to escape without drawing attention to the disaster unfolding before her.

Maggie was only vaguely aware of the flirty tone in the woman's voice, as she discussed a big real estate deal she'd just closed. The other two men were quietly looking over the menu while Maggie tried to recover enough to take their drink orders.

"I can see why this restaurant is becoming so popular." The woman nodded in Tom's direction, then looked up at Maggie.

Her head spinning with trepidation, she waited for her father to glance up as well. How could he not know it was her standing there? Maggie didn't dare look anywhere but at her order pad while she waited to be recognized.

"I'll have a gin and tonic," her father said as he continued to stare at the menu.

Thankfully, her father's infinite ability to ignore women saved the day for her, but the worst wasn't over yet. She might have been given a brief reprieve, but there was very little chance that she could serve a meal to her father and not have him recognize her.

Maggie made her way to the bar where she leaned against the solid wood for support, waiting for her heart to stop its tattoo along her ribs. What would she do now? She couldn't go back to her father's table, which meant she needed someone to take her place.

"What can I get you?" Harry called out over the din of voices and music.

"Gin and tonic, two Bud drafts, and a wine spritzer." She got the words out, but just barely.

"You sick, or something?" Harry asked, his toothpick doing a dance as he pulled on the beer dispenser nozzle.

"No, I'm fine."

"Then, get back to it," he muttered, placing drinks in front of a couple of regulars.

"I'll wait for my drink order."

"Why? I'm gonna be a few minutes," Harry said, filling three glasses at a time.

If Harry wanted to move her, he'd have to pry her hands off the bar. "New customers. Real estate agents. We want them to be happy and spread the word, don't we?"

Harry gave her the once over before starting her order. "You're right."

"I'll have five Coors, if you don't mind, Harry," Tom said at her elbow.

"Get in line behind Miss Manners there." He gave a distracted nod in Maggie's direction.

"How's your shift going?" Tom asked, a pleasant tone in his voice.

"So you've decided to speak to me?"

"Why not? It's clear you got the message."

"Generous of you, I'm sure."

"I'm going to ignore your usual sarcasm in honor of today. I've had a great shift so far, and it promises to get better."

Maggie ignored the curiosity rumbling around her brain. A great shift probably meant some woman had passed her business card to him. Someone he planned to enjoy later, after his shift was done.

But her father was here, now. She considered the chances of Tom helping her out if she cranked up the courage to ask him. She'd rather eat stones than ask Tom for another favor, but the alternative of facing her father's table again was even worse. "I'm glad to hear your shift's going well. Afraid I can't say the same for mine."

"Someone isn't pleasing you? I can't imagine who would be so mean," he said with a droll expression on his face.

Maggie was about to fire off a sassy remark when she caught Harry's disgruntled look. "I just need a little help from you for about fifteen minutes."

"What's it worth to you?"

"What do you mean?"

"I mean, if I'm going to do a favor for you, I want your assurance that I'll get something in return. Nothing's free in this world."

"And here I imagined that you'd given up your nasty ways."

"For you, Princess, I might. Shoot."

If Tom would help her by trading tables with her... "I need your help with table six. If you'll take it, I'll trade you any table you have."

"Table six?" Tom glanced over her shoulder, his eyes scanning the restaurant area. "You mean the suits and the woman with the dress-for-success outfit that does nothing for her in the looks department?"

Leave it to Tom to notice what the woman was wearing and how she looked. Would the lothario ever give it a rest?

He touched her elbow, easing her away from the bar. "Be more specific. Why do you want me to take your table?"

"Do you have to make a federal case out of it? I can't go back to that table."

"Why? Are you afraid someone will recognize you?"

Tom studied the table. "There's a man over there with red hair, a little darker than yours... I'll just wander over and see if he might be who I think—"

"Yes, if you must know, it's my father. For some reason he's having lunch here. I don't want to wait on him. You know why."

Tom looked down at her, the power of his gaze going right through to her nervous stomach.

"Maggie Kincade, you've explained why you don't want to see your father, and you're aware of my opinion on the subject. But we're friends, and therefore I'll take your table...on one condition."

She crossed her fingers. "What's that?"

"I want your promise that you'll talk to your father and get this situation straightened out. I want you to give Jeremy back his life."

"Look, don't do this—"

He pressed his fingers to her lips as he leaned down, his face next to hers. "I don't want any excuses," he whispered in her ear, his breath making her body tingle.

"You're not being fair," she managed over the thumping of her heart.

"Maybe I'm not, but that's how it is." He kissed her cheek.

Heat billowed up in her, taking her breath in one long

swooping gasp. God! How she'd missed his touch, his scent, the way he made her feel! "You'll pay for this."

"Is that a 'yes'?" he asked, laughter rippling through his words.

She nodded.

"Okay. I will take your table so that your father doesn't learn about your employment here until you have a chance to talk to him, to tell him what's going on in your life, and why you felt you had to take this job," he said, enunciating every syllable.

"I will talk to Dad, but please let's get going." She nodded toward Harry who was standing at the beer fridge. "Please don't tell Harry."

"You have my word," Tom said.

# Chapter Thirteen

Whether she liked it, or not, Maggie was again indebted to Tom. He'd taken over her table without another word. Luckily, her father, in his usual fashion, didn't linger over his lunch. She'd finished the day shift without any other problems, then picked up her car from the garage by herself.

She had called Jeremy as soon as she got home, and enjoyed an outing to the shopping mall with her mother and her son before Jeremy's bedtime.

This morning she was back at work doing an extra shift. She'd agreed to do another extra shift because Tom—after helping her with her father's table—had gone back to not speaking to her, and she didn't want to spend time with him at home. Her body overheated every time he came near her. She'd spent hours in the tub with the door locked, fantasizing about the man, but all the marathon bath did was turn her toes puffy pink.

She gave her wig one last pull down around her ears, and opened the back door. The cook let out a curse that echoed though the kitchen.

"It's business as usual," Maggie said to nobody in particular as she pushed the swinging doors open ahead of her and strolled into the bar.

"Not quite," said Harry, his voice a strange mixture of silk and what had to be Harry's version of husky.

Maggie gave Harry a quick once over. The man was sporting a brand new shirt with a brand name insignia on the pocket, a smile on his face that nearly cracked it in half just below his nose, and a strip of pale skin in front of each ear. Harry had ditched his sideburns.

"What do you mean, Harry?"

"Just what I said." Harry smoothed a meandering strand of hair over his bald spot while his eyes trailed around the room before coming to rest on Maggie's face. "You and I have to have a little talk."

Maggie caught a whiff of Harry's new cologne. New cologne. New smile. New Harry? And he hadn't fired her, yet. All good signs. "And that would be about what, exactly?"

"About your work performance."

Maggie's stomach did a tidy lift and rolled over. "My work performance is fine. You said so yourself. See, I'm even wearing my new red t-shirt." Maggie did a half-hearted attempt at a pirouette.

"You've tried your best. You've been mostly willing to go along with my ideas, but there's the whole issue of your reliability," Harry said with what sounded to Maggie like a patronizing tone.

"My reliability? I'm here, aren't I? I'm doing your extra shift, aren't I? I've picked up just about every extra shift you wanted me to do. I even switched to the evenings so that I could fulfill some sexual fantasy of yours, and now I'm not reliable?"

Harry tucked his hands into the pockets of his new jeans, and gave Maggie the once over. "You ran out on your shift the other night, and you've been looking a little tired lately." He pointed at her face. "And there's those bags again."

"What bags?" she asked with all the disinterest she could summon while she fought to keep from glancing at her face in the mirrored bar post.

"Under your eyes. You're not getting enough sleep. Are you and Tom whooping it up after you leave here?"

*Whooping it up?* Hiding out was more like it. "Harry, your eyesight's going. I don't have bags under my eyes."

"Maggie, you gotta be careful. That's how a woman loses her looks."

"Harry, I didn't know you cared," she said, attempting to hold her sarcasm in check. Something odd was going on with Harry, and it appeared Harry's problem was about to become hers.

"This is serious. The other night you took off outta here as if the devil were on your tail, and Tom with you. It can't continue—"

"I came back as soon as I could."

"But you ran off. And you said you don't like working with Tom."

"Tom and I do just fine. What's this all about, Harry?"

Harry tucked his fingers into the curve of Maggie's elbow and steered her to a table near the end of the bar. "I want you to be the first to know."

"Sean's back?" she asked, excited and pleased.

"Not yet, but he'd better get here soon."

"You're leaving?" What would happen to the partnership if he did?

"Funny, very funny. I've found someone, someone who wants me." Harry smoothed the white puffy patches where his sideburns once nestled. "I know you think I'm a womanizer, but that's not true. Not really." Harry sobered. "After my wife died…"

He'd never talked to her like this before. "Harry, I'm sorry."

He sighed. "You know when you're in high school, you believe that love can happen so easily that you don't stop to think about it. But as you get older, you discover that love doesn't come around every day, and when it does, you need to grab it."

She suddenly felt as if she were seeing the real Harry, a man she could get to like. "Harry, if someone's come into your life who makes you happy, you should go for it."

"I really appreciate you saying that, Maggie. You remember Jolene?"

How could she forget? The Spandex Queen. "You found the woman you love and it's Jolene?"

"She found me," Harry said, his smile threatening to divide his face in half again. "Jolene's been working at the Wally Mart, but she doesn't like it."

"I get it. She likes it here. With you."

Harry's eyebrows did a little dance over his eyes. "She arrived the other night when you took off, and she was real helpful."

"Does that mean I'm out of a job?"

"No. It means I want you to show her the ropes, spend a shift or two with her until she feels comfortable. Jolene's a smart girl."

"Smart enough to take over my shift, you mean?"

Tucking his hands into his lap, Harry stared at the table.

So Harry planned to let her go, even though he knew that she needed to hang around until she found Sean. She had to think of something that would appeal to Harry's paranoia. A man his age had to worry that a woman Jolene's age might tire of his aging charms. "If Jolene takes my place on evenings, have you considered how things will be when Tom gets to spend time with Jolene? You're the one who thinks Tom's such a stud muffin. What happens when Tom makes his move on your girlfriend?"

"Won't happen. I'll be here all evening, and I know my Jolene." Harry rubbed his hands along the legs of his new jeans, his smile bright with purpose.

It took all of Maggie's willpower to simply leave and walk away from the old fart. She'd been taken in by his story about love and not letting it slip away, but she didn't feel sorry for him anymore. Who did he think he was, taking her job and giving it to someone else? If she had the paperwork making her a partner she and Harry would have had a different conversation.

When she was a partner, life would be a whole lot different for Harry. In the meantime, she couldn't afford to give up her job, and she needed someone to help her get Harry to see reason. Tom was her best bet for that. He'd helped her before.

She had finished her extra shift, driven home and taken a quick shower before coming back to do her evening shift. If it stayed this busy, Harry might have to consider keeping Maggie on along with Jolene, but she'd get this sorted out once she got a chance to chat with Tom.

"I'll be glad to get out of here tonight," Tom said, flexing his shoulders.

"Me too."

He smiled at her. "Yeah, your second shift today. You must be exhausted." So he'd decided to talk to her again.

"I am." Maggie smiled to herself as she watched Tom. He was one sexy man, and for the most part he'd been a pretty good housemate. Except for the attraction thing. But Tom couldn't help the way he affected women. Well, that wasn't quite true because he knew how attractive women found him. Ever since their night of sex she wondered how he'd gotten to be such an accomplished lover.

Tom settled on one of the stools to tally up his night. Even when he was doing something as mundane as that, Tom looked like every woman's fantasy.

"Tired as I am, I can't go home until I talk to Harry," Maggie said, rubbing her neck.

"You? Talk to Harry? What happened to the Maggie who enjoys giving Harry a verbal thumping before she struts off?"

"I don't strut, and stop kidding. I'm in trouble. Harry wants to cut my shifts. He's hired his latest girlfriend to work evenings. I'm good enough to train her, but not good enough to keep my job."

"Harry wouldn't do that to you."

"You haven't seen how the new, improved, horny-in-love Harry operates. If you don't help me stop him, I'm going to be down to two shifts. I can't live on that."

Tom slid off his stool and edged closer, his fingers doing wonderful little twists and turns down the middle of her back. "I agree. I don't think that's fair, but after all, this is Harry's Place."

"Yes, and if I ever get my hands on Sean, I'm going to punch his lights out."

"Said like a woman with style and class. After you've clobbered Sean, what's next?" he asked.

Tom was standing far too close, the scent of his skin and the warmth of his body fanned the need in her. "I'm going to get my money or my ownership papers to this place, and then Harry and I will be having a conversation as equals."

Maggie clenched her fists, more to keep her fingers out of Tom's black satin hair than anything else.

"I'm impressed. So what do you need me for?"

"I want you to talk Harry into leaving my job as it is. I want you to convince him that his little woman would better serve his needs if she worked the day shift."

"You don't want much, do you?" Tom said, a sardonic twist to his lips.

She met his gaze and her body warmed. "Look at it this way. We need one another until Sean comes back, and if I don't get the work, you'll have to pay more of the expenses. Now is that a good enough reason for you to talk to Harry for me?"

"It is, but there's another problem."

What was Tom saying? "I should have guessed. Fire away."

"Did you talk to your father yet?"

It had completely slipped her mind. She had promised Tom she would talk to her father. "I forgot. It's only been a few days. I've been busy working here."

"Have you tried to contact him, set a time?" he prodded.

"No, I haven't. Besides, he's always busy."

"Ever heard of the phone?" Now Tom was frowning.

"Of course, but I wanted to wait until I was home with Jeremy and could have a real conversation with Dad."

Tom made a derisive sound. "Face it, Maggie. You have no intention of talking to your father any time soon."

She didn't have time for Tom's opinion, but she still needed his help. "Not true."

"Princess, here's the deal. I've bailed you out once already. And in return you were supposed to talk to you father. You didn't keep your end of the bargain last time. I have no reason to believe you'll keep it now," he said.

He nailed her with his gaze and Maggie, for once, didn't have a response. He was right. She hadn't done what he asked. "Look, I promise I'll talk to my father."

"Not good enough. You'll weasel out of it again. Apparently you don't need my help enough to keep up your end of our bargain, not as much as you need to keep your silly pride."

She might concede on the pride thing, but Maggie realized that without her paycheck, she'd have to move home sooner, rather than later. Her father had told her that the next time she moved back, she'd be doing things his way. If she had her money from Sean she'd have a bargaining chip. Without it she'd be at his mercy.

"How can I convince you to help me?" She looked up at him and prayed he'd have an answer that would give her a way to keep her job.

"Like I said, talk to your father, and we'll see."

The old Maggie wanted to throw a four-alarm temper tantrum, but aside from her anger and disappointment, she knew Tom made sense. He'd put her interests—make that her demands—ahead of his own when he took her home the other night. And what had she done? She hadn't done a thing to keep up her end of the bargain. Had avoided it, actually, by taking extra shifts to remove any free time.

While she'd found Tom helpful, she'd taken him for granted—the one man in her life who had been kind. She studied him then, and suddenly realized that in all their time together, he'd told her very little about his life, his plans or what he wanted when he left here. And she was curious, but afraid to ask because she didn't want him to think she was interested that way.

But the hard reality was that she had to find a way to keep her hours, no matter what Tom said, or didn't say. The raw truth was that if Tom had never shown up, it was likely she wouldn't have a worry in the world about her job. It had been only after Tom's arrival that her hours were threatened. Sure, he was good at waiting tables, but so was she. She realized that thanks to Tom, and now Jolene, Maggie was well on her way to being unemployed.

If Tom had left when she asked him a couple of weeks ago, her problem would have solved itself. There had to be something…some way for her to regain her position at Harry's Place. "Okay, you don't want to help me. How about this idea? You and I both work evenings. We could split the shift. Teach Harry's sweetie, and still keep our jobs."

"No way. Harry hired me for my appeal to the patrons, or have you forgotten?"

"And he hired me because I'm ugly?"

"Didn't say that. I'm just reminding you that it's you who has the problem, not me."

"Why don't we toss for it?"

His eyes connected with hers. "For what?"

"Your shift."

"You're out of your pretty skull. There's no way I'm going to let you take my hours by tossing a coin."

And by the look on his face he meant it—but another idea had just occurred to her

*The mechanical bull.*

The old beast under wraps in the back room was a

legend around Harry's Place, if the stories she'd heard from Emmaline were true. According to Emmaline most of the patrons wouldn't take a chance on the hunk of junk because they valued their limbs. But a nice sling on Tom's arm would put him out of commission long enough for Maggie to take over his evening shift. Once she had his shift, she'd be around for Sean's return.

"I wasn't thinking of a coin. I was thinking of the bull."

"You mean we'd ride the bull?" He gave her a blank stare.

"Yeah, and the person who stays on the bull longest wins."

"And I'll bet you still ride the horses at your parents' house. Am I right?"

"You are, but hey, any guy can ride, right? You ride a motorcycle. I mean someone like you wouldn't mind getting on a mechanical bull, would you? Think of the chick appeal. Harry will like this idea—I know he will."

Tom stared at her, his expression one of wry humor.

"Maggie Kincade, you are a witch of the worst kind. I'm not riding any bull. I'm not taking any bets. You're the one with the problem, and I'm not solving it for you." He rubbed his hands over the shadow of whisker on his handsome face, the movement of his fingers, hypnotic.

She stopped her hand before it touched down on the stubble covering his rugged jaw. "Then, what do you suggest I do?"

"I don't know, but let's see… We're both good at our jobs. Are you up for a little healthy competition?"

Maggie didn't like the gleam in Tom's eyes. She looked him over from his head to his toes…to the zipper in his pants, just to prove she wasn't unduly influenced by his sexiness. "Sure. Anything you can do, I can do better."

"Just remember you said that. Whoever makes the fewest tips this Friday night will ride the mechanical bull. Then, we can negotiate the rest of the deal from there."

"What! You're kidding!"

"Why should I be? You're the one who brought it up. Miss Kincade, you can put your money where your pretty mouth is." He leaned closer, his breath hot on her cheek.

How could he do this to her? He'd been so damned busy accusing her of being a bad mother, and now he wanted to prove she couldn't earn as many tips. "I'll decide where I put my mouth," she said as calmly as she could.

"Need help?" he countered as he tucked her hands in his.

His touch made her body quiver. Scrambling to regain her equilibrium, Maggie made the mistake of glancing up into his eyes. They were wide dark pools of lust, fringed by the thickest lashes she had ever seen. "I don't need your help," she gasped.

"And you weren't looking at the zipper on my pants a few minutes ago?"

"No!" She hated the way he could capture her heart and her mind so easily. She hated it and she loved it.

"Are you sure you weren't wanting to have a look behind my zipper?"

"I'm not talking about what's behind your zipper, you egotistical maniac." She dragged in a lungful of air as she pulled away from him.

"Maggie, don't kid yourself. You're after what's behind my zipper. It's all you think about." With that, he patted her fake blond hair and strolled away.

# Chapter Fourteen

riday night at Harry's Place was proving to be a busy one. Tom wove his way between the tables in front of the huge fireplace, preparing another table recently vacated by regulars of his. The women had been more than willing to tip him a little extra, especially when he alluded to the possibility that he might meet them at Smokey's Bar after his shift.

He'd made a point of encouraging the busboy to clean his tables ahead of Maggie's by offering him a bonus for his help. There was no way Maggie was going to win this particular bet. No way in the world.

He could feel the bulge of greenbacks in his waiter's pouch, and knew that Maggie would have to be having one hell of an evening to do better than he was. He helped the busboy clear the table in preparation for the next group.

Tom had to admit that Maggie was more fun than most women, and she was certainly more of a challenge. She drove him to distraction at times, but she did make his life so much more interesting. He didn't think about how he'd feel when Sean returned, when Maggie and he no longer worked together.

He had plans that didn't include her.

Tom made his way toward the bar where Harry was waving his arms wildly. "What's up, Harry?"

"We've got ten women waiting for a table. I've got them in the bar at the moment. But I don't want to keep them waiting." Harry's head bobbed as he licked his lips enthusiastically, fixing Tom with a bright stare. The kind of stare Tom had seen before on Harry's face, one that meant good tippers. Harry had the ability to read people, to know who would be there to spend and who was only there to sip a beer and nibble on a burger.

Tom wasn't into nibblers tonight. He needed good tippers. "Sure, Harry. I'll see what I can do." Tom glanced around the huge restaurant area. He had a table almost finished, and Maggie had one finishing up right next to it.

He found Maggie working one of her back tables near the exit door. Her face was flushed, and there were drops of perspiration on her upper lip. He had to admire how hard she was working. "Maggie, Harry's holding a party of ten at the bar, and he wants them seated, pronto."

Maggie tucked her order pad into her pocket as she turned to glance up at him. "Can't you find a spot for them?"

"Yeah, I can. But it will be awhile, and I don't want to keep them waiting."

"Why not? Everyone's waiting tonight." She rubbed her hand across her sweaty brow, and touched her phony locks.

"Is it hot in that thing?" he asked.

"Yeah, it's hot and hellish uncomfortable. I wish I could take it off." Maggie glanced around the room as she shifted her weight from one foot to the other.

"You will soon, and even sooner, if we get this group seated."

"So, what do you want me to do?"

"If we put our two tables together, we can seat them right away." He pointed to the tables in question.

"Yeah, and who gets the tip money?" she scowled suspiciously.

"We share it equally."

Maggie's expression brightened. "You mean you'd share a table of women and their tips with me?"

He nodded.

She glanced at the tables he was talking about, and back at him. Her expression darkened. "You're up to something, I can tell."

"I love the way you look at me, Maggie. It's enough to make a guy strip to his jockeys."

"Don't start pretending you care."

"But Maggie, I do."

"If you did, we wouldn't be going through with this craziness. You'd be on your bike and out of my life."

Tom held her gaze, and for one tantalizing moment, his body hardened. "Don't do this to me," he said quietly.

"Do what?"

He glanced down. "I don't want the whole world to know how I feel about you."

She followed his glance then looked back up at him. "You mean how a part of your anatomy feels about me."

"You're onto me, Princess. I'm at your mercy."

"Give it a rest, will you? Remember, you want me to share a table of women with you." Her gaze moved along his chest, up over his chin, past his lips, stopping at his eyes. Warmth spread through him as she continued to assess him. "Fine, let's get at it."

"You won't regret it."

"Does this mean we're even?" Maggie asked.

"Not quite, but we can discuss that later tonight."

"You'd better mean it," she warned.

The Friday night crowd was larger and louder than usual, and Maggie was determined to win her bet with Tom. It wasn't about her pride, or her pocketbook. It was simply that she didn't know what to do about her feelings for Tom. Feelings she'd never experienced before. Feelings he would almost certainly make fun of, or take advantage of, if he knew.

She rubbed the growing mound of bills that filled the pockets of her pants, as her gaze followed his every move. Tom had looked so sexy all evening with a smile that never quit. She couldn't figure out whether she'd agreed to

Tom's suggestion to put the tables together out of curiosity to see what he was up to…or because working the tables together would give her a chance to be near him.

It couldn't be the latter, it just couldn't be…

She planted a smile on her face as the women paraded past her to the two tables prepared for them. She wondered which one of these beauties would appeal to Tom? Not the short, dumpy one. Not the one in the designer jeans and the subdued makeup. Tom liked his women red lipped and raunchy.

*Or maybe not.* Truth to tell, she didn't have the faintest idea what kind of woman appealed to him.

A tall blonde wearing skin-tight black pants and a sweater about four sizes too small sashayed past Maggie with a 'he's mine' gleam in her eyes. Maggie gave a 'fill your boots' lift of her eyebrow as she pulled out her order pad.

"What can I get you ladies to drink this evening?" Maggie asked, taking the orders as quickly as possible.

Tom was doing the same thing, and as they headed for the bar, she had to ask. "So, I suppose you've already picked one out of that herd?" She pointed her chin in the general direction of the tables they'd just left.

"Are you doing some sort of survey?" he asked, falling into step behind her.

"Why do you always walk behind me?"

"Because I love the view, Princess," he said, his voice radiating innuendo.

"I repeat. Which of those women interests you?" she asked, firing a glance his way as she reached the bar and the stability it offered. What was it about this man that made her weak-kneed?

"You really want to know what kind of woman turns me on?" he asked, doing his old trick of sliding his body along hers.

Maggie moved away and smoothed her wig while they gave their orders to Harry.

Tom leaned closer, his scent and pure maleness made her breath stop in her throat.

"I like them all, every last luscious one of them. Why settle for a single serving when there's a feast laid on?"

"Of course, what was I thinking? Women always want the old Tom cat."

"Is that jealousy I hear in your sweet voice?"

She didn't know which she wanted to do first; drag the women out by the hair or dump ice cubes on his crotch. "Hardly."

"You could have fooled me." Tom thanked Harry and picked up his tray of drinks. "See you at the table."

"If I have to," she muttered.

"Get that scowl off your face, Maggie," Harry said, putting a twist of lime into the margaritas. "This is what I mean about you. You're always in bad humor about something."

"Really?"

"Yeah, really. If I wasn't operating short tonight, we'd be having a different conversation."

"Good point. And that brings up another. Where's Jolene? Shouldn't she be here learning the ropes?"

Harry's nose twitched. "She's not feeling well tonight."

"An allergy?"

He shot her a look. "Allergy?"

"To work." She was careful to plant an engaging smile on her face as she scooped up her tray and started toward the tables. Maggie knew she was being small minded, but it just felt so right.

As she got closer, she heard Tom joking and laughing with

the women as he passed out the drinks. "Here, let me help you, Maggie," Tom said, taking the margaritas from the tray.

"Over here," called the blonde with the boobs, and Tom rushed to her side with a wink and a smile.

"How can one man have so many mind-blowing physical assets?" asked the short, dumpy woman seated to Maggie's left.

"A freak of nature," Maggie said, thankful to have an ally at this table of swooning females.

The woman looked up at Maggie. "My name's Shelley."

"Mine's Maggie. What can I get for you?"

"A little information. How long has he worked here?" She nodded in Tom's direction.

"Too long."

"No, seriously. Has he been here, say for a year?"

"No. A couple of weeks."

Shelley stared at Tom, her head to one side as she tapped the table. "I've seen him before."

Maggie moved closer. "Where?"

"Well, I was at a club one night, and there was this male stripper troupe. I can't remember what they were called."

Maggie knelt down beside Shelley. "You've got to be kidding! I can't imagine Tom as a male stripper." Not much, she couldn't. It sounded like the perfect job for 'hot hips.'

"Well, he was certainly the cutest, sexiest one in the troupe. I remember he wore these black tights when he first came out on stage. I remember some of the women tried to get up on the stage. He sure could move."

*Skip your sexual fantasies, woman. I know all about them.* She gave Shelley an encouraging smile.

"Now I remember. They were called the Chippendales. They all had these really explicit names and wore these really revealing costumes. I'd hardly forget someone as gorgeous as him."

Maggie certainly hoped not. "Can you remember what his name was in the troupe?"

"No, I can't. I was too busy staring… It doesn't really matter, I suppose," Shelley mused.

If Tom had been a member of a stripper troupe in his past, he had conveniently forgotten to mention that. But it would explain his open familiarity with women, and his self-assurance. No wonder Tom was so at ease around women. It was his business to be just that—someone women couldn't resist.

Maggie watched Tom as he worked the table they shared, the way his hips moved… No wonder the women couldn't get enough of him. His easy charm had every woman ogling him. The glare off their eyeballs was enough to give any sane woman a headache. She glanced away. But looking elsewhere didn't stop her from remembering all the times he'd turned his charm on her. And she remembered the night she'd wanted to jump his bones when she found him asleep in front of the TV.

And what must he have thought of her pathetic attempts to seduce him, the result of her hair-brained scheme to make him think she was a clingy woman? And the night they'd had sex… Had Tom's sexual advances toward her simply been his way of keeping his skills up? Mortified, she felt the blush climb her neck.

Yet, learning the truth about Tom made a crazy kind of sense.

She'd been hot and bothered over a 'professional' who knew what to do when a woman showed interest in him. She'd shown an interest and he'd made the moves he knew would work.

*Look on the bright side. You've been had by the best.*

Maggie took little comfort in the fact that she'd been dangerously close to falling completely for another handsome rogue. She watched him the rest of the evening, increasingly aware that Tom would have more tips than she did by the end of the evening.

It irked her that he would win again. It was enough that

he'd made a fool of her on the sex front, but to think that he would also make a fool of her over money… She needed something, some way to win the bet, or she would literally be riding the bull. And she had absolutely no intention of doing any such thing.

Tom gave her his patented wide-angled, gotcha smile as they passed each other between the kitchen and the bar.

What if Shelley's suspicions were true?

*What if they weren't?*

What if she posed the question to see what he'd say?

At least it was worth a try. Hell, anything was worth a try when all that stood between her and the bull in the back room was a few lousy dollars.

The night was nearly over, and Tom was absolutely certain that he'd won the bet. He was tired, but Maggie looked even more tired. He joined her at the bar.

"I suppose it's time for us to tally up." Tom patted the wad of bills he drew out of his waiter's pouch and glanced at Maggie.

Maggie turned to face him, a strange look of triumph on her face. "Don't count your chickens before they hatch. Or should I say chicks?"

Tom touched one of her phony tresses and brushed a tiny bead of sweat from her forehead. "Was it a hard night?"

She brushed his fingers away. "Not nearly as hard as your night will be before it's over."

"Ah, Maggie. You saw me talking to Samantha, didn't you?"

"Who's Samantha?"

"The buxom blonde from the table we shared."

"No. And I don't care how many buxom blondes you kiss up to. I just want to see you get what you've got coming to you."

Tom noted that Maggie wasn't too tired to put a pout on her luscious lips. He hadn't a drop of interest in Samantha. He had long ago grown tired of women who openly asked him for sex. "Jealousy does not become you, My Dearest."

Maggie's fingers did a mad tap on the polished wood of the bar. "Why should I be jealous?" she asked, a speculative gleam in her eyes.

For a woman who looked as if she would crumble from weariness only moments ago, Maggie seemed surprisingly energetic. "It's late and you're tired. I'm going to be a gentleman about our bet. Why don't you wait until tomorrow to ride the bull?"

"Me? Ride the bull? You'd better think again. You're riding the bull, my cocky friend."

Tom motioned to a table at the back of the bar area, and she followed him. "You're obviously operating under some delusion that you made more tips than I did. Let me be the first to set you straight—"

"We'll just see, won't we?" Her eyebrows did a hip-hop dance.

"Why don't we sit down? That way, you can get a load off your feet and unburden your mind over whatever's bothering you."

Maggie's eyes were framed in a suspicious squint. "Pretty hoity-toity words for a man of your obvious skills."

"Skills?"

Maggie slid into the chair next to Tom and leaned toward him. "You'll never guess what happened to me tonight?"

"A sugar daddy appeared, promising to take you away from all this?"

"Save your smart-assed comments for the bull."

"Wrong, Maggie. He's all yours."

Maggie shook her head slowly, the glint of satisfaction on her face. "You'll be delighted to learn that you've got an interesting night ahead of you."

"How so?"

"Do you remember Shelley?"

"At the table?"

"Did she look familiar?"

"No. Should she?" He shot back, suddenly suspicious.

"Well, she remembers you. She says you had a starring role in a certain male stripper troupe."

Oh…no. "I don't—"

"Don't pretend; besides it's too late. She gave me all the details. Seems she's quite a fan of your butt—or used to be." Maggie dipped her head and peeked at him, a look approaching pleasure now on her face.

The Chippendales had been the best-kept secret in his life. He's spent four years working as a bike mechanic during the day and as a stripper at night to put together enough money for his dream. "What makes you so sure it's me?"

Maggie patted his arm consolingly. "Shelley would be more than happy to confirm the story."

He hadn't wanted anyone to know about his past, mostly because he wanted a clean break from that life. Tom sighed in resignation. "I'd appreciate it if you'd keep this information to yourself."

"Would you, now?"

"Yes, Maggie, I would. Remember we all have our little secrets." He glanced at her wig.

"That we do, but yours is much more interesting and naughtier than mine… Don't you agree?"

"Meaning what, exactly?"

"Meaning that I will keep your little secret, if you take my place on the bull."

Anger slid up through Tom's chest. He should have known his past could resurface, but that Maggie would consider using it against him to win a stupid bet really hurt. "So this is what our friendship is worth?" he asked.

"*What?* This has nothing to do with our friendship."

"Where have you been all your life? In a coma? It has everything to do with our friendship."

Maggie frowned, her lips pulling up into what Tom once considered a cute little pout. No more. She was blackmailing him and he had to go along. He had no choice. When he'd learned about his infant son, Robin, he had vowed to never again be involved in anything that would shame his child. He couldn't change his past, but he could protect his son's future by becoming the father Robin would love and respect. He couldn't let Maggie say anything to anyone. It must never be mentioned again. "Do I have your promise that if I ride the bull you'll tell no one?"

"I promise." Maggie held up her right hand and smiled.

He didn't return the smile. He couldn't. It made him feel sad as well as angry to think that someone he liked, and had come to trust, could do something mean like this. "As usual, you're going to get what you want, Princess."

"Did you really think that no one would find out about your past?"

Maybe it was wrong of him to hope that no one would find out, but he believed that with enough time, no one would really care about his past. Especially if he became a responsible father and member of the community where he planned to have his bike shop. "No. I just never imagined that you'd use it against me. For the record, I never intended to hold you to the bet. I just wanted to tease you, and have a little fun."

Maggie's smug expression drooped. "You didn't?"

"No, but it doesn't matter now. I don't need people like you in my life. I'll ride the damned bull, and I'll be out of here by tomorrow."

"*No!* I mean you can't do that! What about the money Sean owes you?"

"Maggie, you don't get it, do you?"

A blush crept up Maggie's face as she met his angry gaze. "Don't get what?"

"Life isn't about money. It's about caring for others, doing the right thing by the people who care about you."

"I do care!"

"No, you don't. All you care about is money. My congratulations to your father. He did a fine job of raising you to be just like him.

# Chapter Fifteen

*L*eaving tomorrow. Maggie's hopes and dreams slammed headlong into her new reality.

Tom wouldn't be there, wouldn't be a part of her world. It wasn't…wasn't right. He couldn't go. He couldn't leave her like this when there was Sean, and Harry's Place to worry about. She needed him as an ally. Sure, she didn't like him, and she had reason, but still…

*What were those reasons again?* She twisted a phony curl as her mind scrambled for the reasons.

He was arrogant. But he could also be so sweet, so adorable.

He always looked out for number one. But hadn't he looked out for her as well? Hadn't he taken her to see her son twice? And he'd even come back looking for her that awful night when her car quit.

Now he said he was going to leave her because she might tell someone what she knew about his past. But to leave had been his intention all along, hadn't it? Maybe he was angry and didn't really mean what he said. Maybe he just wanted his secret kept. But did he really believe she'd give away his secret? She would never have done that. She could be trusted with something that important.

But she had threatened to expose his secret.

No! She hadn't really meant it. Yet, if she wanted to find out more she could have waited until they were alone at the house to confront him about his past. That would have given him an opportunity to share his past with her. If so, this evening might have turned out differently. She should have waited.

Tom said he never intended to have her ride the bull, even though he knew he would win the bet. She warmed at the thought and then felt really bad. Tom did care about her. Maybe not in the romantic way... Maybe more like a friend, and she had willingly accepted his friendship. Then threatened to blackmail him. He said he was leaving. Before Tom, she'd never had a male friend, and now she needed one in the worst way.

Maggie wanted to kick her own ass for being such a fool. Tom was right. She shouldn't have brought up his past. Worst of all she shouldn't have threatened to tell on him. But it was too late now to change what she'd done.

She saw a crowd forming near the end of the bar, and knew with a sinking heart what was about to happen.

"Hurry up you two. Everyone's waiting," Harry said, the tufts of hair on the top of his head dancing, his smile spreading like oil across his wrinkled features. "The back room is filled to overflowing and everyone's betting that you can ride the bull, Tom. You've come up with one hell of an idea. We should have done this before. What a showstopper! My favorite waiter riding the bull. Glad I didn't trash the old thing," Harry said, rubbing his palms together.

Tom's expression darkened as he turned to Maggie. "You were so sure you would win the bet, you told everyone I would ride the bull even before you talked to me..."

Maggie's stomach crashed into her belly button. "I only told Emmaline."

"And Emmaline told Harry and so on and so on. Maggie, how dumb and uncaring could you be?"

He was right about the uncaring part. She'd been so

determined to win the bet she'd hurt someone who had tried to be her friend. "I'm not dumb."

He snorted. "We'll argue your IQ later."

"What's going on with you two? I've got paying customers waiting out back. Let's get a move on." Harry's cheeks flashed a bright pink as a woman from the earlier busload wove into sight and gave him a smile and a wink.

*Another woman in Harry's life?* Maggie couldn't keep track, and besides she didn't care. All she cared about was getting Tom to stay, at least for another day. "Look, I'm sorry about all this. I didn't mean—"

"I don't care what you meant, Maggie. I'll ride the damned bull, and then I'm out of here."

Maggie spirits fell as she followed Tom to the back room. The narrow space was filled to overflowing with a bunch of the regulars. Maggie spotted a couple of the guys who were always on the lookout for a quick feel. She was so completely fed up with men who thought that it was open season on her butt. Worst of all, the one man she wanted to encourage was about to do his bodily parts serious damage—all because of her.

Tom made his way to the bull. Maggie's breath caught in her throat. He had no experience riding horses, let alone a mechanical bull. Tom was going to get hurt and it would be her fault. What had she been using for brains all evening? Maybe she was an idiot, as he claimed. If Tom were injured, she would never forgive herself.

Watching him climb up into the saddle, Maggie knew in a moment of insight that she couldn't let him go through with it. Shoving and pushing bodies aside, she made her way to the bull. "Tom, please don't do this."

Tom gave her a frosty glance. "This was your idea, remember?" he asked, his glance sweeping over the rowdy customers crowding around him.

What she wouldn't give to relive the past few hours, to make up for her mistakes. She wanted Tom in one piece, and in her life. He may be Mr. Wrong, and she was certainly the worse judge of men in the world, but maybe her luck had changed in the man department. "You were right. I was wrong. This was a stupid idea. There I've said it."

"Louder," Tom said.

Oh Lord, he was going to make her grovel. But what choice did she have?

"Getting you to ride the bull was a stupid idea," she yelled above the din.

The room went silent. From somewhere behind her, she could hear the clop of Harry's cowboy boots on the wooden floor. "What's going on here?" he asked, throwing a disgusted glance between Tom and Maggie.

"I don't want Tom to ride the bull. I don't…"

Her words trailed off as her gaze locked on Tom. He was even more gorgeous sitting astride the ridiculous imitation bull. Warmth rushed her; her cheeks glowed with shame.

"Continue Maggie. Why don't you want me to ride the bull?" Tom's glance never left hers, and suddenly she knew in her heart that the one man she cared most about in this world was going to leave and she would never have another chance to tell him what he meant to her—what she felt for him.

"Come on, we've all placed our bets. Let's get on with it," someone yelled from the back of the room.

"Tom, these people are expecting something for their money. You can't back out now." Harry's nose twitched as he rubbed his jaw. "Maggie, why don't you get out of here? Go finish up your work. This is a man thing."

Maggie unlocked her gaze from Tom's as frustration snapped through her. She wanted to grab Harry's bald head and rub it along the floor. "Harry, I'm sure you've made a few bets, and you hate to part with your money, but Tom is not riding this piece of junk."

"Can I be allowed to speak?" Tom asked.

"Certainly, but make it fast. This crowd isn't going to wait much longer," Harry urged.

"Since everyone here is a betting man, and since I'm the one who has to make it or break it on this contraption, I want you to guarantee me half of tonight's receipts."

Harry's head jerked up. "You can't be serious. That would be hundreds of dollars. I have to pay expenses, including your wages, and you're asking me to share half of what remains with you. Why would I do that?"

"Take it or leave it," Tom said as he began to dismount.

Harry's glance went to Maggie. "You did this."

"No, I didn't. But I wish I'd thought of it."

Harry switched back to Tom. "Stop. Don't get off just yet. Give me a minute to think about this."

"You've got thirty seconds," Tom said.

Harry's eyes did a pinball bounce. "This isn't fair; you know that."

"Harry, if I ride the bull tonight, these gentlemen will be back for many nights to come because they'll all want to see someone ride this bull, and make bets among themselves, as they're doing now. I'm about to make you a lot of money."

Harry's beady eyes took in the room full of people. "You got a deal. But make it good, you hear?"

"Do I get a say in this?" Maggie asked, desperation crowding her words.

"No, you don't." Harry glanced past her to emphasize his point.

"I'm not leaving. Tom will get hurt if somebody doesn't stop this craziness."

"Out of your hands. Now move," Harry said, taking her arm.

"Tom, I'll be right here," Maggie yelled over the roar of the crowd.

"Let's fire up old Ferdinand, and see how he hangs," Harry yelled as he reached for the switch.

Maggie watched in horror as Tom's body rose and bucked in the air, his head snapping back, his face fixed in a grimace. For what seemed like hours, Tom clung to the raging mechanical monster while Maggie cursed herself for being so stupid as to suggest this in the first place. So utterly dumb. And by suggesting she'd blackmail him unless he did this she'd let her best friend down. Her very best friend in the world.

Then Maggie heard the distinct crunch of bone as Tom pole vaulted over the bull's head and hit the floor. Hard.

# Chapter Sixteen

<br>

"Please Tom, honey. You're in the hospital. I'm so sorry. You'll never know how sorry I am unless you open your eyes. Please wake up," a voice crooned as the cobwebs began to clear from his mind.

Tom's head ached and his arm felt like it was on fire. "I'm awake," he mumbled, glancing in the direction of the voice. *Maggie.*

"I'm so sorry. You can't imagine how bad I feel. I could have prevented this. I should have stopped this." There were tears in her eyes as she stared down at him.

*Maggie in tears?* It didn't fit. Maggie was all about money, about winning the bet. "What happened?" he asked, reaching for the side rail of the hospital bed, only to have shards of pain shoot through his arm.

Maggie's hands pushed him back down in the narrow bed. "You have a mild concussion. You hurt some part of your shoulder. They've put a sling on your arm and given you something for the pain. Does it hurt a lot?" Maggie asked, her voice trembling.

Tom met Maggie's anxious gaze. "Are you sure you're all right? I didn't think you cared," he croaked, his head pounding like a runaway jackhammer.

"I do. I really do. I'm worried about you. Tom, I've

been a stupid, silly idiot. You're hurt and it's all my fault."

"Maggie Kincade apologizing to me? I must be dreaming."

Maggie went to the door of the hospital room and closed it. "I need to talk to you."

Tom adjusted the pillow under his sling with Maggie's help, and watched in disbelief as she smoothed the sheets and turned his pillow for him.

"Don't keep me in suspense. You're fussing over me, Maggie. Not a good sign. Am I dying?"

"Please don't joke with me. Tom, I never wanted you to get hurt. You made me so angry. I just wanted to pay you back for the way you made me feel." She glanced at him, her eyes swimming with tears.

Despite her tears, he had never seen her look more beautiful—a beautiful woman with an agenda. "Maggie, I don't get it."

Her fingers toyed with the bedsheet, folding and unfolding the cotton material. "I don't care about the money or the bet or anything." She took a deep breath and met his gaze, her face tight with anxiety. "This is so hard for me to say."

*Was Maggie Kincade, of all people, having a change of heart?* "Take your time," he said, reaching for her hands with his good hand.

She worked her fingers around his. "Are we holding hands?" she asked with just a hint of the old Maggie.

"We are," he confirmed, watching the way her glorious red hair fell in lustrous waves around her face. She'd been upset enough to remove her wig. He let the implications of that wash over him, and all sorts of great ideas blossomed in his aching head.

"Tom, I don't want you to go away. I've been difficult, I'll admit that."

"Try impossible," he said, snuggling his hand into hers.

"Okay. Impossible. But I can change all that. You're

right, I'm a spoiled brat, and I want my way all the time, but I really do want to make a life for Jeremy and me." Her lips worked. A tear fell on his hand. "I don't want you to leave tomorrow. I would like for you to stay on at Sean's with me. As long as you can…"

Her words slipped from her lips as she moved closer.

Holding his breath against the pain, Tom moved over on the bed. "Here, Maggie, climb up here with me. But I have to warn you, no sex until I figure out how to maneuver this sling," he said, attempting to be humorous. Maggie wasn't laughing, but the look in her eyes, a defenseless look, went straight to his heart.

He smiled as they snuggled together. Despite his injury and the exhaustion caused by a long night and being thrown by a mechanical bull, Tom had never felt better in his life. "Maybe we should try this more often. I like lying next to you, Maggie."

Maggie rested her head on his good shoulder. "I never told you this, but I feel closer to you than any man I've ever known."

"Including your ex?"

"Yeah, especially my ex. Mac wasn't someone you could get close to." She smiled her quirky smile, and in that instant something inside Tom stirred and lifted, filling him with more happiness than he'd felt in a long while.

"What are you thinking?" she asked, as she cuddled closer.

"That you and I may have something special going on between us."

Maggie touched his chin, her fingers warm and comforting. "I hope so. I really do. I want you to stay with me…until Sean comes back."

"I probably will, but after that I have to go. I've got things I have to do."

"Things? Don't you think it's time you told me what's going on in your life?"

*Could he tell her about his son?* He nearly had a few days ago, but he'd caught himself in time. Robin meant everything to him, and he did not intend to let anything stand in the way of his plans where his son was concerned.

But Maggie had exploited his past to her advantage. And she'd blackmailed him to ride the bull. He looked at her. Studied her.

She said she was sorry, but could he be sure?

A part of him desperately wanted to tell her about his son. Make her understand. And because he'd be leaving when Sean got back, what harm would it do if Maggie knew about Robin? Besides he needed to share his enthusiasm about being a father. "There's someone special…"

Tom heard Maggie's sudden intake of breath as she eased away from him. "Someone else?"

Sadness and longing filled Maggie as she searched Tom's face for the answer to her question. She wanted to climb inside his skin. She wanted to be with him, be part of his life. When he landed on the floor, bucked from that ridiculous bull, Maggie had been afraid for Tom. No, make that terrified.

She recognized the symptoms. She'd fallen for him, for a man who was on the move, who planned to walk out of her life. And who now admitted to being involved with someone else. At least this time around, the man she'd fallen for had been honest enough to tell her the truth. She sat up, wrapping her arms around her midriff. "So, let's hear it."

"Hear what?" he asked.

"Who is she?" she ventured, feeling a little lost and a whole lot insecure.

Surprise flooded his face, followed slowly by a smile that lit his handsome features. "You got it all wrong." His eyes were dark as he met Maggie's questioning look. "I have a son who is six months old. I want him to be a part of my life. That's why I want the money Sean owes me. I want to get my motorcycle business started as soon as possible. I have the location all picked out. It's in an industrial park south—"

"You have a son and you're telling me you're starting a bike business?"

"Yeah. I thought I told you about that."

"You didn't." Maggie struggled to remain calm.

"Maggie, my son deserves to have a respectable father, a father he can rely on."

The air whooshed from Maggie's lungs. "Let me get this straight. You have a son, and you're starting a business," she repeated.

He nodded. "Just outside Boston."

It was all too much, too painful. "Where is your son?"

"He's with his mother, but she's agreed that I can be a part of Robin's life."

"Robin…"

Maggie couldn't make the connection. Tom wasn't the father type, was he? Still, he'd been really sweet with Jeremy. "So that's why you were so concerned about Jeremy?"

"Yeah, partly. I haven't had any experience with children, but I want to be a father. A good one."

He smiled, and a heavy feeling that had plaguing her since his fall slid away from Maggie's heart. Seized by the thought that Tom Rawlins was opting for the family plan, a shiver ran through her. "And his mother, what about her?"

"It was a one-night stand. At first I didn't believe her, but she had the testing done, and I'm definitely the father. I didn't know what to do. All I knew for sure was that my son deserved a father, and that no child of mine would be raised the way I was. Robin's going to have everything I can give him."

A tinge of jealousy, followed by crazed feelings of loneliness flooded through Maggie at the thought that Tom could care so much, and could be so open about it. Maggie finally understood why Tom was so quick to offer advice on raising Jeremy. He had a very personal reason. "And you love Robin?"

Tom's eyes warmed. "It's funny. The pictures of Robin seemed almost unreal. Loving a child will be a whole new experience, and I'm looking forward to it."

Tom was sharing his feelings with her—Maggie Kincade. He was showing her she could be trusted with his private life. The whole thing took her breath away, and scared her speechless.

Did she want this newfound sharing?

His closeness made her feel so much a part of him, his life, and what he cared about most in this world. She wouldn't have missed being here for anything. She reached for him, her fingers connecting with his cheek.

"Tom, I…I don't know what to say. You'll make a great father. The only problem I can see is, what if Robin doesn't want to ride a Harley when he's old enough to walk?" she teased, anxious to keep the tone light. In truth, she felt somehow set adrift by the knowledge that Tom had a life waiting for him in Boston.

Tom gently kissed her hand. "My son riding a Harley seems like someone else's life, not mine… I love the thought of having a son I can do things with. I want to be there, to be part of his growing up. There's so much I want to do with my son."

Envy pinged through Maggie as she listened to Tom. Jeremy would never have a father like Tom, and that was her fault. She had been a lousy judge of men. Yet her poor judgment had given her a wonderful little boy. "All I've ever wanted, since the first day I held Jeremy in my arms, was to give him a good life, to love him and care for him. It was selfish of me to want to keep my father out of my life, but I needed space to make it on my own. I wanted Jeremy to be proud of me too."

"We're not so different are we? We want our children to have good lives. A year ago I would have run away from the family thing, but the first time I held Robin in my arms…" Tom sighed.

It was suddenly very important that she share her feelings with Tom. She wasn't sure why, but she was not going to miss out on the chance. "If my father had his way, I'd marry someone from his social set. Someone who would provide for me, and in return I'd be just another lonely housewife, waiting on a man whose needs would always come first.

"I know women like that. They pop pills for fake happiness and have no sense of who they are or what they want. I can't do that. I need to find out what I'm really good at. I'm pretty sure I could be really good at running a business like Harry's Place. You know with a little work and planning the steakhouse could be turned into a great restaurant, a family restaurant. And the backroom would make a great playroom for children while the parents had their dinner. Of course, it would need to be completely refurbished, but with my banking experience I know how to obtain bank financing."

"Maggie, so you've been thinking about what you want to do with Harry's Place? If you don't get to be a partner in the steakhouse, you'll find another restaurant."

"It's odd that you should say that. My father has always talked business to me, even when I didn't really understand what he was talking about. I guess some of it stuck."

The words were out before she felt the impact of what she'd said. She'd listened to her father and taken business courses he'd recommended. Because of his business acumen and her need to please him, she had a clear sense of what it took to make a business work. Had her father and his beliefs held the answer to her independence and happiness all along? "Isn't this weird? You and me here, together talking about our lives, about our children and what we want for them. I've never done this before."

"You mean lying in a hospital bed with someone?"

"No, silly." Then she saw his smile and realized he was kidding.

They cuddled together, comfortable with each other in the quiet of the hospital room.

Finally, she murmured. "Robin is going to have a lot of fun with his dad."

"You think so?" Tom's smile of pleasure spread happiness through Maggie.

"I know so." Maggie wrapped her arms around Tom and kissed him, finding his lips warm against hers. She kissed his face, his cheeks…then her fingers trailed along his throat. "This is so nice," she whispered between kisses. She placed her hand on his chest and felt his heart pounding beneath the flimsy cotton of the hospital gown.

"Finally, there's something we can agree on." He pulled her closer, his lips claiming hers.

Where had this man learned to kiss? Cancel that, she didn't want to know. Jealousy could be a dangerous thing. While she let his tongue have its way in her mouth, she moved her hands over his chest, down toward his waist and under the blankets.

He encased her hand in his. "Be careful. You don't want me to be lying here with a raging hard-on when the doctor comes in to discharge me."

"Oh yes, I do," she said, her tongue playing along his lips and dipping into the hot recesses of his mouth.

"Maggie," Tom groaned, pulling her across him with his good hand. "I'm at a distinct disadvantage."

"I love a man in a sling. I get to have my way with him," she teased.

# Chapter Seventeen

aggie's head felt like a basketball. No, make that a watermelon. Her stomach wasn't much better off. They'd gone back to Sean's house and stayed up talking like old friends. She'd found a bottle of bourbon stashed in the kitchen and they celebrated Tom's safe return. Tom hadn't had anything to drink because of his head and his meds, but that didn't stop her from imbibing.

Despite his sling, Tom insisted on going to work in the morning. And she insisted that if he did, it would be in her car, not on the Harley because she didn't trust him to drive and she couldn't have survived the loud noise created by the Harley engine.

When they reached Harry's Place it was totally silent. Tom checked the beer fridges while Maggie refilled the pop cooler, and still not a sound, except for the distant rumble of the cook's muffled curses.

"Where is everybody? I expected to see Harry in here counting his money. Or lack of it. I can't wait until he pays you what he owes you. Half of last night's take should be a tidy sum," Maggie said.

"Are we talking about money this morning?" Harry asked, coming through the saloon doors from the back entrance.

Maggie turned, ready to go on the defensive. When she

saw the look on Harry's face she stopped. "What happened to you?"

"Love, that's what happened." Harry did a little jig around the bar area. He came to a stop in front of Maggie, and his fingers did a playful tap on the wooden counter.

Visions of men in white, carrying wrap-around jackets popped into her head. She noticed Harry's flushed face, his eyes that actually twinkled. Something about sex-junky Harry didn't fit. "Love?"

"Yes, I'm in love."

Maggie could feel Tom standing behind her, his sling resting on the bar, as she braced for bad news. "You and Jolene?"

"Hell, no. Jolene's long gone." Harry patted the tuft of hair plastered to his bald spot. "I didn't realize how tired I was of all those young ladies. What am I saying? There wasn't a lady among them. And I was no gentleman."

*Had someone put something in the water? Had Harry found religion?*

And why was Harry telling her, the person with the least desire to know? She glanced at Tom, but he looked as dumbfounded as she was.

"Do you *want* to be a gentleman?" she asked Harry.

"I want to be more than that. I want to turn my life around. I've found someone very special."

Maggie moved closer for a better look. "You found someone. Have we met her?"

"No. I was cleaning up after the bull ride last night, when a woman came up to me. At first I didn't recognize her. She said hello, and asked me to buy her a drink. We started talking and it turned out to be Francine Doherty from my high school days. She had a crush on me back then, but I didn't know about it. I loved her the first time I saw her, but I figured I wasn't good enough for someone as classy as Francine. Funny how things can become so complicated, and to think we missed out on all those years when we could have been together. Not that I regret my marriage to Annabelle, but all the same, it is great to connect with Francine again."

First there was Tom who shared his past and his future plans with her last night. Now Harry was confiding in her. Maggie didn't know how many more surprises she could handle. "That's nice. Go on."

"We spent the night together. We're in love and I'm moving to Danbury."

*"You're what?"* Tom asked, the surprise in Tom's voice reassuring.

"Yeah. Francine owns a craft store, and she wants me to move there and help her run it. I couldn't be happier." Harry beamed.

"We're happy for you," Tom said, "but what happens to Harry's Place?"

"I'm willing to sell my half to the two of you."

Dumfounded, Maggie considered what that might mean. The place had a steady clientele, a good location, and with a little work it could be a good business to own. And hadn't she already put her inheritance into it? All for the wrong reasons in the beginning, but after working here, she had to admit that Harry's Place had potential.

"What about Sean?" Tom countered.

"What about him? He's gone off, leaving me to manage the place. I don't want him to own my share of the business. He'd run the place into the ground."

"But doesn't Sean have to agree to you selling your half?" Maggie asked.

"No. That part of the agreement was to help Sean." Harry rubbed his jaw. "Back when Sean recognized that he had a gambling habit. He didn't want to be caught in gambling fever and be able to put his half of the business into the pot, so to speak."

Tom and Maggie looked at one another, then at Harry. "So you can sell us your half, free and clear?"

"I can, but I want to do it soon."

"Can we get back to you?" Tom asked.

"Sure, but don't take too long. Francine's leaving for Danbury in two days, and she's not leaving without me."

Maggie and Tom stared in shock as Harry broke into song, something about a four-leaf clover and overlooking someone.

"Well, what do you know? Harry's in love and ready to move on," Tom said, his mind rooting through the possibilities.

"And ready to sell Harry's Place." Maggie pulled her wig down farther over her ears and adjusted the two blobs of fake curls lying along her cheek. "What do you think we should do?"

"If we had the money, or could raise the money, it might be something to consider. There's a good opportunity here for someone willing to work hard."

"I agree. All it needs is someone who has money and determination. We'd have to get Sean—"

"I'm beginning to think that Sean isn't coming back." Tom rubbed his jaw in frustration.

"What do you mean? Did he call you?"

"No, but we need to find out what he's done with our money, so we can make plans."

"You're right. Maybe Harry will come clean now. I'm sure he knows where Sean is, regardless of what he says. I'd like to work out a deal with Sean," Maggie said, tapping her fingers on the counter as she eyed Tom.

Tom saw the anxiety in Maggie's eyes as well as the insecurity behind her words. She wasn't nearly as sure as she pretended to be. He could relate to that. "Easy, Maggie. We need to consider our options. If we can come up with the money, and buy Harry out, we'll have controlling interest."

"How do you know so much about all this?"

"I listen to people when they're talking business."

"We could be quite a team, if we tried," Maggie said, her smile wavering.

"Maggie, we talked about this last night—"

"I know. In a couple of days you'll be gone, right?" Defiance filled Maggie's eyes.

Yet, something about the way her head tilted when she asked the question told Tom that the answer mattered. A few days ago, he would have flattered her, strung her along for a while before telling her the truth about his intention to leave regardless of how she felt or how good an opportunity Harry's Place might be. But seeing her like this, knowing how much she wanted to prove her worth to her father, he couldn't give her any reason to think he'd be part of her plans. "You'd like to own this business, and it's a great opportunity. I'll do what I can to make things work out for you."

"Except stay." There was a sorrowful tone in Maggie's voice that Tom had never heard before.

He had to make Maggie understand that he couldn't stay here. He'd come to get his money from Sean. Money that would help him start a new life. Until he had his life in order, his business up and running, Tom wasn't interested in a romantic relationship. "I can't stay."

"Coward." Maggie turned away giving her full attention to the napkin holder she'd been filling.

Tom flexed his fingers under the sling as he considered his answer. "Maggie I know my limitations."

"Whatever. Here's hoping your son can get used to the revolving mommies in his life."

Tom scowled. "That's a pretty low blow. What do you think I am?"

"A man like you who enjoys a healthy sex life would have to be very discreet." Her glance flicked over him. "Just how long will it be before you have to explain to Robin why there are different women coming and going in the house?"

What had gotten into her? She had to know how mean

and intrusive her words were. "Maggie, you don't have to worry about me or about Robin. He has a good mother, and a good father. We both want what's best for him. I'll keep my private life private."

She turned to face him. "Don't make promises you can't keep. Believe me, I know."

Was that a tear glistening on her cheek?

"You're being unfair, Maggie."

"I call it the way I see it," Maggie said as she turned back to the tray she was filling with the over-stuffed napkin holders.

Tom watched her turn away with the loaded tray, her head high.

"If I were the marrying kind—"

"You'd marry me, right?" She tried for a grin as she tossed the words over her shoulder and made her way between the tables.

"Yeah…" What was he saying… Tom had to shake himself free of the home and hearth notions simmering in the back of his mind…thoughts of Maggie and him curled up together while their children slept in matching twin beds across the hall.

*Yeah, right!*

Living with Maggie would mean having to trust her with every part of his life. He had never trusted any woman completely. Not since the day he turned sixteen and his mother told him to get out and earn a living. "Smarten up," he muttered to himself, turning his attention to Sean and how to find him.

Maggie's knees shook as she made her way across the room toward the fireplace. She had seen the look in Tom's eyes, a look she'd seen before. Mac's eyes had held the same look when he beat a hasty retreat from their marriage.

Like him, Tom would walk out of her life without a backward glance, without so much as a decent good-bye. There would be no more friendly banter, no red-hot sex, only her deep-seated need to say anything, promise anything to make him stay. A pain rose in her chest, so sharp and hard it took her breath away.

Fighting to ignore it, she plunked the tray down on one of the tables and set about methodically putting a napkin holder on each table. Life was repeating itself. Like some b-rated movie, she'd trusted someone again, and they had let her down. But this time there had been no promises, no vows. So why did this hurt more?

Maggie had no idea why she kept repeating the pattern, but until she changed her ways, she would always be vulnerable to some man with a great body and a careless heart. She was past due for a change, starting with Tom Rawlins. She'd show him. She'd get this business, not only to prove her abilities to her father, but to make Tom wish he'd stuck around.

She sneaked a peek in Tom's direction. He was leaning against the bar watching her. His shirt was open at the neck, displaying the gold chain and 'spoil me' charm he always wore. Maggie's fingers twitched at the memory of how it felt to weave her fingers through his hair, to stroke his skin while she watched arousal play across his face. A tingle started somewhere south of her belly button as their gazes locked. Even in the muted light of the restaurant, Maggie could feel the electricity crackling between them.

It was as if he were memorizing her face, her hair, her whole body. Maggie closed her eyes for just a moment and drank in the feeling his gaze summoned. Her nipples hardened and she ached for his touch.

But there would be no more of Tom's touches. In a few short days Tom Rawlins would be a memory. A wonderful, bittersweet memory.

There was that pain again—just beneath her ribcage. It had to be indigestion. Tom might be the single most gorgeous man to walk into her life, but he was also about to be the single most gorgeous man to walk out.

Why him, and why now? She couldn't really have deep

feelings for Tom, beyond attraction. She just liked him. What woman wouldn't?

*Face it. You're under the influence of lust.*

She knew better than any woman that lust was powerful, overpowering, all consuming, and capable of creating havoc in her life—especially when the object of her lust was about to leave. What she was feeling had to be some kind of early withdrawal.

Had to be.

She couldn't ask him to stay because of her desire and she had no defense against her pain if he turned her down. Could she offer him a business arrangement, something he couldn't resist? He said he'd help her, and having him involved in a business with her would mean she would have someone whose business acumen she could trust. Or was she simply looking for a way to keep him in her life?

Was she that desperate?

Somehow, her shaking legs made it back to the bar where she braced herself against its polished edge. "Tom, what would you think of us forming a partnership? We could both own the business. I'd be managing partner. I'd do the books, and get your advice on any necessary changes or additions to the business. You could run your bike shop somewhere here in town. What do you think?"

Tom wouldn't look at her. *What did that mean?* As she waited for and agonized over his possible answers, hope bubbled up in her at the crazy thought that some part of Tom could remain in her life, still be part of her dream.

"It's a great offer, Maggie. But I'd have to think about it." His eyes were dark pools of resolve, mingled with regret. "Whatever we decide to do, I promise to help you any way I can."

Maggie felt suddenly weak, unable to cope. "You've already said that."

"And I mean it. I want you to be happy in your life. We've had a great time, and I'll never forget you."

If that wasn't a swan song she didn't have red hair. Maggie couldn't look at him, and witness the apology in his eyes as he rejected her offer. Determined to salvage her pride, she concentrated on staring at the antlers over the fireplace. He couldn't be allowed to see how much she wanted him to stay. It was very clear that Tom's heart and mind were in Boston with his son and his bike shop venture. "So, it's thanks-for-the-memories time, is that it? You're out of here?"

Tom grimaced. "Don't do this."

She saw Tom's statement for what it was. The conversation was as far as he was concerned. But knowing the pain that lay ahead for her, Maggie couldn't let him leave without trying one last time to change his mind. "You're overlooking a great business opportunity in your rush to get out of here."

"Maggie, I told you before. I made a promise. I have a son who needs me…" His voice held a hint of exasperation.

Maggie quietly gathered the hurt clinging to her heart to the pain tucked deep inside her. There was nothing she could do, no argument she could make that would win against Tom's need to be with his son—and his need for freedom. She understood that. She couldn't blame him, admired his choice actually, but it did nothing to ease the hollow feeling creeping around inside her. "Well, I guess that's it," she said.

Tom's gaze moved past her, a look of surprise on his face. "Not quite. I believe the lost has been found."

# Chapter Eighteen

Tom held out his hand. "Well, if it isn't the long lost Sean O'Toole. Where have you been?"

Sean shook Tom's hand as he gave Maggie the once over. "Hi, Red. What are you doing here? And where did you get that hellish looking wig? Ruins your looks. My neighbor told me you moved in. Why would you do a thing like that?"

"I'm only living there because I can't afford to live anywhere else. I'm waiting for my money, you creep," Maggie said grimly as she started around the edge of the bar. "I want my money back. All of it."

Tom grabbed her just before she launched herself at Sean. "Easy, Maggie. Let's hear what Sean has to say." He tucked her into the curve of his good arm and was relieved when she didn't resist. He had a sudden jolt of awareness as her body curved to his and her breast nudged his rib cage. She felt good there, like she belonged…

"Sorry I wasn't around when you got here, Tom. I was in Vegas."

"Gambling. We know," Maggie snapped.

Sean ignored Maggie, a dangerous thing to do in Tom's opinion. But Sean was a big boy and he could look after himself.

"My luck was off." Sean rubbed the back of his neck, ran his hands through his thick brown hair as he stepped around them and went behind the bar. Plucking a beer out of the fridge, he snapped it open and took a long drink. "I've got to get my hands on some serious money."

"Meaning you don't plan to pay us what you owe us," Maggie said, her voice deathly calm.

This time Sean looked at her. "Don't put a knot in your thong, Red. I'm going to pay you. I just won't be any time soon, that's all."

"That's not fair. You owe me the money. You cheated me out of a partnership here."

"I never promised you a partnership."

"You did so." Maggie slipped from Tom's arm and stomped around the bar. She lifted the divider, letting it slam down behind her as she marched up to Sean.

"Maggie, come back here," Tom said, knowing it was pointless to try to stop her. Maggie was ready to do battle, and deep down he didn't blame her.

"In a minute, Tom," she said, anger blazing in her eyes.

"One of the things I've come to admire about you is the way you're willing to fight at the least provocation, but why don't you rethink this?" Tom asked.

"Too late," Maggie said, turning to Sean. Pointing her magenta painted fingernail at him, she said, "I don't care what you have to do, I want my money, or I want to be a partner here. You're not going to get away with playing me for a fool any longer."

Tom could feel the heat of Maggie's words clear across the bar.

Had Maggie been involved with Sean? She'd denied it, but who wouldn't? Sean wasn't the kind of guy you'd take home to your mother, and Maggie had admitted to being a poor judge of men. Tiny pinpoints of jealousy wafted through Tom at the thought of Sean and Maggie together.

Had Sean used Maggie's vulnerability against her when it came to getting her to invest in his business?

"Help me out here, buddy," Sean said, looking to Tom for support.

Seeing Sean's indifference toward Maggie's plight put a sizable dent in his friendship with this man. Whatever had gone on between them, Maggie deserved better than what Sean was offering. Added to that, it looked like neither Tom nor Maggie would get their money back. Tom shrugged. "Afraid I don't know the history between the two of you. That makes this your battle, Sean."

Sean glanced quickly at Maggie before turning back to Tom. "Ah, come on."

"Sean, you owe Maggie and me a lot of money. How do you plan to make that right?"

Sean frowned. "Well, I talked to my accountant on the way into town, and he says that the receipts are up, that business is good. If we give it a little time, we can all get our money."

"We're not stupid. That won't happen if Tom and I don't have any say over how the money's spent. You and Harry have check signing authority. An open invitation to a gambler like you." Maggie barked out the words.

Tom watched Maggie's flushed face, and the fierceness in her eyes, suddenly realizing he loved the way Maggie fought for what she believed and went after what was hers. He caught the hint of anxiety in Sean's eyes as he moved back to lean against the beer fridge. Tom could have told him that was a bad move. Maggie liked nothing better than to have her opponent cornered.

But Sean was a big man, powerfully built, and Tom feared Maggie could be hurt. "Sean, I have an idea that might work."

"As soon as you call off your woman, I'll listen."

"I'm not his woman," Maggie snapped, taking another step in Sean's direction. "And you're not going anywhere until you give me my money. And no more stories about not having it. You can go to your bank."

Sean gave an exaggerated sigh. "Leave it to a woman to think in such simple terms."

"You twit!" Maggie yelled, moving even closer to Sean.

"Maggie, come out of there before you get yourself in trouble."

Maggie gave Tom the benefit of her determined smile. "I'm not going to get myself in trouble. I just want to be sure that Sean's paying attention when I speak to him. That's all."

Tom met Maggie's lying gaze.

"Yeah. Right. Maggie, get out of there, now. I have a solution to the problem. One you'll like," Tom said.

"Let's hear it," she said.

"First, do as I ask, Maggie."

Maggie hesitated, giving her bottom lip a good chewing as she did so. "All right." Maggie made her way to Tom's side. "This had better be good."

Relieved, Tom turned his attention to Sean. "You know Harry's getting out of the business, do you?"

"Yeah, I talked to him earlier. He's offered to sell his share to you and Maggie. I'd like to buy his share, but I can't raise that kind of money."

"Would you consider selling your share to Maggie? You owe her money, and this would be a way to pay off your debt to her. Your accountant can figure out what your part of the partnership is worth…"

There Tom went again. Making her feel special. She wanted to believe Tom meant what he said, because if he did, he might be willing to be her partner in Harry's Place. And a business partnership was better than no partnership.

She glanced up into his face and saw raw determination

in the set of his jaw. Tom wasn't going to back down from Sean, which made him her best chance when it came to getting her money back. In a way, she was lucky that Tom stood to lose his investment, just as she did.

Instinctively, Maggie moved closer to Tom. Tom responded by wrapping his good arm around her, drawing her against him. She could feel the steady beat of his heart through his shirt. His body felt familiar, like home. Being next to him was the one place in the world where she'd always feel safe. "Tom has a good idea, Sean. I'd be willing to work something out."

"Listen to her, Sean. Maggie deserves a chance."

His words slid over her like warm cream. They made her feel so good, so valued.

*But why was he doing it?*

He didn't want to be part of her life. He'd said so. She glanced up at him again, luxuriating in the warmth passing between them, at the way his body curved toward hers, at the way he towered over her in such a protective way.

"You're great. Thanks," she whispered against the crisp cotton of his shirt.

"Did I hear right? Was that praise coming from your lips?" he asked, glancing her way, a smile crinkling the skin around his eyes.

Another thing she liked about Tom—he could see humor at the strangest times. "Thanks for coming to my defense."

He smiled and returned his attention to Sean. Maggie got to watch his chin…his fascinating jawline. Everything a woman could want in a man's jaw. But wasn't that true of so many of Tom's physical attributes? Yet he was so much more than simply the sum of his physical assets.

He was doing all the things she wanted the man in her life to do, all the things she'd never found before in a man— all those things that could make love grow. And to top it off, Tom Rawlins was fighting for *her* dream.

"So Sean, what do you say?" Tom asked.

"I'm sure Red would be great as a manager. But I want to change and make this business work. Gambling is wrong. It destroys everything. Look at me. I'm broke and I'm going to have to start over." Sean's voice rose as he toyed with the lever on the beer dispenser.

"Sean, remember me? I'm the friend who helped you out the last time. I'm the one who listened to your pleas for understanding. You wanted my help and you got it. Now, we're right back where we started. Sean, I have plans and need to be paid back too, and you need professional help."

"And I'm going to get it. I'm going to contact one of those groups that help gamblers get over their addictions. I want to build the business up even more."

"Sean, if you're serious about getting help for your gambling problem, you've got enough on your plate. Let Maggie buy your share of the business, and you focus on getting your life back in order."

"Don't tell me what to do. I'm going to work this out for myself." Sean's eyes radiated anger.

What right did Sean have to be angry? Maggie wondered. His gambling was the problem. Tom was simply trying to help a friend.

Maggie decided she'd had all she could take of this arrogant man and his excuses. "Face it. You're a gambler who needs professional help with your addiction. Or are you going to con someone else out of their money, maybe ruin them too, just to feed your bad habit?"

There was a moment of shocked silence, followed by Sean's half-hearted laughter. Sean and Tom exchanged looks—the kind of look that men share when the little woman dares to speak up. Tom and Sean were making it clear that she was not in on the discussion. Mac had used that strategy hundreds of times, and it pissed Maggie off. She had to keep something in mind. Tom and Sean were buddies, or Tom would never have loaned him the money.

*So, what was she doing here?* Feeling left out and alone, she headed for the door.

"Where are you going?" Tom asked.

"You two need to talk. I've got things to do."

"Like your nails, or maybe you need to shampoo your wig?" Tom asked as he caught up with her.

She was just about to tell him what she thought of him and his friend when she saw the concern in his eyes. "Tom, don't tease me. I'm not in the mood."

Tom matched her stride. "I'm not either, but I had to get your attention somehow. Let's talk."

"About what?" she asked without stopping.

"Don't give up so easily."

"I'm not giving up. I'm facing facts."

She stopped and Tom nearly ran into her. "Haven't we done this before?" she asked, remembering that morning when she first met Tom, and he'd followed her down the hall to her bedroom. What she wouldn't give to turn back the clock. It wasn't until right now that she realized just how much fun she and Tom had living together.

"You're right. We've done this before, but the circumstances were much different." He touched her cheek, letting his fingers trail along the smile lines and across her lips. "I remember thinking how much I wanted to kiss you, and how much you wanted me to kiss you."

Her body trembled at his touch. She needed him to make love to her, to wipe out all the strain and worry building in her. If only she could slip into Tom's arms, and convince him to take her away from all this.

But it couldn't be. She had Jeremy and plans to make a future with him. Tom was leaving and she had no power to stop him, nor did she want to keep him from his son. She swallowed against the tears and glanced up into his eyes. "Our kissing days are over. Remember? We're just friends. There's nothing left for us to do but find a way to get our money from Sean."

Maggie pulled her wig off, and felt a strange sense of freedom. "The game's over. Sean won't keep his promise about making me a partner. I would have to borrow the money to buy Harry's share. If Sean can't pay us what he owes, I'm done. I'll have to face my father, let him remind me of my failures, and go on from there. I've wasted all this time and effort for nothing."

"Don't say that, Maggie. There's us. We've been a great team, and we're friends."

She wanted to tell him she couldn't be his friend. She couldn't watch him live his life separate from her. She couldn't face the thought that he would find someone else to love. Her heart and her pride wouldn't let her. "Sure. Why not?"

"Then let this friend help you."

"By hooking up with Sean?"

"Maggie, you need to have a little faith in me. Have I let you down yet?"

How could she tell him just how let down she felt by the prospect of him leaving? She needed Tom in her life, his caring, his willingness to be good to her. She needed all of him, not just his friendship. "No, you've been there for me. You've been a good friend."

Tom took her shoulders in his powerful hands, his fingers warming her skin. He lowered his face to hers. All-encompassing desire rose in her chest as she caught his soapy, clean scent.

"Maggie, I'll stop Sean if I can."

"Stopping Sean is only part of it." She blurted out the words and prayed that he wouldn't ask about the other part. Loving Tom, who didn't love her, was not a topic for conversation.

"Dammit it! I mean it. I want you to be happy."

She met his gaze. Sparks of excitement snapped between them. "I want me to be happy too."

"Fine. Then come back, and let's talk to Sean. I have an idea how to handle him."

"Tell me."

"Not unless you come back with me while I put my idea to him. Come on, Maggie, you're dying of curiosity. I can see it in your eyes. Did you realize that your eyes get kind of beady and small when you're curious or suspicious?"

Hardly the words of someone smitten by the love bug. "They do not. I don't have beady eyes."

"Go look in the mirror...after you hear my idea." He tipped her chin up and kissed her nose.

She edged her lips toward his, her fingers creeping up the front of his shirt. Her breath caught in her throat as he kissed her, gently at first, and then with more authority. Pulling her closer, his lips tasted hers in the most incredibly sexy way. He ran his tongue over the cupid's bow of her upper lip. "Have I convinced you to do as I ask?"

Her body strained against his as a humming sensation started in her lips and traveled the length of her body. Could she handle any more of this man today, any more of the raw sexuality that he could command so easily?

*Definitely not.* She'd be so much better off if she went back to Sean's house, packed her stuff and left. "I don't think that will work."

"Come on. What have you got to lose?"

*My heart, to yet another man who's walking away.* But if Tom's idea had any chance of recouping her money... Dare she hope that Tom might come to her rescue one last time? "Okay, if you say so," she said.

Reluctantly, she slid her arm around Tom and they walked back to the bar, the fit between them perfect. Recognizing that this was probably the last time she'd be this close to Tom, she let her fantasy float unfettered and clung unashamedly to him.

Holding Maggie close, Tom approached the bar. "Sean, I have another idea."

"Fire away," Sean said, looking up from the account book he held in his hands.

"Why don't we settle this another way?"

Sean arched one eyebrow. "I'm listening."

"You're a gambling man. Why don't we place a little wager?"

"On what?" Sean brightened, putting the account book aside.

"I'm suggesting we each ride the mechanical bull."

"Ferdinand? You got to be kidding." Sean gave Tom a quizzical glance while the beginnings of a smile tweaked the corners of his mouth.

"Ferdinand would certainly be an interesting way for us to settle our differences, and add a little risk, don't you think?" Tom asked.

"What's the deal?" Sean asked, his tone one of frank curiosity.

"If I win, you will give your share of Harry's Place to Maggie to settle what you owe her. I'll recoup my loan from her when she can pay."

"Brave man," Sean said, his gaze shifting to Tom's sling.

Fear for Tom tore through Maggie. "Tom, you can't do that! You have a sling on your arm. You'll get hurt again."

"Don't you worry your pretty little head…" Tom smiled at her, and Maggie was immediately suspicious.

What did he have up his sleeve? "Forget it. I don't want a share in Harry's Place that badly."

Tom took her arm and steered her to a table away from the bar. "Maggie, Sean's not going to be able to pay us. If we can get his share of the business, and find a way to buy Harry's share…"

"Neither of us has the money or a banker willing to back us, which means your little plan won't work," she whispered, afraid that Tom was making a terrible mistake. Had Tom's bang to his head made him crazy? Or did he have a personality change? Either way, she had to come up with something to stop this insane scheme. "Why are you doing this?"

"I want you to have a chance to succeed. And if Sean's telling the truth, and the receipts are up, we might just be able to put together some sort of partnership."

The plan was nuts, but it did have a certain charm, a special upside. His suggestion implied he'd be her partner in the business, which meant they would stay in touch. "You'd be willing to be my partner?"

"Your long distance partner…certainly."

She had to think fast. It was insane for Tom to even consider riding that bull with his bad arm… But there was another way. Her father had the cash and if she could get his backing, Tom might not have to get hurt. Her father had his I-told-you-so button polished to a high sheen. It would mean she'd have to face him, and talk to him. It would be difficult and painful, but she had some really good reasons to do it. She wanted to be successful, to earn enough money to raise her son on her own, and get her father off her case. But she could not have Tom hurt again because of her. "There is another option."

"And that would be?"

"I'll talk to my father, like I promised. You don't need to ride the bull."

"Maggie, you don't want to have to go to your father about this. Not this time. You and your father have a lot of issues to settle before you ask him for money. Besides, you've put so much effort into being your own person. I won't hear of it now. Riding Ferdinand will be a piece of cake."

"Piece of cake! You'll land in the hospital, just like you did before. Only this time, you'll break bones."

Tom's gaze lingered on her lips as his good hand cupped her jaw. "Maggie, I'm going to do this tomorrow morning before opening. There's nothing you can do to stop me," he whispered, before letting his lips slide over hers.

At his touch, her heart took flight, swooping skyward with her pulse racing. Her fingers reveled in the feel of his muscled hardness beneath the cotton of his shirt. "We'll see about that," she murmured, breathless.

"It's a done deal," he replied.

She wanted him with every fiber of her being. She pulled him tighter. He held her fast with his sling as he lifted her chin and deepened the kiss. They stood there, joined, warmed and wanting what each held for the other. Maggie had never been happier.

Tom lifted his head, easing his lips from hers. "Maggie, I'd like to continue this, but let's get Sean out of our lives first. Then we can have one last round; just you and me."

The thought of Tom making love to her sent her pulse dancing in the clouds. Raw heat rose in her, starting between her legs. She wanted him, no matter what the cost. No matter that this was a last round…

With her weakened knees about to pitch her forward into Tom, Maggie sighed. "If you say so. I want you to understand that you don't need to ride the bull. You're free to go."

*What!* She didn't mean one word of it. Body heat had fried her brain! She wanted him to stay, to be her partner in more ways than one. And the worst part of all, she had finally learned what it meant to love somebody. She would do anything for Tom, including talk to her father. She'd make any concessions needed to make Tom's life easier, to be part of his plans for the future.

And afterwards, the love she felt for Tom would simply be left to die, invading every part of her life as it slipped away. When she'd discovered a true friend, and the one man, the only man she wanted as a lover and a friend, she was losing him.

# Chapter Nineteen

Maggie went over to Sean's house later that day to find Tom and Sean parked in front of the TV. She gathered her things and put them in her car. All the time she was getting ready to leave, she watched to see what Tom was doing, if he would send her off on her not-so-merry way. Instead, her knight in tarnished armor and Sean were watching some mindless game and barely acknowledged her while she made one last trip through the house, checking for more of her belongings.

Tomorrow would be their last time together. Not much of an ending. She'd get to watch Tom injure himself *again* on a silly bull. Not a smart move in her opinion. But since arriving back at the house neither man showed the slightest interest in her opinion.

Despite his earlier offer of sex, she didn't approach him. Loving Tom was not just about sex. It was about all the other things that made him so special. Too bad she had to learn all that too late.

To think that after all the doofus men in her life, she'd finally found the one for her. She stood at the patio doors, looking out across the lawn toward Edna's house.

She had first set eyes on Tom right there. She remembered how it felt when she saw him, how gorgeous he was in his black leather pants and jacket. The way her body had responded to him… As lonely as she was going to be in the days ahead, she wouldn't have wanted to miss that moment when he'd walked into her life.

"Are you coming in to watch the game with us?" Tom called from the den.

She had zero interest in some stupid game. "No, I'll see you tomorrow."

She went down the hall one last time, gathered her suitcase and her jacket from the bed, and started toward the kitchen.

"Where are you going?" Tom asked as he came up behind her.

"I'm going home. I need to see Jeremy and talk to my parents."

Tom caught her wrist in his powerful grip, his flesh warming hers, reminding her of why she had to escape…

"I don't want you to leave," he said.

"Sean's back. The TV works." She shrugged.

"I get it. You're in a snit over the game."

She wasn't in a snit. She was pissed off. There was a distinct difference, one he wouldn't understand. "Refresh my memory, but wasn't it you that said I needed to talk to my parents, straighten things out with my father?"

"Is that what you're doing?" Tom tipped an eyebrow.

"Yes. It probably won't work, but I'm willing to give it another try."

Tom smiled and Maggie felt warm all over. "Maggie, you're not doing this for me, are you?"

"The ego of some people." She managed a smile to cover the lump pressing into the back of her throat.

"Like I said when we first met, what you see is what you get. Will you be there tomorrow morning to cheer me on?" He moved a curl off her cheek, his smile teasing.

Nothing would keep her away, but if she succeeded in what she had planned this evening, there would be no reason for him to ride the mechanical bull. No reason at all.

"Nothing could keep me from seeing you make a world class fool of yourself. But let's look on the bright side."

He teased her cheek with his fingers, driving her crazy. "And that would be?"

"You'll make one hell of a chick magnet with both arms in slings."

Tom moved closer, his gorgeous body fanning the heat rising in her.

"Maggie, face facts. You can't get enough of me." He gave her a cheeky grin as his hand slid over her butt, squeezing and rubbing her eager flesh. Despite all her well laid plans to resist him, her body molded to his hand, moving with him, setting up a rhythm neither could stop. Unbidden, her hands began to stroke his chest, edging higher toward his neck. Her breath caught in her throat as she met his inquiring gaze.

"Kiss me, Maggie," he said, holding her tighter and forcing his growing erection against the softness of her belly.

Maggie concentrated on how his body felt against hers, how much she loved the skin of his neck, while she kissed her way to his lips. His mouth took hers, demanding more as they moved closer. Nothing else mattered as blood rushed in her head, her heart hammered her ribs and a wash of lust so powerful she couldn't get her breath claimed her.

She wanted everything his lips offered, though she knew without a doubt that Tom would never be hers. That it had been a fantasy from the first kiss to this.

As her body molded to his, a thought wiggled its way between them. She could no longer settle for less than what she wanted. All her life she'd dreamed that there would be a man in her life who would love only her. A man who would make her the focus of his life. A man who would stand by her through thick and thin. And she'd do the same for him.

She gently pushed him away. "We can't do this anymore."

"Why not?" he asked, his lips toying with her cheeks, leaving a tender trail of warm kisses.

"Friends don't do this sort of thing." She moved away from him, and without looking back, she gathered up her things and walked out the door.

Maggie parked in front of her father's three-car garage. Glancing around, she had to admit that the brass carriage lamps added an elegant accent to the wide block sandstone construction of the garage's exterior.

For the first time in a long while she hoped her father would be home enjoying his first of two very dry martinis before dinner. She focused on what she was about to do, taking comfort in knowing her father's rigid routine.

Opening the side door leading to the kitchen, she was met by a scream of excitement from Jeremy. The sight of her son, so full of life and so cute, with his head of copper curls and dimpled cheeks, filled her with joy. "Hey, big guy," she yelled as she scooped him up, luxuriating in the tight urgency of his little arms.

"I love you with all my heart," she whispered into the warmth of his neck.

"I luff you too, Mommy," Jeremy whispered back as he squirmed out of her arms. "Grampy wants to get me a pony. Can we, Mommy?" His eyes danced with excitement as he pressed his hands together and gave her a smile she couldn't resist.

"We'll see, pumpkin. Grampy and I will discuss it." She wished her father had talked to her before mentioning it to Jeremy, but they hadn't talked for a long time—her fault as much as his—she admitted. Yet she could hardly blame her father for wanting to spoil Jeremy. She found it hard to resist those dark brown eyes.

"Hi Mom, how's it going?" Maggie asked as she chose a chocolate chip cookie off the cooling rack on the counter.

"Great. You'll stay for dinner?"

"I'll stay all night, if it's all right with you. I've moved out of Sean's house."

"Why?" her mother asked as she slid a roast of beef into the oven.

"Sean's back. And he isn't prepared to pay me the money he owes me."

"That scoundrel!" Rowena was immediately sympathetic, reminding Maggie that her mother had been there through everything, despite her reservations over Maggie's plan.

Maggie told her mother all that happened around Harry, the bull, and Sean's arrival, while keeping any mention of Tom out of the conversation. Her feelings for Tom were off limits.

"Sean is a miserable man. What are you going to do?"

"I thought I might talk to Dad. If I could get a loan to buy out Harry and Sean, I would own the business."

Her mother closed the oven door, and turned to Maggie, a look of surprise on her face. "What about Tom?"

Maggie focused all her attention on the cooling cookies. "Tom will look after Tom. Besides, he's headed out of town any day now."

Rowena wiped her hands on her flowered apron. "I'm sorry to hear that. You liked Tom. And he was kind to you."

"Yeah, we're friends, I guess. He's got a business he's starting in Boston."

Rowena gave her daughter one last questioning glance and turned back to the sink full of vegetables she was preparing for dinner.

"Can I help, Mom?"

"No, talk to your father."

Maggie glanced at Jeremy, playing with LEGO at the kitchen table. "Okay... I'm not that sure that Jeremy should have a pony."

"Have you forgotten? You had one at his age," her mother said, without turning around.

*How could she forget?* She had loved Sachmo to distraction

and had tried to convince her parents to let her share her bedroom with the pony that had captured her heart. "Yeah, but he seems too young to ride a pony."

Rowena turned around to face Maggie. "Don't decide about the pony until you talk to your father. And if you move home, it means that Jeremy could have his pony right here with the other horses."

"I know. I know." Maggie sighed and headed for the living room.

She slipped through the butler's pantry, through the dining room with its mahogany table gleaming in the afternoon sun and into the living room where her father sat in a leather wingback chair.

"Well, if it isn't the late Maggie Kincade, entrepreneur," her father said, glancing up from his newspaper.

In the interests of civility, Maggie ignored her father's challenging tone. "Hi, Dad. How's it going?"

"I'm doing fine." He moved his cocktail glass to make room on the side table for his newspaper. "What about you?"

Should she tell him what a mess she was in? If she did, and he made fun of her, and her business abilities… Forcing herself to remember why she had come to see her father, she plunged in. "Things haven't turned out the way I had hoped."

"Go on," he said, his eyes following Maggie as she sank into the champagne-colored damask of the sofa opposite her father.

She'd made the choice to leave her father out of her business, and now she was back trying to explain. Her father would never let her forget this mistake. But for her sake as well as Tom's, she had to take a chance. "I've lost my investment."

Her father rested his hands on the arms of his chair, his gaze never wavering from hers. "I'm sorry. I know how that feels."

"You do?" Maggie searched his face, and instead of disdain and impatience, she saw understanding. Maggie couldn't decide whether to be thankful or fearful.

"Maggie, I've known all along what you were up to. You swore your mother to secrecy, but we've been married nearly forty years. We have no secrets."

Maggie's heart slid sideways. "You let me make a fool of myself, and you didn't say a word?"

"I didn't do it to make a fool of you. Far from it. I wanted you to give the whole business thing a try. I've known Sean O'Toole since he bought into Harry's Place."

"You have? Why didn't you tell me he had a gambling problem?"

"Because you didn't want my help, and I thought it was better for you to learn from your own mistakes."

"You let me risk Jeremy's future?" Anger welled up in her. This was not going well at all.

"Jeremy's future was never at risk," her father said, emphatically.

She wasn't going to get into another argument about Jeremy. Her father had always wanted a son, and Jeremy was as close to a son as her father would ever have. For that reason, she had always avoided any confrontation over Jeremy. "But you thought it was okay for me to be tricked by Sean?"

"Of course not. I wanted you to learn something of value. You and I have had our differences, but you're my daughter. You believe I've been hard on you, but if you're going to make it in the world of business, you have to learn to be able to assess a situation, to look for the hidden agenda."

*Not another business lecture.* Maggie tapped her fingers on the arm of the sofa, debating whether or not she should simply cut her losses and leave. "Dad, I made a mistake." To hide her embarrassment, Maggie let her gaze follow the pattern of afternoon light stretched across the ceiling.

"We all can learn, even me."

Surprised, she glanced his way. "You?"

"Yes. I had a call from someone I hadn't heard from in years."

"Who?"

"Someone who's a lot wiser than I. She sat me straight on a couple of things." He glanced at Maggie and there was an honest-to-God twinkle in his eye.

Someone setting her father straight? Maggie wanted to meet this person. "Come on, who was it?"

"Edna Cotter."

Maggie giggled. "Edna?"

"Isn't she a hoot?" he asked, his face wreathed in a smile. "I've known her for years. She used to own a bar downtown, in the old plumbing supply place on Amond Road. Everyone went there, including my father."

"Yeah, Edna said Gramps was wound too tight."

"And he was. He was." Her father picked up his glass and drained it. "My father, Jonathan Kincade, Senior, was a real mean-spirited man."

Her father was going to admit something like that? The sky must be falling. "Edna said that?"

"That and a whole lot more. She told me I needed to change my attitude where you were concerned. I should smarten up and see just what a fine person you are."

"Edna Cotter?"

"Yeah," he said, a half-smile creasing his face. "She's one feisty old lady. And smart too, I might add."

Maggie couldn't believe it. "I didn't even know she liked me."

"It seems she does. She told me all about you and your young man living together in Sean's house."

*Oh, no. Here comes the lecture on morals and not being a good example to Jeremy.*

"I'm not living there anymore."

Her father eyed her. "Does that mean you're moving home?"

"For now. Once I resolve my financial problems, I'll be looking for a place of my own."

Her father leaned forward. "Why don't you and I call a truce? I've been difficult, but so have you. We're more alike than you realize, Maggie. And it would please your mother immensely to have you here."

Awkwardly, her father touched her hand. "I want to help you and Jeremy any way I can."

Maggie saw the sincerity in his eyes, and felt her throat tighten. "Dad, I'd like that, but I don't know if we can make it work."

"Neither do I, but I'm willing to try. We tend to shoot from the hip and then go off to lick our wounds and hurt feelings without resolving anything."

*These words were coming from her father?* "True. I always feel like I don't measure up around here." She let her gaze drift around the room, to the impeccable furnishings, to the very expensive works of art her father had collected over the years. "Remember the last time I lived her? I still can't keep house."

"And you sure as hell can't cook," her father said, but there was affection in his words.

"And sometimes I'm not a good judge of people." She shrugged, her glance colliding with his.

"And I expected too much and didn't appreciate all your other qualities." There was a gentle tone to his voice Maggie hadn't heard before.

"You expected me to be just like you. And I'm not."

"But you want to have your own business, and be your own boss. You got that from me," he said with pride.

Her father seemed to want to call a truce. Had Edna had that much influence? And did it really matter as long as they had reached this point? She'd come here hoping to convince her father to help Tom. And they were having a pretty good conversation, considering how things usually went between them. Take a chance, a voice inside her head whispered.

"Dad, I'm glad you and I are talking. Before, I felt like you were criticizing me about everything I did." They were hard words to say and even harder emotions to admit to. And yet she felt as if a load had been lifted off her heart.

He nodded in agreement. "Sometimes I was really hard on you. And I will be again, but I'd like us to take a little time and work through what's going on between us."

*He was serious.*

Could she let her guard down? "I made a mistake in trusting Sean. He told me that my investment in his business made me a partner. I found out I wasn't. I never felt so stupid in my life…"

"Maggie, did I ever tell you about the time I invested in a laundry?"

She shook her head.

"It was my first attempt at going into business on my own. I was working at the bank—"

"You never said a word about working at a bank."

"Why did you think that I was so keen that you work at one after you quit college? I wanted you to become familiar with how banks operate, because in today's business world, you need to know."

"So like you, Dad, to be trying to run my life," she said, only this time she couldn't keep the smile off her face.

He offered a wry smile. "Anyway, I bought the business, only I knew nothing about washers and dryers. All the equipment was old and had to be replaced. I had to rewire the building to meet code, which meant I had to do some construction. I lost my shirt on it."

"How come you never told me this before?" she asked, feeling a closeness to her father that she hadn't felt in a very long time.

"Because we never seemed to be able to connect, and I confess I didn't want my daughter to see me as a failure."

"Not wanting to admit to failure must be a Kincade trait."

He laughed, making her smile. "We all make mistakes, especially starting out. I'll lend you whatever it takes to have you own Harry's Place."

"What? You're serious?"

"I want you to succeed. You deserve to have a business of your own, if that's what you want."

"I do want it. Dad, I want to be a success."

"Not just to prove something to me, I hope," he said, leaning back in his chair.

She couldn't believe her ears. *Her father? Doing this for her?* "In the beginning I wanted to prove I could succeed, but something's changed…"

What was it? Could Tom have anything to do with her change in thinking when it came to proving herself to her father? She knew the answer… Too late she knew exactly why she saw things differently—Tom Rawlins. Maggie wanted to cry. Instead, she wrapped her arms around her father's neck. "Thanks, Dad."

He smiled and patted her back. "You're welcome."

"Dad, do you mind if I leave for a couple of hours? I have to speak to someone about the business, and it's important."

"Why not? Your mother will hold dinner. I'll take Jeremy out for a walk."

Her father was taking his grandson for a walk? Would wonders never cease? She wanted to tease him about breaking his routine, but she couldn't take the time. She had to get to Harry's Place and tell Tom her good news. Her news might provide a second chance to get things right where Tom was concerned.

Meanwhile, back at Harry's Place, Tom was a little bit worried. After his first disastrous ride on the bull, he'd decided to take a look at the motor and gear mechanism.

What he'd found explained why he'd done a head plant over the bull's head, and he intended to make a small adjustment.

He'd been working on the bull for about an hour, but he hadn't made much progress—probably because he couldn't concentrate on anything but Maggie. Every time he thought about leaving her, a pain started deep in his chest. What the hell was the matter with him? He'd known lots of beautiful women, and he'd left lots of women like Maggie when they tried to tie him down. He knew what he wanted in his life, and he planned to have it. Granted, waiting for Sean had caused a few problems, but nothing he couldn't handle.

Still, he wanted to see Maggie. *Where was she?*

"Hello Tom," a woman said from the door of the storeroom.

Tom glanced over, and his breath caught. "What are you doing here? Is Robin all right?" he asked, striding over to where Nina stood holding his son.

"He's fine. We came to see how you were doing," Nina said, her blond hair skimming her shoulders, her smile inviting him closer.

She was a good-looking woman, and Tom had always liked blondes.

Yet, seeing the look in Nina's eyes and hearing the intimate tone in her voice made Tom suddenly feel awkward. "Here, let me take him," he said, to cover his sudden awareness that Nina might be looking for something more from him. But Nina knew exactly what kind of relationship they had. They both loved Robin, nothing more.

"He needs his daddy to hold him," she said, passing Robin over, but not before she brushed up against Tom.

With his attention on Robin, he listened as Nina told him all the details of his son's daily activities. Robin's smile was so wide, and his dimples were so huge. Were all kids this cute? He'd never noticed before.

"When are you moving to Boston?" Nina asked.

He hugged his son against his chest, reveling in the warmth of his little body. "Any day now."

"Tom, I'm thinking about moving to Boston."

Surprised, he glanced at her as he shifted Robin to his hip. "Why would you want to leave your family and move to Boston?" he asked, although he had a pretty good idea what her answer would be.

"Because I want Robin to be close to his daddy. Every child needs his family, and I could be a big help with your business. I've taken a bookkeeping course, and I've been working part time in my dad's auto parts business." She glanced at him, her need to please him evident in her too-bright smile. "A motorcycle shop and an auto parts business have a lot in common. I'd be a big asset to your operation."

Tom hugged Robin to him while he thought about what to say and how to say it. He didn't want to hurt Nina. She'd been kind to him, and she was a good mother, but that was as far as it went. As far as it would ever go.

"Think about what fun we'd have together, watching Robin grow up," she urged, her lips beginning to tremble.

He had to admit he could do worse than a woman who cared about him, loved his son, and had offered to help him get his business up and running. "Nina, I don't know what to say."

Nina crossed the narrow space between them. Placing her hands on Robin's blond curls, she stood on tiptoes, and kissed Tom. "Don't say anything for the moment. I'll take Robin now, and you call me when you're finished here. I'm at the Midtown Motel, and I'll wait to hear from you. We'll *both* be waiting to hear from you," she said.

Maggie had raced through town, roared into the parking lot at Harry's Place, to be told by the cook that Tom was in the back room. She strode down the hall, her excitement brimming over at the news she had for him.

In the weak light of the windowless space, she saw a woman kissing Tom, and a baby in Tom's arms. Some part of her mind snagged on the fact that the love in the woman's eyes was meant for Tom. She stopped. "Excuse me," she murmured and began to back out of the room.

"Maggie, come back. I want you to meet Robin," he said, carrying the child over to where she stood.

*Was that relief she heard in his voice?*

As Tom came near, Robin snuggled into his father's shoulder. His blue eyes watched her. "He is so cute," she managed to say, while her mind went over all the possible reasons why Robin's mother would be kissing Robin's father—a kiss that definitely had not been platonic.

"And I'm Nina, Robin's mother." Nina appeared from behind Tom, resting a proprietary hand on Tom's arm. "And you are?"

"A friend of Tom's."

"We both work here at Harry's Place," Tom said and the blonde stepped closer to him.

A flood of jealousy made Maggie's stomach churn. But what right did she have to be jealous? Tom had made it clear that they were only friends, and now she understood why. Nina and Robin were his family. She wanted to be nasty about it, but the look on Nina's face said it all. The woman was in love with Tom.

*And why not?* He was easy to love, though a coward when it came to telling her the truth about his relationship with his son's mother. But still, he was a very lovable man.

"Yes, Tom and I share the evening shift," she said, feeling like a fifth wheel on a tricycle.

"Nina and Robin were just leaving," Tom said, his expression neutral.

There was no way Nina was leaving, not if the look in her eyes was any indication. And Maggie had no reason to hang around eavesdropping on a private conversation, or peeking over Tom's shoulder while he planned his new life. "Please don't leave because of me," Maggie said, seeing how good Tom and Nina looked together—a handsome couple. "I only dropped in to say good-bye to Tom," she said, heading for the door before she did something really dumb—like cry.

But where did all this understanding on her part come from? As recently as a few weeks ago, she would have created a scene over how she'd been treated. Always up for a challenge, she would have fought to get Tom back, despite what pain it might have caused Nina or her son.

But this time she saw the situation from someone else's point of view. It made her palms sweat just thinking about what this might mean.

"Maggie, I'll talk to you in a few minutes," Tom said, but she didn't answer him. She needed time to think about what was going on here.

One thing was certain. She would not wait around for Tom. He had a whole new life waiting for him in Boston, and she had a business to run…without him.

Tom saw Nina and Robin off at the door with a promise to call as soon as he was free. Although Nina wanted to hear more about Maggie, Tom ducked her questions. Seeing the agony in Maggie's eyes when she saw Nina told Tom all he needed to know. Maggie was in love with him, but not nearly as much as he was in love with her. It had taken him only seconds to realize that as they stood together with Robin. He wanted to chase after her, but didn't want to tangle with Maggie and her stubborn streak right now.

He was putting the metal cover back on Ferdinand's motor when he felt Maggie presence in the room. "Stop lurking," he said, hoping that her being here meant she was willing to talk.

She walked over, a look of optimism on her pretty features. "I talked to Dad."

So she didn't plan to rehash meeting Nina and Robin, and for that he was grateful, although a little surprised. "And he said what?"

"I can have the money I need to buy Sean and Harry's interests in Harry's Place."

"That's great."

"No, stupid, that's more than great. Like I said, it means you don't have to ride the bull. I've got it taken care of."

Tom looked at her, at the way her chin was set, and her eyes focused so intently on him. "Maggie, I'm really happy for you, but I have a couple of issues I need to settle."

"The family thing," she said.

"No, I need to get my money back somehow."

Maggie rolled her eyes. "I'm willing to help you, silly."

"That's fine, but I want my money to come from Sean."

"But aren't you the one who's been telling me it's not always about money?" She stared at him for what seemed like forever.

He stared back, wanting to remember every detail of her, from her perfectly oval green eyes to her beautifully proportioned body, and all the luscious areas in between.

He also saw her loneliness for the first time, her need for people, for him. In that moment of recognition, something shifted in him. He wanted to win this bet with Sean for his own purposes, but deep down he now realized he was doing it to gain Maggie's respect.

He'd never forget the look of disdain in her eyes when she confronted him over the stripper thing. He'd known then just how straight and uncompromising Maggie could be... That underneath her show of bravado lived a very proud, determined woman. "You're right. This isn't just about money. I want you to remember me."

"Really? I thought we agreed to be friends. And I promise you're going to have trouble forgetting me. I'm going to call you every time I have a business problem, especially if we're partners. And we will be partners, no matter what kind of squirming you do to get out of it." She gave him a scowl as she pushed the baseball cap off her forehead.

"Why the cap?" he asked, tipping the peak of the cap back over her gorgeous face.

She tilted her chin up and giggled. "Can you imagine this? My head feels cold without the wig."

He was going to miss this feisty woman who could laugh, cry and love…

"Cold head, warm heart. Is that it?" He touched her chin, and heard the tiniest of sighs escape her lips.

She stepped closer. "What can I say to convince you not to ride the bull?"

"We've been over that."

"No, *you've* been over that," she said.

Could he tell her his other reason for riding the bull? Now that she'd gotten her father to commit to the financing needed, it wouldn't be easy. But when had being around Maggie been easy? "If it makes you feel any better, there's another reason why I'm doing this."

"What possible reason could there be for you to risk your neck on an old mechanical bull?" she asked, her face a mixture of curiosity and disbelief.

Resting his good hand on his hip, he met Maggie's gaze. Her smile made him feel happy. Her smile lit up her face. And the way she tilted her head when she wasn't sure about something, or wanted to make a point…

There were a lot of things about Maggie he'd never forget. There was a whole lot about Maggie he'd been missing in his life…

"Maggie, I want to win this money." He shrugged, feeling suddenly very vulnerable.

She opened her mouth to say something. Something smart and funny, he was sure, but he put up his hand to stop it.

"I'm sure this sounds a little crazy, but I want you to respect me. I've changed, and I want to start by proving it with you. I'm going to ride the bull no matter what you say, because I want you to understand that I'm different now."

Why would he do that now? When he was leaving? Didn't he know she loved him the way he was? Maggie's stomach was full of butterflies fluttering to find an escape. "Tom, I already respect you. You're a little nutty at times, prone to wanting your own way, obviously. But other than that…"

"I want you to believe in me. The man who once worked for a stripper troupe has changed."

"I know. You told me you wanted to change for Robin's sake. That's great."

"I've also changed my attitude toward women."

"Now, that I don't believe. You'll always see a woman as a conquest."

"Not true."

She stared at him, disbelief and hope at war in her heart. "Tom, you don't have to pretend with me. Twenty-four hours ago, you were ready to pack up and leave. You told me that you had to have your freedom. You couldn't be tied down."

"Yeah, I did. And maybe it's still part of who I am, but I want to change that. Every one deserves the chance to change. Look at your father. You said he would never help you out, that he always criticized you, and look what happened?"

Why was she arguing with him? If he said he'd changed, then maybe he had. But nothing could change the fact that he was leaving for Boston, for a life with his son…and Nina.

"You're right. My mistake. I appreciate the fact you want to impress me."

Tom touched the peak of her cap, then moved his hand away. Sadness rushed through her. Tom and Maggie—the best table waiting team at Harry's Place—was over.

"Not just to impress you. I'm not going to play with your emotions any more. Hell, I spent a lifetime learning how to make women want me. It was my career, but not now. I want us to be the best friends any two people could be. Then we'll see…"

Maggie's breath stilled. *Was Tom suggesting they had a chance? Was her dream all these long days about to come true?*

*No.* She squared her shoulders. She was not going to buy into that fantasy again. If Tom wanted her, he could say so now. No more waiting around for a man to decide her fate. Been there, done that. "What are you telling me? I can sit home and pine for you while you and Nina play house?"

Tom looked crestfallen, and for a brief moment, Maggie wished she'd kept her big mouth shut. "I'm sorry for bringing Nina into this, but from what I saw—" The sting of tears silenced her. Why did she have to cry and ruin everything?

"Maggie, Nina is Robin's mother. End of story."

"Please don't try to protect my feelings. I'm all right with you being with Nina," Maggie countered, feeling the tension build inside.

"Maggie Kincade. Tell the truth. You love me."

She couldn't let him believe that, not when he was leaving town. "No, I don't. Who could love someone like you?" she asked, mortified to hear the tremor in her voice. Before she did something completely dumb like kiss him, she escaped out the door.

"You'll be here to see me ride the bull, and don't be late," Tom called out after her.

# Chapter Twenty

The next day dawned bright and promising—the exact opposite of how Maggie felt.

"Don't look so sad," Tom said as he tweaked Maggie's nose. His smile that could melt icebergs was crushing the life out of her. They were standing together beside Ferdinand. There wasn't a sound, only the rattle of pots in the kitchen as the cook got started for the day.

"I'm not sad for you. I'm sad that a smart man like you wants to break his bones. Did you ever consider that you might be one of those weird people that like to hurt themselves?"

"Maggie, you've got to stop worrying about me. I'll be fine. It's Sean you should worry about." Tom gave her a wink.

Her suspicious mind kicked in. "What are you up to Tom Rawlins?"

"Nothing. Nothing at all. I'm going to win the praise of Sweet Maggie, and then I'm going to pack my bags."

"Who's packing their bags?" Sean asked, coming up behind Maggie.

The last thing Maggie wanted was any contact with Sean. She moved to one side. "Tom's leaving after this."

"After I beat the pants of you, buddy," Tom said, adjusting the sling on his arm.

"You're not going to be going anywhere if you injure your other arm," Sean said.

"There's a thought," Maggie said. "Tom may be forced to stick around."

"Just watch and see," Tom said with far too much cockiness in his voice to suit Maggie. But no one was trying to suit Maggie, she thought, glancing around the musty storeroom. Certainly not the two males she was keeping company with at the moment.

"I heard the cook talking this morning about what happened the last time you were on this bull. You sure you want to do this?" Sean asked, a nasty smirk on his face.

"I'm with Sean on this one," Maggie said, but Tom didn't seem to notice.

She watched Sean as he talked to Tom and wondered what she had ever seen in the man? She wasn't attracted to Sean and sex had not been a factor in her decision to give him her savings. So, it had to be something else. Ego maybe? Sean could be so charming when it suited him. Or maybe it had been her need to impress her father by teaming up with Sean in a business venture on her father's home turf, in her hometown.

Maybe what had been missing was a deeper need to connect with a man, to feel valued...equal. Yeah, that was it. She had always wanted to feel special, to experience the feelings her mother described when she talked about her father.

Her throat hurt with unfamiliar feelings of worry and foreboding as she watched Tom get up on the bull. If only she could prevent this latest mistake-in-the-making, and stop Tom from being injured.

"When you're ready," Sean said with excitement.

"Now," Tom yelled, bracing his knees against the sides of the bull.

"Here you go, buddy, for the best two minutes of your life," Sean said as he hit the switch, sending Tom toward the ceiling.

Tom's rear-end connected with the phony bull's back in a bone-grinding thud, but he was still on the bull and still able to breathe. Chalk one up for his earlier experience and all the times he'd worked out. The bucking jarred his teeth, but so far it didn't seem as bad as the first time, or maybe it was his mechanical skills that made the difference. Still, his shoulder throbbed, and his head pounded with renewed intensity.

He braced his knees against the sides of the bull, dug his fingers into the saddle pommel as he fought to stay on the mechanical animal. He could see Maggie watching him—worry lines etched in her beautiful face, her skin pale.

Her worried gaze met his. His bouncing eyes spotted tears shimmering in her eyes. He couldn't look at her for fear of losing his concentration and ending up on the floor. His shoulder pained with every jolting movement, but so far he was still on the damned bull. His eyes returned to Maggie as the bull began to slow to a stop. Tom's heart did a painful push against his ribs as he saw the loneliness in Maggie's eyes. She would miss him when he left today…and he would miss her.

She'd stood by him today during his second ride on the bull. She'd been there when it would have been much easier for her to leave and return to her wealthy family, to her son. When he'd made it plain he wouldn't give her any reason to stay with him.

How could he really leave this woman? But, if not, how could he possibly stay? Staying meant making a commitment, and he'd had no problem last night when he'd talked to Nina about his feelings for Maggie. Nina had wanted to know if Maggie was his reason for refusing to consider starting a relationship with her. He'd denied it, but now seeing the look in Maggie's eyes, he knew he hadn't been honest with Nina or himself.

He breathed a sigh of relief, mingled with another feeling he couldn't identify. Longing? Loss? He eased his leg over the bull and stepped down onto the floor.

Before he knew what was happening Maggie was in his arms. "Don't you ever do anything so completely dumb like that again! Do you hear me?" she demanded. As she ran her fingers lightly over his injured arm, she got as close to him as she could.

"It's over. I'm fine," he reassured her, though he wanted to howl from the pain radiating up his arm.

"Promise me you won't do that again," Maggie insisted.

"Hey honey," he stroked her hair, and smoothed the tears that clung to her cheeks. "Is this the same Maggie? Or has someone taken over your beautiful body?" he crooned, kissing her surprised lips.

"Don't joke about this. You could have been seriously injured. And where would you be then? I thought you wanted to make it to Boston, to your—"

"Hush." Tom kissed her. A kiss meant to silence the words on her lips. A kiss that dragged him into the feelings buried beneath all the playful joking and teasing he'd done over the past weeks. As his body molded with hers, his mind was consumed with one thought.

He'd used all his skill to keep Maggie at arm's length, to avoid the emotional entanglement that could lead to commitment. He'd intentionally ignored what staying with Maggie would mean. In the beginning, she'd been just like all the women he'd known. But now, he knew he could trust her with his feelings and his life.

As he stood holding Maggie, his good arm wrapped firmly around her, he realized something else even more important. For him, there would only ever be one woman.

Maggie. Unable to cope with the rush of feelings, he pulled away.

"Are you okay?" Her expression was one of concern, shot through with surprise.

To cover his uncertainty, he gently led her to the back of the room. "Let's watch Sean. Then we'll see."

"About what?"

What was the man talking about? And what had he tried to do by kissing her nearly senseless? Her body ached for him, for what she would lose when he walked out the door.

And now there they were spending their last minutes together, watching the gambler who'd ruined both their lives, ride a mechanical bull… She tried not to think about that as she watched Sean soar high over the bull's head…and land on his behind. *Ouch!*

She felt a little sorry for Sean, but not enough to help him up off the floor. All she needed now was Sean's signature on an agreement that would give her his ownership interest in Harry's Place.

And now that it was finally over, all she was emotionally capable of was relief. Tom would be okay and he was ready to start his new business—her throat tightened. Desperate to shake off the feelings of loss, she forced herself to concentrate on the future with her son and her new business venture.

Not wanting to have either man see her sadness, she glanced around the storeroom. What would she do with this space once she owned it? The bull would definitely be removed, but after that she wasn't sure. It didn't seem important now.

She turned to go, and ran smack into Harry.

"Well, pretty lady, where did you come from?" Harry's eyebrows were doing a come-hither glide above his eyes.

"Don't try to put the moves on me, Harry Washburn."

"Maggie?" Harry gulped and his Adam's apple jumped. "I didn't recognize you. What did you do to your hair?

It looks great. Better than the blond job, but how did—"

"Never mind, Harry. Is my father here?"

"Your father... Now I get it. That's why Jonathan Kincade is in my office with a load of papers, and a suit with an attitude. He and his lawyer said they had business to discuss with me. He said he was looking for you, but I never made the connection. You're his daughter?"

Dad hadn't wasted any time, but then again, he never did. "Yes, he's my father."

"Well, he's offering me a very reasonable price for my share of this place, and I plan to take it."

"I'm pleased," Maggie said.

Her father walked into the room, and for the first time in years she honestly looked forward to talking with him. She wanted his ideas on what changes she should make in the business, and to share her plans for the restaurant area. "Hi, Dad. I didn't know you were here."

"Yeah, we've got the deal pretty well finalized with Harry. Now, I need to talk to Sean and your friend Tom. Once the financial aspects are completed, we can concentrate on getting clear title to the property." Her father was all business as he glanced in Tom's direction. "What were they doing?" her father asked.

"I'm about to get the papers signed to get Sean's part of the business."

"How did you do that?" her father asked, a mixture of pride and surprise in his voice.

"It's a long story, Dad," Maggie said with a small sigh. She watched Tom, the man she loved help Sean to his feet. Tom was a very kind person—kinder than she was for sure.

Jonathan Kincade eyed his daughter, and a smile started at the corners of his mouth, creeping up to his eyes. "Maggie, you're in love with this man, this Tom Rawlins."

Maggie swung her gaze to her father, denial hot on her lips.

"Don't deny it. I've seen that look on your mother's face

for years. It was the look that made me the luckiest man alive."

"You think I love Tom Rawlins?"

"Guaranteed." He surprised her with a hug.

Tentatively at first, she hugged him back as feelings of happiness began to rise up in her. Hugging her dad was so nice. "You're right. I love him."

"So, what's the problem?"

"He's moving to Boston. He won't be back."

Her father held her at arm's length. "Listen to me. Don't let him go without a fight. Get him alone and tell him how you feel, how much you love him." He ducked his head and looked straight into her eyes. "Sometimes a man needs a good kick to see what's right under his nose. It was the case with your mother and me. Don't let Tom go."

*Her father giving her advice on love… Color her speechless.*

She was still fumbling for words when Harry returned. "I'm so glad your plan worked," Harry said with far too much glee in his voice.

"What plan are you talking about?" Maggie asked as she watched Sean hobble out of the room under his own steam.

"Ferdinand can be a little temperamental sometimes. Calm as a pussy cat one day, uppity and feisty the next. Something to do with the motor I suspect," Harry said, eyeing Tom.

"Tom, you didn't monkey around with Ferdinand, did you?" Maggie asked.

"Me? Why I'd never do something like that. No, I sure wouldn't." Tom offered the denial as he grinned at Maggie and shook hands with Harry. "It's been nice knowing you, Harry."

Harry pumped his hand. "Likewise. I'm going to clean out my desk."

"Harry, thanks for everything," she said, feeling a weird kind of kinship with Harry at this point, despite the meanness she and Tom experienced as his employees. The sky must be falling, or possibly a realignment of planets?

She was still thinking about Harry when her father whispered in her ear. "Maggie, are you going to introduce me?"

Maggie made the introductions, and watched while the two men in her life sized each other up. Tom had never looked more handsome, and Maggie felt really proud of him as he held his own while talking business with her father.

"Young man, I'd like to know what your intentions are where my daughter is concerned—"

"Dad!" Heat rose in her cheeks. She couldn't look at Tom. She couldn't bear to witness the embarrassment on his face.

The silence dragged on while each man stared at the other. Maggie fought the urge to scream. But all she could do was stand there, waiting for whatever came next. As the silence continued, Maggie's mortification grew. "Why don't you tell him you're leaving?" she said barely above a whisper.

"Sir, I'd like to talk to your daughter about that," Tom said, his eyes sweeping her face, his expression one of need and caring.

"You're leaving for Boston. What do we have to talk about?" Maggie asked.

"I was, but I want to talk to you about an idea of mine. It popped into my head while I was on the bull."

"Do you often get ideas that way?" Maggie asked Was Tom about to change his mind? But he couldn't. He had his plans all made, plans she knew didn't include her. It didn't make a bit of sense, but the whole day didn't make sense. She glanced at her father who was watching Tom.

She turned her attention to Tom who appeared uneasy, tentative, so unlike the man she knew.

"This is a bit out of the blue, but I don't want to leave here without some hope that you and I have a chance at a relationship," he said, his expression serious.

"A relationship? Of course. *We're friends.* That's what you wanted… Unless you've changed your mind." Maggie's thoughts raced. "You're going to be living in Boston, and I'll be here."

Tom glanced at Jonathan Kincade. "I want to be with your daughter, sir. But first, I have to work a few things out. I rode the bull so that Maggie would be free to buy Harry's Place on her own terms."

Her father scowled. "So what's in it for you? After all, most people wouldn't risk getting hurt like you did simply to prove a point or to help someone else."

Tom rubbed his neck with his good hand. "In the beginning, I wanted to help Maggie, so I could leave with a clear conscience."

"You'd have done a good turn for a friend, is that it?" her father asked.

"Not completely. You see…my relationship with Maggie is a little more complicated than that. I want Maggie to be proud of me."

"I am," she interjected.

"I understand." Her father nodded his head slowly, a smile on his face. "I'll leave you two to work on your lives. Meanwhile, I'll get the paperwork sorted out and ready to sign." He shook Tom's hand. "It's been nice to meet you," he said, and there was a don't-hurt-my-daughter look in her dad's eyes.

Maggie couldn't let her father leave without thanking him. She put her arms around his neck. "Dad, thank you for everything. You won't regret helping me. I promise."

"I know I won't. But we have something else to discuss when you get home."

"What's that?" Maggie asked, her curiosity making her anxious.

"Your mother and I want to give Jeremy a pony for Christmas."

"A pony." She eyed her dad as she prepared her

argument against such a gift. Then she remembered her mother's comments about her own pony. "Jeremy would love a pony."

Her father's happy expression connected them in a way words couldn't. "I'll get right on it."

With Tom's good arm draped over her shoulder, Maggie watched her father leave. Funny how her relationship with her father had changed. But change was everywhere. She turned to Tom. "So, tell me what's going on?"

"I never thought I'd be the one to say this, and I know we agreed to share space at Sean's house and that was all. No romantic involvement."

"A good decision at the time." And one she regretted.

"You think so?"

Unwilling to expose her fantasy where Tom was concerned, she shrugged.

"I was on the bull, wishing I could be anywhere else, when it occurred to me that you and I make a great team. Maggie, we're good together."

"Obviously, *good together* isn't good enough."

"Let me finish. I realized, as I crashed around on the bull, that the rest of my life would mean nothing if I had to spend it without you."

Maggie froze. Her heart pressed against her throat, blocking her breath. "Are you saying that riding the bull gave you the time you needed to figure out that you love me?"

His eyes searched hers. "I love you, Maggie Kincade."

Maggie wrapped her arms around Tom's neck. "I'm going to have that bull bronzed."

Tom exploded in laughter, his body rocking back and forth as he held her in his arms.

"I'm serious," she said, trying for a stern expression. "Without Ferdinand, you would probably never have had your epiphany."

"Oh, yes I would have. Ferdinand just helped me along."

Tom stroked her cheek, kissed her forehead, and let his lips linger on hers. Maggie drew in his s cent, enjoying every ounce of his attention. "We're two very different people, and we will have to learn to compromise, but it could be worth it."

Maggie waited, her lips trembling inches from his. "*Could* be worth it? Tell me what *could* be worth it."

His dark eyes searched hers. "You. I want you. Maggie Kincade, will you marry me?"

"Marriage? Tom Rawlins, the commitment phobic, wants to marry me?" she said, trying for a joking tone to ease the mound of excitement crushing her chest.

"Okay, picture me eating a bowl of crow, but yes, I want to marry you. I want to have kids, a house, and at least one dog."

Everything she had ever dreamed of… "But without the bull?"

He nuzzled her neck. "No bull."

She luxuriated in the tingling sensation his lips made on her neck. "I was kidding. The bull doesn't really worry me," she said, working her fingers under his shirt.

"Me neither." He returned her kiss, making her head swim.

"I will marry you on one condition," Maggie murmured, her body humming with anticipation.

"And that would be?"

"You promise to spend the rest of your life with me."

"We're talking forever, here," Tom mused.

"Forever. Take it or leave it."

"I'll take it," he said, hugging her close, his lips trailing along the sensitive skin of her cheek, setting up the now familiar hum in all her body parts.

Dear Reader,

I hope you enjoyed reading *Finding Mr. Wrong*. If you have the chance to visit my website www.stellamaclean.com, please get in touch with me. I would love to hear from you and what you thought of this book.

*Finding Mr. Wrong* is the first in the Liberated Ladies series. These are women whose lives are turned upside down by events beyond their control. On the path to putting their world back together they discover men who fit their individual need for the perfect hero.

Maggie Kincade found hers in Tom Rawlins.

Here's just a hint of what to expect in the next book, *Cookie Carmichael Takes A Man*.

Cookie Carmichael has spent her life being the perfect wife and mother, and taken her husband's philandering ways in stride to keep what the rest of the world thinks is the perfect marriage. She's taken care of her grandmother, taken her mother's advice even when it was wrong, taken her turn knitting scarves and mittens for the school fundraisers. She's taken so much in her life, including the arrival of her husband's latest squeeze on her front doorstep.

Now it's Cookie's turn to take back her life, take back her respectability and take the man of her choice. Shea's not sure he wants to be taken, given how much he enjoys the smorgasbord of women who pass through his life. In fact Shea sees himself as a man who takes control of any situation. That is until the day Cookie shows him her secret weapon— her caring and support during the greatest crisis of his life.

*Cookie Carmichael Takes A Man* is due out in November 2016.

Enjoy your life and the people you love.
All the best,
*Stella*

# Other Books By Stella Maclean

Heart of My Heart
Harlequin Superromance

Baby in Her Arms
Harlequin Superromance

A Child Changes Everything
Harlequin Superromance

The Christmas Inn
Harlequin Superromance

The Doctor Returns
Harlequin Superromance

To Protect Her Son
Harlequin Superromance

Sweet On Peggy
Harlequin Superromance

Desperate Memories
Romantic Suspense

Unimaginable
Romantic Suspense

# About the Author

STELLA MACLEAN has been writing for years. She likes the close relationship she has with her computer, and her furry friends, Jethro and Sully. Stella also likes what she does with the hours she spends hiding out in her office making up stories about the lives of imaginary people. Imaginary people are the most fun because no time is wasted on fact checking, library research visits or any of those other jobs that slow a writer down. Besides, with the stroke of a key any character you don't like or have grown tired of can be easily removed. Stella enjoys telling stories about people who, like many of us, find love elusive.

*Finding Mr. Wrong* is one of her favorite stories.

Stella loves to hear from her readers, to have discussions about writing and reading and anything else that is of interest to those people who enjoy her books.

She can be reached at her website: www.stellamaclean.com
Or you can find her on Twitter: @Stella_MacLean
Or on Facebook: http://tinyurl.com/7ls3ere

www.ingramcontent.com/pod-product-compliance
Lightning Source LLC
Chambersburg PA
CBHW050757080726
47590CB00020B/289